MOUSSE AND MURDER

MOUSSE AND MURDER

Elizabeth Logan

BERKLEY PRIME CRIME
New York

BERKLEY PRIME CRIME
Published by Berkley
An imprint of Penguin Random House LLC
penguinrandomhouse.com

Copyright © 2020 by Penguin Random House LLC
Recipes copyright © 2020 by Penguin Random House LLC
Penguin Random House supports copyright. Copyright fuels creativity, encourages
diverse voices, promotes free speech, and creates a vibrant culture. Thank you for buying
an authorized edition of this book and for complying with copyright laws by not
reproducing, scanning, or distributing any part of it in any form without permission.
You are supporting writers and allowing Penguin Random House to continue to
publish books for every reader.

BERKLEY and the BERKLEY & B colophon are registered trademarks and
BERKLEY PRIME CRIME is a trademark of Penguin Random House LLC.

ISBN: 9780593100448

First Edition: May 2020

Printed in the United States of America
1 3 5 7 9 10 8 6 4 2

Cover art by Elsa Kerls
Cover image: Bull moose by Doug Lindstrand /
Design Pics / Offset / Shutterstock
Cover design by Judith Lagerman
Book design by George Towne

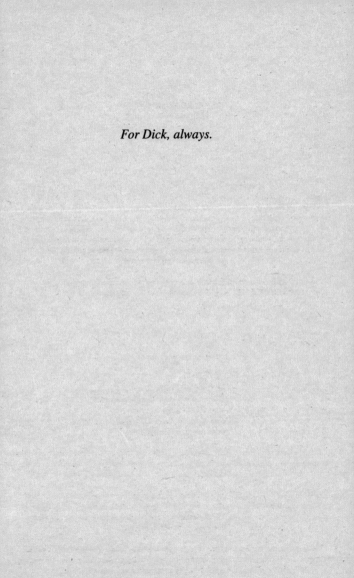

For Dick, always.

ONE

I DISCONNECTED THE PHONE CALL, WAITING FOR THE sirens, ready to be arrested and thrown into the women's side of the tiny jail in Elkview, Alaska. A fine way to settle back in my hometown after a few years away.

I had just lied to my mother. Worse, I'd done it while looking into her eyes on FaceTime. Trusting, beautiful brown eyes that almost perfectly matched her hair. My hair, too. How had that falsehood rolled off my tongue?

The last time I'd lied to Evelyn Cooke, I was six years old and I'd blamed cousin Petey for starting the fight in his backyard. And that was technically not a lie, because we'd shoved each other into his sandbox at the same time.

But this afternoon, at thirty-three years old, I'd told a whopper. Was it because I was distracted by warnings of the freezing rain heading our way, icy rain that would keep tourists away from the Bear Claw Diner? My diner, as of almost a year ago, when Mom decided to retire and travel with Dad, who was still giving management workshops all over the world. To think how thrilled I'd been that Mom would entrust everything to me—the diner, the staff, her recipes, her great following of regular patrons, and even Eggs Benedict, aka Benny, her beautiful orange tabby.

"How is everything going, Charlie?" Mom had asked from the deck of a cruise ship headed down the Danube. Or was it up the Danube? I hadn't had much time for travel myself, what with a brief, ill-advised stint as a law school student in nearby Anchorage, followed by culinary school down in San Francisco, three thousand miles and one time zone away. And now I had full responsibility for a twenty-four-hour diner.

"Is Oliver okay with the new recipe you suggested?" Mom asked, catching me off guard.

"Absolutely," I'd answered, passing over the knock-down-drag-out in the kitchen right after lunch. "He loved the idea."

In truth, an imbroglio had begun when I proposed a simple change to our signature bear claw recipe. My position was that adding a bit of chocolate to anything was an improvement, but I should have known better than to suggest a change to my head chef.

Oliver Whitestone, whose fiftieth birthday bash I'd just missed last year, had been with Mom since the early days of the Bear Claw and had always resisted any variation in the menu. Who was I, too green in his eyes to even be called a rookie, to mess with success? I was a mere child, in middle school, when he was hired at the Bear Claw. Never mind that I'd grown up there, doing my homework after school, twisting on a red vinyl stool, trying to see my reflection in the bright chrome trim, sometimes pushing the limit of the legal age for waitressing or kitchen work. And never mind that I'd been to culinary school, though admittedly not in Paris, where Oliver was trained.

Oliver liked to remind us that he could be cooking anywhere in the world, emphasizing his point by spreading his sadly short arms to encompass Europe, I guessed.

"But you chose us," I'd say, and spread my own much longer arms to take in our retro black-and-white tile with seating for fifty, as long as a few of the customers were skinny. I wasn't always sure Oliver understood my sarcastic tone. Just as well.

Today I'd inadvertently escalated the rift between us. I'd brought in a chocolate bear claw recipe to show the staff and suggested they give it a try over the next few days. An innocent experiment. Oliver had taken the paper from my hands and torn it into tiny pieces.

I wasn't proud of the shouting match that followed, within easy earshot of the remaining lunch crowd. The rest of the kitchen staff, used to these sparring contests, carried on with their work. The disruption lasted several minutes and ended, as usual, with Oliver storming out of the kitchen and slamming through the back door. He'd tossed his white jacket and hat over the chopping table, grabbed his parka from a hook, and muttered something about any new recipe in connection with his dead body.

It wasn't the first time he'd left in a huff, though not always because of me. He'd once disappeared for an hour during a rush because one of his helpers showed up eating a cheeseburger from Chief Beef, a new fast-food place in town.

Who knew where Oliver was now? Probably with his new girlfriend, a construction worker on the old drive-in movie renovation project down the road.

I walked around the empty diner, refilling the ketchup, mustard, salt, and pepper containers, with my eyes on the door, ready to welcome Oliver back and issue an apology if needed. A temporary truce would be better than nothing. It wasn't as if I needed chocolate bear claws tomorrow, or at all, if it came down to that.

I'd known it would be tricky working with Oliver, who'd been used to one boss for many years. If my mom could even be called the boss, she was so mellow. Besides being on opposite ends of the spectrum height-wise—I towered over her from when I turned thirteen—Mom and I were also very different in terms of temperament.

I found part of a meatloaf sandwich behind the fake jukebox and smiled as I remembered the little boy who'd sat there earlier, probably annoyed that the only real jukebox was the large electronically operated console at the back of the diner. Oliver didn't mind upgrades that weren't edible.

Fortunately, it was already after three o'clock in Elkview, and the Danube was ten hours later. Mom had probably been too tired to catch the lie I was sure was written all over my face. The fact that she'd said simply, "Good," and then "Love from Dad, too. Talk tomorrow," meant I was home free. For now. *Phew.* Both a good "phew," because I didn't have to worry my mom with a tantrum story that was all too familiar to her—Oliver had been her second-in-command for as long as I could remember—and a bad "phew," because I'd have a hard time sleeping knowing I'd kept the truth from her. I'd done it so it wouldn't ruin her trip, I told myself.

So you wouldn't look like you couldn't handle your new responsibilities was hard to own up to.

I continued my hit-and-miss cleanup—filling the metal napkin holders in each booth and along the counter, adding environmentally safe straws and clean place mats as needed, still trying to justify my lie, which I'd managed to reduce from "black" to "little white." I finally realized it might be more productive if I talked to someone other than myself. In a happy coincidence, my childhood friend Annie Jensen had also moved back to Elkview, to manage her family's inn down the road from the Bear Claw. Even happier, we had promised each other at least two movie dates a month as soon as the drive-in reopened, no matter the state of our respective businesses. I called up Annie's number and got voicemail.

Too bad. But a useful offshoot of the failed attempt to contact Annie came to me. Thanks to the orderly arrangement of my contacts list, I had a stabbing reminder of a meaningful action I needed to take, one long overdue. JENSEN was immediately after JAMISON on my screen. I gritted my teeth and highlighted *Ryan Jamison*, my ex-fiancé, and one of the reasons I'd fled from San Francisco. Ryan, the SF Bay Area lawyer who saw greener pastures with one of his paralegals and neglected to inform me in a timely fashion. I hit DELETE and felt a shiver of glee, as if I'd punched him in the gut, but without the assault charge.

I knew my next option for companionship would be no-fail, even if remote. It was love at first sight for Benny and me. Sure, it might have been because I'd arrived in his life armed with an automatic feeder programmed to dispense his favorite food throughout the day whether or not I was home. There was nothing wrong with a little bribery—motivation?—to win over a beautiful orange and white tabby. Benny, renamed by Mom, was a reluctant castoff from a friend of hers who had moved overseas. I wondered which country didn't accept American cats.

"Kind of defeats the purpose," Mom had said when she saw Benny's feeder. "I gave you Benny so you wouldn't stay at the Bear Claw twenty-four-seven. Now you're telling me you're going to feed and pet him through your phone?" She shook her head.

I'd dissuaded her of the remote petting idea, though I thought it couldn't be far off, given how quickly technology changed these days.

It wasn't only Mom who thought I went over the top when I added a camera to the system, one that included two-way audio. How many ways can a cat say *meow*? A lot, it turns out, depending on his mood. I had come a long way, mastering Benny's meows, trills, purrs, and the occasional growl when he was unhappy.

A selection of games that pets could play were all accessible from the app on my smartphone. I called the unit "the Bennycam." So far, I'd tested the laser game only once and was still a little wary of hurting Benny if the beam he was supposed to be chasing around the floor went astray and chased him back.

Today I tuned in and waited a few minutes for Benny to get within camera range. I'd set the camera up in the open space between my kitchen and dining room, giving me video access to the area where Benny spent the most time when he was awake. The app had already given me the feedback that he'd consumed three ounces of food since I saw him last. I'd made a quick visit home to Benny right after my blowout with Oliver, ostensibly to pet my cat, but more for my own benefit, for him to comfort me.

When Benny pawed his way to the camera, I gave myself a virtual pat on the back for being in sync with my pet and watched as he checked out the feeder tray and nibbled. I allowed him a semiprivate moment for noshing, then started in on my roster of concerns, starting with, "What am I going to do if Oliver doesn't come back in an hour to prep for the dinner shift?" Although Benny might not have been aware of it, he answered with, "Call Victor and lure him in as a substitute, with a promise of time and a half." As usual, "Now leave me alone while I nap" was implied by his tone.

I could promise Victor a less-than-full crowd this evening. It was Monday, typically slow to begin with, but with the added deterrent of constant weather warnings on radio and television. We'd probably be feeding only the poor tourists who were unaware that winter could still be raging through March in Elkview.

Travelers from all over the world came here to walk amid icy glaciers and snow-covered mountains along the scenic Glenn Highway. We Alaska natives always found it amusing that many of them would act surprised or even complain about the cold weather. The word was that the clothing store on Main Street did a thriving business from tourists who had an immediate need for a heavy sweater or jacket, and woolen caps flew off the shelf.

I left Benny napping in a cone of sunshine on the living room floor and got back to my diner issue. I texted and emailed the delinquent Oliver, plus the few friends of his whom I knew, and then, giving up, texted Victor. As a backup to the backup, I headed for the freezer myself and pulled out a large tray of our original-recipe individual shepherd's pies, along with another tray filled with corn muffins.

When the small bells over the front door tinkled a few minutes later, I held out hope for Oliver, but a glance through the serving window showed Elkview's finest, Alaska State Trooper Cody Graham. The lawman, simply "Trooper" to those who knew him well, headed for his favorite booth at the rear of the train-car-shaped diner. So he could sit against the wall, facing everyone, his back to no one? Not that he would admit it. I smiled, thinking about how I'd pictured him here earlier, arresting me for fibbing in the first degree.

"Are those shepherd's pies I smell?" he asked.

"You can't possibly smell them, Trooper. They're still frozen solid."

"Did you put out a call for your MIA chef?"

I was chuckling now. "Yes. How did you know?"

"Then you're on kitchen duty until you can bring in reinforcements."

"Right."

"Then those are shepherd's pies I smell."

"I'll get one started," I said.

TWO

TROOPER GRAHAM REMINDED PEOPLE OF EVERY WEST-
ern movie they'd ever seen. Tall, lanky guy with a deep
voice and a big hat. It was hard to tell how old he was, but
he seemed no older than when he'd helped me with my
math homework many years ago. Later I learned he hated
math and his trick was to coax the right answer out of me.
His empire consisted of two patrol cars and one deputy,
fresh from training. In a pinch he'd press his wife into service. June Graham was equally tall and thin, but without
the big hat.

Now the trooper needed his food. I put a shepherd's pie
in the small oven and walked around to the dining area,
picking up a dinner salad and two mugs of black coffee—
one for me—on the way. Flexing my waitress muscles.

"You might as well pour another one of these," Trooper
said, pointing to the heavy white mugs. "Chris was right
behind me. He's pulling up now. You can always hear that
rattly old pickup. You'd better grab the cream," he added.

Anything for Chris Doucette, the town's favorite newspaperman. One of the town's few newspapermen, and a pretty cute guy as well, without the fussy, landscaped facial hair that Ryan was so fond of. Chris had hardly any scalp hair, in fact, having kept to his military crew cut, whereas Ryan . . . *But Ryan who?* I asked myself, making my way back toward the kitchen.

I knew that Chris, not one to seek out veggies, would snag a couple of pieces of cut-up pastry from under the plastic wrap on the tray in front. I came back around the counter with a small pitcher of cream, and sure enough, Chris was already working on a chunk of bear claw. I was surprised he took the time to hang his parka on the coatrack first and take a seat across from Trooper before diving in.

"How would you like one of those with a hint of chocolate in the filling?" I asked him.

Both the trooper and Chris made faces and uttered different forms of "Euww."

I made a face of my own. "Come on."

"Just teasing," Chris said. "But why mess with perfection?"

"We heard about the fight over it," Trooper said.

"I'll bet you didn't leave your high salary and prestige at a big-city restaurant only to fight a small-town chef," Chris noted, as if he were getting ready to write a feature article. "Wasn't your menu listed as one of the top ten in San Francisco?"

Times like this, I was glad I wasn't a blusher, because flattery from Chris would have done it. Not that I was crushing on him, but I wouldn't have minded a little personal time with him. Maybe that was crushing. I'd have to check with someone under twenty.

"Thanks. Top five in the whole Bay Area, but who's counting?" I said. "Just don't let Oliver hear you call him 'small-time,' or 'small-anything.' But how did you guys hear about our fight? There was hardly anyone here at the time."

"Remember what Ben Franklin said?" Chris asked.

The three of us spoke in unison. "Three may keep a secret if two are dead."

The saying was even more true of a small town like Elkview, with a population hovering just under one thousand people, depending on whether Mary Jane Chapman had twins or triplets.

By the time Trooper's shepherd's pie was ready, I'd forgotten all about the missing Oliver and the nonresponsive Victor. I joined my friends for some Elkview gossip: how Jeb and Sam got into it again in the bar on Main Street over the weekend, how the Martin girl took a job as the nanny for the ever-growing Chapman family, whether the junior hockey team would make it to the finals, and other breaking news. It was times like this that I loved being home again.

Then a familiar sound interrupted our conversation: Trooper's pager, a remnant from the past that many law enforcers still used as backup.

Trooper stepped into the small hallway in the back of the Bear Claw, where the restrooms were and the pay phones used to be. Small town or not, he did his best to keep police matters private. His integrity could be a bit annoying to a curious person like yours truly, and even more so to a journalist like Chris.

Chris twisted his very fit body in the booth he'd been sharing with us, apparently trying to provide a better angle for his good ear. I would have followed suit, perhaps even heading for the kitchen to be closer to the hallway, but the rattling of the assembly of doorbells caught my attention.

A veritable crowd entered the diner: A shivering young couple with cherry-red faces, followed by two men with unkempt beards and none-too-clean heavy jackets. Each pair took a booth toward the front, and I smiled broadly as the population of the Bear Claw more than doubled.

I greeted my new patrons and urged them all to try the shepherd's pie with complimentary corn muffins and free refills on the coffee. As often happens, people behaved against type, and the scruffy guys were more pleasant than the gentrified couple who probably hailed from an East Coast city.

That last thought had me mentally shrinking from my mom's disapproval for the second time today.

"Don't be so quick to judge, Charlotte Agnes," I heard her say in her scolding voice, taking me back to every childhood reprimand that began or ended with my formal name. Adding my middle name, in honor of my sainted aunt whom I'd never met, gave immeasurable weight to the rebuke.

I moved in to take the order from the couple in designer parkas, navy blue for him, baby-doll pink for her.

"It's sleeting out there," said the male, as if he were personally affronted by the weather, unaware that he could be in Fairbanks, Alaska, the coldest city in the United States, by dinnertime.

"Not exactly," I said. "Sleet is a mixture of rain and snow. What we have here is freezing rain, which happens when rain that's in below-freezing air hits the ground." I illustrated with a vertical clap of my hands.

"Who knew?" he asked, in a tone that said he didn't like being corrected. I immediately regretted my little meteorology lecture. At least I hadn't gone on about where ice pellets and hail fit into the winter precipitation scheme. I reminded myself that while pretty much everyone in Alaska was a weather junkie, these folks wouldn't know that.

I cut my losses and made my way back to the kitchen with orders for four pies, four muffins, and four coffees.

"Hot, please," the pink parka called after me, as if in this weather I'd have assumed cold, with a side of ice.

I'd glanced at the brochures on the table between the pristine parkas. The National Scenic Byway. Denali National Park. The Musk Ox Farm. The Matanuska Glacier. If they'd been more sociable, I'd have told them about the wedding I'd attended on the glacier. On the ice. Transportation by helicopter. A delicious cold buffet. And a spectacular photo album that had been featured in a travel magazine.

I'd worked at the various visitors' centers attached to the parks one summer during college when Dad convinced Mom that I needed a break from diner work, if only for my résumé. I'd memorized every Fun Fact about the sites and loved to share them with my patrons.

"Did you know," I'd begin, "that the ultra-fine qiviut fiber on the musk ox is softer than cashmere and eight times warmer than wool?" I didn't share such amazing knowledge with this couple, however. Their loss.

When a truck I recognized as belonging to Al Messner of Pilgrim Packing Company pulled in at the edge of the parking lot, I knew I'd better take out a second tray of pies. Big Al could be counted on for a double order. I was ready to rehash the funny bit we usually shared about how far off track those Pilgrims had gotten. I felt comforted that a regular customer had arrived. Al would be happy to sit through talk about the weather as long as I kept his mug filled and didn't stint on the Dutch apple pie.

I was so swamped for a few minutes, I didn't notice that both Chris and Trooper Graham had left—through the back door, or I would have seen them traipse down past the stools. What does it mean when a trooper gets a call and he and a journalist leave together? My mind whirled with the possibilities.

A GROUP OF CLIMBERS HEADED FOR DENALI CLEANED me out of pies and muffins, but it was worth it to eavesdrop on their talk of ski plane landing sites and the best climbing routes. It was five thirty before I had a minute to breathe. Even better, help had arrived. It had been a while since I'd played cook, bottle washer, and waitress.

First, Annie showed up, her thick pale green down coat adding ten pounds to her already chubby frame. Annie and I were friends all through Elkview schools, hardly lost touch though we attended different colleges, and enjoyed being neighbors again.

"You'd better put me to work," she said. "I had a call from a tour bus leader with a group on their way from Anchorage to Fairbanks. She's looking for food and lodging for about thirty people, in case they all wanted dinner in a diner." Not for the first time, Annie thought that was a pretty funny line and laughed accordingly, but then, she was always in a good mood.

"How come you're not home making up beds?" I asked.

Annie shrugged. "We're okay. All the cottages are made up and Maria's got the house under control. I might need to borrow some towels, however. Oh, and how about four dozen bear claws for tomorrow's breakfast? That will cover the strays and singles, too."

"Why are we standing around wasting time?" I tossed Annie an apron.

Annie had inherited her parents' inn—there was a lot of

that going around our little community. Her property housed a midsize Victorian with a row of small cottages on either side. Like the Bear Claw, Jensen's Elkview Inn survived on the tourist trade. I smiled, thinking how the ice climbers, another category of regular patrons, would recoil at being lumped in with "tourists." Regardless, taken together, with all the mountains, parks, and other natural attractions in the area, it worked out pretty well for food and housing businesses.

Finally, Victor arrived, and I no longer had to be head chef.

"No Oliver yet?" Victor asked.

I shook my head.

Victor's dark hair was tousled, as if he'd come straight from his bed. His eyes always seemed at half-mast even when he was in a cooking frenzy, blending sauce ingredients with one hand and building a multilayered sandwich with the other. As he wrapped an apron around his slight frame, I pointed to his chest.

"That doesn't mean you can use his apron."

He laughed and ran his fingers over the stitching along the top edge. "Oh, is that what 'O. W.' means?"

I tsk-tsked my disapproval, knowing Oliver would be furious. "It's your funeral," I said.

"You said double time, right?"

"Time and a—oh, sure, double time."

For that rapid pay increase I earned a high five, though the exuberance was slightly one-sided.

I left the menu to Victor while Annie and I followed directions.

"Moose and pork meatloaf and mashed potatoes. Tossed salad and custard pie," he announced. "And we have about six servings of mac and cheese, in case there are kids, plus

French fries if the mashed don't work, and maybe three or four plates of wings. But push the meatloaf. Special recipe, only the best moose meat, unique to the Last Frontier, et cetera. You know the drill."

A great cold-weather menu. Victor dug into the meatloaf prep; Annie was assigned to peeling potatoes; I raised my hand for salad duty, cutting up lettuce, carrots, tomatoes. Victor's sister was a Bear Claw part-timer, and he called her in to help serve. Nina, a business student at a local community college, was like her brother: small, dark, and quick.

Annie and I had no trouble chatting while we worked. There was always an interesting guest or two at her inn, and today's was a Frenchman, no less.

"He's so charming," Annie said. "From Switzerland. On his way to see the northern lights. His name is Pierre. Pierre Fournier. Isn't that a great name?"

"Of course."

"Sort of musical."

"Uh-huh."

Annie had obviously forgotten how we'd both struggled through high school French, and at the time "musical" was not the term we gave it. In fact, "It hurts my nose," she'd said, more than once.

"He's writing an article for some travel magazine. But his rental car broke down and Max's is saying they can't get the part we need. Well, he needs. So he's staying with me. Well, not with me, but maybe with me."

It was always a challenge to unwrap Annie's syntax. Fortunately, she almost never required a direct response.

"He has this great chart," she continued. "It shows sunrise and sunset for any day of the year for any city in the state, even the teeny ones. Teeny towns."

"Is that so?" I refrained from reminding Annie that

she probably had a similar chart, as I did, as most Alaskans did.

"He said he's always wanted to chase the aurora." She smiled as if he'd claimed to want to chase her. But maybe I was reading into it, since Annie was an easy mark for a pretty face and a healthy dose of charm, especially an exotic French specimen. "He talked on and on about ox, and how Fairbanks is home to the only captive research herd of musk oxen in the world. He really wants to see them. Wouldn't that be something?"

This time, I declined to answer.

We moved out to the dining area, checking condiment containers and restocking napkins. I wondered if Annie would have been as interested in the musk oxen if it had been an old guy from Juneau who went on and on about the animals. I doubted it, but there was no need to bring it up while she was free labor in my diner.

A new tinkle of the bell over the door brought in a woman I recognized as Oliver's girlfriend. She wasted no time, but came up to Annie and me, one hand outstretched.

"I'm Gert Marcus, Oliver's friend," she said, going for my hand first. "I was here once before and I remember you." She moved over to Annie and introduced herself, then got to the point, speaking loudly enough to reach Victor and Nina in the kitchen. "I'm looking for Oliver. Anyone know where he is? We're supposed to be going to the movies tonight down in Wasilla."

Annie shook her head; Victor yelled, "No." I started to explain that I hadn't seen Oliver since just after lunchtime, but Gert had already turned and headed for the door.

"Woman on a mission," Annie said. "She must be the construction worker; she's built like one. We should have asked when that old theater is going to reopen."

"She didn't leave a lot of time for that."

Annie got a call saying the tour bus was on its way, with thirty-three adults and three children. They'd be here in about twenty minutes. I checked my watch. Just after six. Except for a brief visit to Benny after lunch, I'd been at the Bear Claw since eight in the morning.

It was a good thing I'd filled Benny's feeder. According to the promos for the product, he could go a week before a refill would be needed. I hoped I'd never have to test that promise. But if Annie was serious about needing bear claws for her breakfast crowd, I'd have to plan on being here a couple of hours after dinner. I looked out the window and tried to decide if it was worth dropping in at home again. But the diner was so warm and cozy that I decided to check in on Benny again remotely. I hoped my mom would never find out how weak her only child had turned out to be.

I took a seat on a stool across from the pass-through window and clicked on the Benny app. I felt daring enough to start the laser game with him. Benny saw the bright red dot immediately and began chasing it around the floor to the rhythm of my finger movements.

My laughter brought Annie and Victor out to the dining area.

"What's this?" Victor asked. When I explained, he grabbed my phone. "You have to give him a challenge and some real exercise," he said and shot the laser dot up the wall to about four feet, then made rapid circular motions.

Benny's head jerked up as he tried to paw the image. He jumped to a level higher than I'd ever seen him reach. Victor lowered the dot quickly and had Benny racing around with it in what I thought was a panicky state. I grabbed my phone away from Victor, gave him a don't-you-ever-mess-with-my-tabby-again look, and wished there were a way to travel through space and help Benny calm down. I had to be satisfied with audio only.

"It's okay," I told Benny, in my most soothing voice. "It's going to be okay." From all appearances, Benny was calmer than I was, but it would be a while before I turned that laser on again, and certainly never in Victor's presence.

I resisted making some "bad Victor" comments, because I still needed the uncompromised services of my sous chef. Benny leapt up on a sweatshirt I'd left on a chair and kneaded it, his orange and white tail twitching, his green eyes darting toward the camera, sensing my presence, virtual as it was. I relaxed when he switched to licking his paws, starting his long grooming process.

As Benny continued his ritual, the sleek white tour bus pulled up in front of the Bear Claw. A line of tourists, huddled in mittens, scarves, and hoods, stepped down and rushed toward the door. About ten passengers into the unloading, Annie nudged me.

"Charlie, Charlie. There's Pierre," she whispered, a wide grin taking over her face. "I was hoping he'd decide to join the tourists for dinner."

I had the feeling Annie was going to be the first one at Pierre's booth and that he'd get excellent service.

As for me, I noticed Trooper's patrol car pull up, with Chris's old jalopy close behind, as expected. From their grim faces, I sensed they didn't have good news. The question was, how long could I wait to hear it?

THREE

THERE IS NOTHING LIKE A DINER FULL OF CHEERFUL sounds and mouthwatering smells on a bustling evening. Especially if you own the diner and want it to succeed.

The clanking of heavy platters on the through-window shelf competed with the chatter of satisfied customers, who were spilling over onto stools and sliding into booths. Victor's happy whistling added a nice touch—fortunately, he had forgiven my scolding over Benny and the laser dot game—as he filled the air with the aromas of his spicy moose and pork meatloaf and the baked stuffed bell peppers he'd magically produced as an extra offering. I wondered how long Victor would stay at the Bear Claw. He was young enough to want a career that was "going someplace," as he'd put it to me more than once, though he wasn't willing to make the effort of earning a culinary school certificate.

With Victor here now, I had it easy, taking orders, refilling drinks, and manning the register as needed. I also sold a few Bear Claw Diner T-shirts and several logo mugs, all emblazoned with a friendly-looking cartoon bear designed ages ago by one of Mom's employees. About once a week a customer would ask to buy one of our heavy white plates with the same design. One of these days, I'd get around to adding them to our modest souvenir case under the cash register. Oliver was convinced that customers had been sneaking out the plates their food was served on, under their down vests or in their backpacks.

"Might as well sell some clean ones and make money to replace the stolen ones," he'd said. Once in a while Oliver thought calmly and clearly—but only when he wasn't talking about changes to the menu.

How quickly I circled back to *Where is he?*

Annie and Nina did the heavy lifting this evening, back and forth to the kitchen with overloaded trays. To her credit, Annie lingered only a short while at Pierre's booth with each trip.

"Come and meet him," she said to me at one point. "He's going to have a drink with me in the parlor when we get back. His idea." She'd patted her chest at heart level to indicate what she thought of the idea.

I smoothed my apron and tucked a piece of long hair behind my ear as if I were preparing for an interview. *He's the one who should consider himself on the hot seat,* I told myself. *He needs my approval, especially if he has designs on my BFF, Annie, who deserves only the best.*

Pierre stood, as much as anyone can stand in a diner booth, and shook my hand. His hair was squared off on top, very high and very blond. I'd never seen an Irish knit sweater so stylish, as if it were custom made to fit a broader-than-normal chest. My judgment, taking it all in? A rock star or a runway model, not an accountant.

"Annie has told me so much about you," he said, with just enough of a French accent to be adorable. "And your friend, Benny. And how you play with him from here, from your excellent diner."

He pronounced my cat's name as if it were spelled *Ben-EE*, with the accent at the end. The diner became *dine-ER*. Otherwise, his English was very good. I wondered where he'd learned it, but I held back comments like *Don't you have a cadre of girlfriends in Zurich?* and *You'd better not hurt this amazing woman.*

"Your research sounds fascinating," I said instead. "I understand you're heading for the northern lights, but you're not with"—I swept my arm in a half circle, to indicate the diner population—"these folks." I also took the opportunity to greet Pierre's tablemates, not surprisingly all female.

"*Oui.* The magazine is paying for my trip. I've been on my own, but my rental car is out of, what do you say, whack? I'm thinking of joining this group for some of their activities, if they'll allow me." As he smiled his way around the table, I had no doubt that he'd be welcome, and I could tell he had none either.

"You can bunk with us," said a young woman in a down vest, eliciting giggles from her companions.

Annie cleared her throat. We'd been ignoring her. But, all things considered, she was doing very well, especially in the face of the competition in the booth. I hoped she wouldn't decide to join the tour herself, though I couldn't have said why I cared. "We can certainly accommodate you until Max can fix your car," she said. "If you decide not to join the tour."

I was glad to hear Victor call out an order before I had a chance to ask who "we" might be.

As usual, once everyone was served a main course, chewing and swallowing took over. Talking and requests from patrons died down. I was about to check on Trooper and Chris, then remembered an important factor: the regulars, who wouldn't be expecting their preferred stools or booths to be occupied. In my excitement over a full house, I'd forgotten them.

I had a stark reminder when two semis pulled off the road and into my parking lot at almost the same time. Moe and Jack had arrived, minus Manny this evening. I couldn't remember when I learned that those weren't the real names of the three truckers who came around as often as anyone who lived in town. I had to wrap my brain around the reality that there really was a famous trio with those names. They were the advertising icons for a company of automotive service centers dating back a century and still thriving. Not quite as much of a myth breaker as Santa Claus or the Easter Bunny, but close.

My particular Manny, Moe, and Jack were Arnold, Steve, and Dave, in that order, and their truck cabs were blue, green, and red, in that order. There was definitely not the same lyrical quality to their real names as the car guys could boast. These were truckers with different companies who often traveled together. I decided I'd better head off Moe and Jack before they invoked a phrase or two that was not family friendly.

First, however, I had to pave the way for an idea I hoped they'd buy into. I made a quick trip to the kitchen, pulled Nina aside, and gave her a new rush job, then rushed myself out to greet the two truckers as they filed in.

"No Manny tonight?" I asked, as if that were the reason there wasn't an available booth nor three or even two empty stools together.

"He's been running late all day," Moe, aka Steve Carter, said, talking around a toothpick. "But, hey"—he switched the toothpick to the other side of his mouth—"what's happening here?"

Moe had his hands on his hips. I had the feeling he was ready to do battle, perhaps arm-wrestle over a spot.

I leaned in to diesel-scented jackets. "Tour bus," I said in a quiet voice. "But follow me. I have something special for you."

I walked toward the kitchen slowly, to give Nina as much time as possible to carry out my plan. When I saw what she'd been able to do in a matter of minutes, I mentally raised her salary. Earlier, I'd heard her explaining the subjects of the framed photographs and sketches on the walls to a family of four. Most of the photos, like the ones of Vitus Bering, the Danish explorer who was the discoverer of Alaska, were older than I was. I remembered as a kid memorizing scripts for each photo and it seemed that Nina had done the same. I could see that she had a future in the diner business.

Next to the wide metal table in the kitchen was a smaller wooden one we used for sides or temporary storage. Nina had found a tablecloth, probably left over from an office party of yore. She'd set it with three plates, glasses, a crystal-like pitcher of water, and a carafe of hot coffee. I could have sworn she'd also combed her hair. Her smile was wide and welcoming, as was that of her brother, who stood proudly behind her, ready to cook up dinners before their eyes.

I crossed my fingers behind my back to ward off the evil spirits of inspectors who might call this an infraction of a diner zoning rule, seating customers in the kitchen. *Desperate circumstances call for desperate measures,* I thought as I placed my hand over my heart to complete the ritual.

"We figured this would be more comfortable for you,

what with that crowd and all." I tipped my head toward the main dining area. The only dining area, usually. I wasn't as embarrassed as I should have been with such deception, but then, I did always try to put the customers' needs first. Mom would have been so proud, maybe even enough to erase my lack of civility with Oliver earlier in the day. I doubted he would have accepted this creative seating arrangement. Though I did miss him, I could see that there were advantages to his absence.

I stayed to chat with the flannel-clad drivers (Nina had hung up their jackets—Ritz-Carlton-style service) until their special meatloaf orders were ready. She placed their platters in front of them with a flourish.

Moe lowered his face to his plate and took a noisy whiff. "Moose, right?" he asked.

Victor nodded and placed a bottle of ketchup on the table, something Oliver would never acquiesce to. It wasn't long before Manny, aka Arnold Quinlan, the stockiest of the trio, as well as the oldest and most ready to retire, came in the front door. He was more disheveled than usual, looking like he'd had a bad day. Nina escorted him back to where his friends were ready to extol the special service this evening.

"Where's Oliver tonight?" Manny asked.

"Night off," Victor said. "But the same great moose-loaf," he said.

More meatloaf, more ketchup, and I excused myself to return to the main area to help Annie clear the plates and take dessert orders.

Another ordinary evening at the diner.

It always amazed me how many people called a bear claw dessert rather than a breakfast pastry. *They would qualify even more as a dessert if they had a layer of chocolate in their core,* I mused.

I was ready to approach the last booth and visit with—
i.e., query—Trooper and Chris. Imagine my surprise when
I looked back and found not my two so-called friends, but
a new crew of parka-clad millennials, three of them on
each side of the booth, also equipped with Denali literature.
More strays, like Pierre, driving on their own, I guessed.

Trooper and Chris must have used their booth as a meeting place, then once again escaped through the back door. I
saw that they'd had coffee only. Too bad they didn't have the
courtesy to leave when they saw that Moe and Jack needed
a place to sit. Not that I was peeved with them. They had
overpaid, after all, for coffee they'd hardly touched.

THE TOUR LEADER'S SECOND-IN-COMMAND AN-
nounced the end of dinner and told everyone to settle up at
the register and climb aboard the waiting vehicle. He'd
been sitting on a stool flirting with Nina for a lot of the time
and must have decided to call it quits when Nina went home
with her brother in what we called "the oldest jalopy in
Elkview."

Annie had a different plan for Pierre, having offered to
drive him to the inn in her pickup. I told her yes, of course
she could leave, since this wasn't her place of employment
in the first place, and, by the way, she wasn't getting paid,
except in food and drink.

"I'm taking him up on his suggestion of a nightcap," she
whispered to me. "He has photos of this ox where it's dig-
ging a hole to put some food in. Or something. I'm sort of
interested in those facts"—she waved her hand in the air as
if brushing off fleas—"but I'm hoping he'll tell me more
about his place in the Alps and all."

I didn't need to know the "and all," or anything else the

nightcap might bring about, though I knew I'd eventually hear details whether I asked for them or not. Annie had been through a series of unpleasant breakups, though none as recently as I could claim, and none where she had to return a ring.

I waved as Annie and Pierre left. She was the most easygoing person I knew, and I hoped she'd find someone who would appreciate her, no matter what country he lived in.

NOT FOR THE FIRST TIME, THE PROMISE OF A BIG storm didn't materialize, at least not by Alaska standards. The freezing rain had been reduced to mere snow flurries that hardly stuck to the ground. I was especially happy for the eager travelers who'd marked up their brochures and needed safe driving to make their trip pleasurable. The tourists I'd entertained this evening still had miles to go before they hit their destination. The bus would make a few stops, each one with spectacular river and mountain views and wildlife.

I still had a lot of baking ahead of me. Annie had ordered double digits of bear claws for those who chose to stay at the main house and enjoy a continental breakfast in the morning. In spite of that, I decided I could afford a nap.

As soon as the place cleared out, I put a sign on the door that said, in so many words, wake me up if you really, really need anything. The sign was designed by a friend of Mom's and thus had the seal of approval—Mom might take a nap now and then, but I couldn't remember a time when she'd actually closed the diner. She hired a string of students from the local community college who were only too happy to work the graveyard shift, serving a few stragglers while having most of the time available for doing their homework or surfing the net, and getting paid for it. I was happy for the mutual benefits.

I checked the schedule and noted that Tammy and Bert were due at one a.m. Perfect. Tammy was one of the few in the crew who knew how to bake. I could get her started on the bear claws and go home for a few hours. I hoped she didn't have a term paper due.

I rolled out the most comfortable chair in the kitchen, an old office chair that had seen better days but seemed perfectly contoured to my long torso. I plugged my phone into its charger and turned the chair so that my back was to the blinking diner sign—the red neon BEAR CLAW DINER in vertical array. Once I was comfortable, I hit the Benny app. He was fast asleep on a pile of blankets, including one king-size quilt, on a living room chair, his paws wrapped around his face, his feet tucked under him.

I told him I was sorry I hadn't gotten home since early afternoon and promised to head back as soon as I set Tammy up in the kitchen. I was asleep before I could hear his answer, though I thought I saw his tail twitch in approval.

AT FIRST I THOUGHT I WAS DREAMING. THUNDER? Loud music from a pickup? More like insistent banging on the front door of the diner. I shook my head awake, turned my chair around, and saw the source of the noise. Trooper Graham. He stood so the gold stripe down the length of his pant leg caught a reflection from our red sign, resulting in a strange orange glow. It wasn't unusual for him to show up at this hour, but he rarely woke me unless he was desperate for a cup of coffee and a bear claw, or simply bored. I regretted that there'd be no pastry tonight. The tourists had cleaned me out. Maybe he'd be satisfied with another corn muffin.

I hoisted myself from my pseudo-bed and made my way to the door.

"I should have saved you a bear claw," I told the trooper once he was over the threshold.

"Not here for that." His somber voice cued me to his grim face, and I remembered seeing the same look when he and Chris had come by during the tourist rush.

"What's up?" What I wanted to ask: *What was that page that had you and Chris rushing out of here all about?*

He motioned me to the first booth. "Have a seat."

Uh-oh.

I slid in across from Trooper, wishing I'd made a fresh pot of coffee, a touch of panic setting in. Was he bringing me bad news? Mom and Dad were thousands of miles away, having a good time, as of three o'clock this afternoon. Had things changed? Had they left the trooper's number as an emergency contact? Not likely, but I had no idea what international protocol might be. I had no other relatives to worry about. And I was between boyfriends, I thought, optimistically. Was Annie in trouble? Had that Frenchman . . . ? Was it Benny? My house? I lived only a stone's throw away; if my home had burned to the ground, I would have heard fire engines or even seen the flames.

Who or what else could bring about this serious turn? It dawned on me. I leaned forward, elbows and arms on the table.

"Oliver?"

"Why would you think that?" Trooper took out his notebook.

I gulped. "He's been gone all day." I looked at my watch. Twelve forty. "Actually, almost twelve hours. Was there an accident? The roads are—"

"No accident."

I frowned. "What, then?"

"Murder."

I pressed my back against the booth, as if I could sink into it and end up in another reality, one where Oliver was at the door of the Bear Claw, ready to cook, ready to bark about how someone had left his kitchen a mess, someone had served mustard, someone had added salt to his perfect recipe.

"How?" I thought I said, but my voice seemed to be echoing through my body.

"Were you here all day, Charlie?"

"Yes, with Oliver gone, I had to stay to be sure—"

"You didn't leave the diner all day?" he asked, scribbling something in his notebook.

"No, I—"

"Not between, say, one and two?"

I paused. "Oh, right. I stopped off at home to see Benny for a few minutes."

I strained to see what he was writing.

Trooper closed his notebook, slapped it on the palm of his hand, and slid out of the booth.

He took a long, loud breath as he walked away. "Just, don't leave town, okay, Charlie?" he called over his shoulder.

"Where would I go? Why—"

But the door closed behind him.

I was left with more questions than before he arrived, the biggest one being: Why was the trooper, who'd known me since I was a kid, treating me like I was a . . . I could hardly bring myself to finish the thought . . . a murderer?

* * *

THERE WAS NO GOING BACK TO SLEEP. I COULD EITHER
sit and stare at the Big Dipper on the state flag draped on
the wall, or do something useful. Like search the net for
information that wasn't forthcoming from my alleged
friend Trooper Graham.

My first efforts were futile. Oliver Whitestone's death—
murder—was apparently too recent or too unimportant to
make my local news feed or any search engine. A shudder
ran through me, traveling from my toes to my head as I
tried to absorb the reality that a person I knew well was
gone. I closed my eyes and focused on my breathing. I'd
been relatively lucky in that I'd never lost anyone close to
me, even from natural causes, let alone through violence. I
was a baby when my grandparents died, and my one deceased aunt, my father's sister, lived most her life and all of
mine in Florida.

I went back and sat on the chair I'd been napping on. My
gaze fell on the same booths, the same stools, the same
photos of our beautiful state—whale sighting in the Bering
Sea; the forget-me-not, our state flower; glaciers on the ma-
jestic Denali, the tallest peak in North America, at more
than twenty thousand feet. All were familiar, except now
everything had changed and the photos seemed blurry and
out of whack. Askew on the wall, or in my head? I looked
toward the through-window to the kitchen, my eyes swell-
ing with tears.

One thing I knew—I needed to leave the Bear Claw,
where Oliver's shadow hovered everywhere, sometimes
chiding me for wanting to change his menu, other times
laughing with me when I told him a Benny story, like the
time Benny's day-long toilet-flushing antics had run up my

water bill. One thing for sure now, I needed to get home to Benny, wake him up if I had to, talk to him.

I nearly kissed Tammy when she arrived about ten minutes early. She looked as cool in leggings as anyone over six years old could, with a bright green tunic top that might have taken first prize in last week's St. Patrick's Day parade. I remembered how Oliver would claim to be five percent Irish so he could take the day off and head south to Soldotna for the parade and a pub spree.

Was everything from now on, even a common color, going to remind me of Oliver?

As I'd waited for Tammy, I'd wrestled with whether to tell her about Oliver's murder. They seldom crossed paths in the Bear Claw, and I didn't see the point of concerning her for no reason.

I needn't have given it a second thought.

"Horrible thing, huh, Charlie?" Tammy said. She took a clean apron from the kitchen closet and tied it around her waist.

"How did you hear?"

"My boyfriend—he drove me here tonight—he has the police channel. I couldn't believe it. Do you know what happened?"

"What did they say on the radio?"

"Not much. You know how they say everything in code." Tammy shrugged. "Just that his body was found outside of town and they had no witnesses. Oh, and they gave a number to call if you have a tip, yada yada."

I couldn't fault Tammy's casual approach to Oliver's violent death. She hardly knew him, except for notes he would leave her. Reprimands for leaving the oil uncapped or failing to clean the grill to his standards or putting her notebooks on surfaces in contact with food.

I didn't trust myself to entertain murder theories with Tammy, or any human at the moment. I needed my tabby. I was saved from making the choice when a family of four that included two preteen boys came through the door. Usually when folks stopped in at this hour, they were looking for a restroom and a warm place to sit for a while. Tammy hopped to it and suggested hot chocolate for the boys.

When Bert arrived a few minutes later, I felt I could leave the diner in enough good hands. The two college students got along well and would work together to fill Annie's bear claw order. While they dealt with the recently arrived nuclear family, I wrote a detailed note to whip up a batch of four dozen bear claws, besides the inventory for the usual breakfast crowd. "Call if you have any problems," I added.

I extracted my jacket and keys from the back of the kitchen and headed for the back door. As I approached the exit, I heard Bert take the opportunity to engage in a game of punk-the-tourist.

The punk always started with a question from a customer, this time one of the young boys.

"Are there any elk in Elkview?" He smirked, unaware of what was coming, thinking he was the first to ask the question.

"There's one in the booth behind you," Bert said.

Before they could think about it, both boys gasped and jerked their heads around. Then they laughed, but not as hard as their parents.

At least some people were having fun.

FOUR

MY OUTBACK STILL HAD THAT NEW-CAR SMELL. I'D HAD
to wait for my color of choice, black, or "crystal black," as
the dealer called it. I could have had a white vehicle immediately, but even the salesman laughed at that idea for
driving in Alaska. Unless you didn't care that you might
lose your car in a snowstorm, a possibility any time except
the three summer months, white was a ridiculous idea.

I took my usual route home, through the main shopping
area of Elkview. At another hour of the day, old Lucas
would have been sitting on his porch, freezing, but unable
to give up his people watching. His souvenir shop sold nug-
gets, antler buckles, Native American crafts, I SCALED
DENALI shirts, quilts, assorted antiques, and maps.

For an extra dollar you could buy a map that was marked
up by Lucas himself, with suggestions for where to see an
elk; how to navigate ice; what the best turnoffs were if you
were hungry, thirsty, or ready for a spectacular view of Denali itself. I'd lost track of how much Lucas charged for

taking your photo with your head through a hole in a board, kissing an elk or a moose, or driving a dogsled.

I passed more gift shops on both sides of the broad street, made broader for lack of sidewalks. Who wanted a curb, a hidden stepping hazard when the snow came and blanketed the town? As I drove by my go-to coffee shop, I could have sworn I smelled Aly's famous Nutella crepes. Oliver had once brought a container of the crepes back to the Bear Claw and tried to reverse engineer the recipe, to no avail. Not even a generous pour of birch syrup could save Oliver's version. I didn't like competing with our local businesses and had been glad that Oliver's experiment failed.

It was not a good idea to think of Oliver while driving on the main road, even though the street was deserted. I took a left at the adults-only explorer's shop, where every sharp instrument known to climbers was for sale. The side street was easier to navigate, without all the paraphernalia left out by shop owners on the main road—broken wagon wheels, flags, sawed-off barrels, bushel baskets, oversize wood carvings. All odd pieces that passed for lawn decorations and were often left out all night.

My small house was on a lane parallel to the main shopping street, lined with western hemlock trees. I'd grown up in a four-bedroom, two-story Elkview rarity, where I kept expecting the baby sister or brother who was never to be. Now, every so often, my parents would talk about how they needed to downsize, but it never happened, and once I moved back to town they didn't even pretend anymore. They assumed I'd eventually move back into my old bedroom. I tried not to dwell on the idea that it might be up to me to populate the old homestead.

I rounded the corner onto my street, eager to get home to Eggs Benedict, who responded to both his formal name and his nickname. I expected him to bound from his likely spot on the top shelf of my bookcase as soon as I opened the door. If he didn't, I'd have to think twice about his loyalty.

I passed the one house that stood between the corner and my driveway, picturing my neighbor Earlene and her family in presumably worry-free sleep. I prepared myself to greet Benny and talk to him, get him up to speed on Oliver's passing, seek his advice on how to deal with the upsetting situation.

I had a long list of questions for him: When and how to tell Mom? How to locate Oliver's family? Who had killed him? That was a big one.

And an even bigger one: did Trooper Graham really consider me a suspect? No, I convinced myself. The only reason the trooper had asked me to stay in town was that he might need my input. Which was why I needed to gather my wits and pull together all I knew about Oliver's personal life. First thing tomorrow, I decided, I'd go through the files in Mom's home office and find Oliver's job application. Mom never threw anything out, so I was sure there was a folder somewhere from his first day on the job.

I was surprised to realize how little I knew about my head chef. We overlapped at the diner when I was thirteen and he was in his early thirties, so we didn't exactly become friends. We almost never interacted outside of the diner, except for occasional chance meetings downtown. And now we never would, I thought, a lump forming in my throat.

Oliver lived on the outskirts of town, near the airport, while I lived close to the main streets. I recalled a time when a man claiming to be Oliver's brother came to the Bear Claw looking for him. Of course, I wouldn't give him Oliver's address, but I did share his expected work hours.

When the man finally came in at a time when Oliver was in the Bear Claw's kitchen, the two had an argument that was over-the-top volatile, even by Oliver standards. Other than that incident, I'd never met any of Oliver's relatives, if indeed that man was one. The alleged brother was tall, thin, and fair-skinned, none of which could have been said of Oliver, who would never answer any questions about the man.

I'd met Oliver's current girlfriend only once besides this afternoon. She'd come to pick up Oliver one of the times his van broke down. I was sure Trooper would have figured that out by now, although I didn't know when "by now" was, since I didn't know when exactly Oliver's body had been discovered. Or by whom. Or where. Tammy had mentioned a police radio saying "outside the town." Elkview was less than thirty square land miles. According to the tour books I'd had to study for my visitors' center jobs, the state of Alaska registered more than six hundred thousand square miles. That was a lot of "outside the town."

I was ready for the deep sigh of relief I released when I pulled into my driveway. *Home at last.* But my headlights landed not on my pale green stoop, newly painted for the coming summer months, but on a man, an official guardian of the Forty-Ninth.

Trooper Cody Graham.

Trooper was perched on the edge of the Adirondack chair on my porch, bent over, his winter uniform jacket zipped to his neck, his hat on his head. Where was his vehicle? The one with the cartoon bear's head on the door. Probably parked around by my back door. Did he think I'd flee if I saw the patrol car out front? Start a wild car chase through Elkview and out to where I had a getaway bush plane waiting?

"Trooper," I said, exiting my vehicle.

"Charlotte."

Charlotte. This was not a social call, then. As if the hour for the visit wasn't my first clue. He hadn't come looking for a leftover bear claw. He wasn't shivering, so he couldn't have been sitting out very long in what my car's dashboard said was twenty-three-degree weather.

"Would you like a cup of coffee?" Pretending everything was normal. It was one thirty in the morning and my chef was dead, murdered, but the state trooper and I were going to have coffee and a snack.

"Sounds good."

So far, so good. No handcuffs clanked, awaiting my wrists. He didn't read me my rights. We stepped inside. For all I knew, Trooper had already been inside. I still did not lock my door very often, though an increase in the tourist trade only a block over had changed the habits of many Elkview residents.

"Can't trust the rabble from those states," old Lucas would sometimes say about the people who kept him in business. Never mind that Alaska had been one of those states since 1959, ushered in by President Eisenhower. I wouldn't have been surprised if Lucas had been one of those who had opposed the propositions for statehood.

As I'd hoped, Benny was waiting on top of my bookcase and leapt down. He made his way to my ankles. He had clearly heard my car and was ready for some serious petting, which usually started with his own expert weaving around my legs. He knew Trooper Graham well enough not to be intimidated by him. I picked him up, giving him a better shot at crawling around my shoulders. I knew that his automatic feeder still had a good supply of food, but with my free hand took a can of his favorite meal from the cabinet anyway. Before I headed for the can opener, I held the can up to Trooper in a silent do-you-mind gesture.

"Go right ahead," he said. "He's the mayor, right?"

"If Talkeetna can have one, why not Elkview?"

I got Benny settled with his midnight snack. While I got the coffee ready, Trooper and I spent a few minutes rehashing the story of nearby Talkeetna's famous cat, Stubbs (he who was without a tail), a pale orange tabby who'd reigned as the town's mayor for twenty years until his death a few years ago. One legend had it that Talkeetna, an unincorporated Census Designated Place, like Elkview, couldn't come to a consensus on its human representatives, so someone started a write-in campaign for Stubbs.

"They were all sleazy pols," Trooper reminded me, naming a few of his favorites.

"Stubbs won by a landslide." I laughed. It was nice to have a shared history, especially when entertaining a law enforcement officer about to interrogate you.

I arranged assorted cookies on a plate, from the enormous batch Mom had made before she left for the cruise. As if I needed another reminder to call her.

"Told your mother yet?"

I shook my head no, wondering how Trooper seemed to always be able to zero in on my thoughts. At the moment, that would be a good thing, I reasoned, since he'd be able to see, quote-unquote, that I was innocent of any harm that had come to my chef.

"I don't want to ruin her trip."

"What time is it there anyway?" he asked.

I checked my kitchen clock. "Ten hours ahead, so it's getting toward noon in Germany."

"She's up."

I groaned. "So she'll be getting news on her phone."

"But Elkview news?"

"I think my dad added a *Bugle* app before they left."

Why was I trying to talk myself out of contacting my mother myself?

"You don't want her to hear it from someone on the ship. You have no idea how they get news from home. Your mother mentioned that a couple from Palmer would be on the cruise with them, right?"

"Uh-huh. Stella and Barney Russell. Dad knows him from a conference panel they were on. Then they all got together afterward and have stayed friends."

"Palmer's only about an hour away. If the Russells talk to their family here, there's a good chance the crime will be part of that conversation."

The crime. Panic was on its way. "I need to call them."

"And your mother will have your father, plus the Russells, to talk to if she needs that support."

"Maybe if I knew more details." A ploy, but I needed one badly.

As soon as he'd finished eating, Benny hopped on my lap. He ignored the cookies—second-rate compared to the gourmet meal he'd just consumed—and curled around my torso like a bulletproof vest.

I noticed Trooper sliding cookie after cookie off the plate and into his mouth and realized he probably hadn't eaten since that pot pie hours ago. Unlike me, he didn't work in a diner, able to sneak a slice of meatloaf here and a slab of pie there. And unlike Benny, he didn't have an automatic programmable feeder available in his office or patrol car. Besides all that, Trooper's wife, June, a sometime-deputy to her husband, had been out of town for a couple of weeks, visiting relatives on the Panhandle. He'd probably run out of the meals she'd stocked up for him.

And still he'd let me feed Benny before feeding him. No wonder I had a soft spot for him, even though he'd practically accused me of committing murder.

Without asking, I journeyed to my fridge, releasing Benny in the process, and brought out everything that was within its best-by date—deli meat, cheeses, crudités. I added bread and condiments and placed the offerings on the table.

"Now we're talking," he said, constructing what my father used to call a Dagwood sandwich in the days before he started counting calories.

"Does that include you? Talking?"

"He was found in the bush, away from his house, around three yesterday afternoon." He took a wide-mouthed bite of what might have been a three-inch-thick sandwich. I tried not to picture what "found in the bush" was like.

I was grateful, however, to have some real information. If I'd known that all he needed was food, I'd have fed him a lot sooner. "There's pie, too," I said.

He almost smiled. "Doc guessed it happened a couple of hours before he was found." Another bite of sandwich while I took in this information. Oliver was killed very soon after he left the diner. *Stormed out of the diner,* I reminded myself. "Covered with a tarp, some branches," Trooper continued. "Not a big effort to hide him. Probably in a hurry."

I gulped, almost sorry I'd asked for details. I let out a long sigh, struggled to keep back tears. "How—?"

"Doc says it was more than one bullet to his chest. He says someone who was not a good shot."

Which might have been anyone over twenty-one in

Alaska. We had no other requirements for owning a gun—no permit, no registration, no concealed-carry law, no waiting period for the purchase of a handgun, rifle, or shotgun.

"You own a gun, Charlie?"

Again, reading my mind. "No, I don't." *But thanks for getting back to calling me Charlie.* "You know Mom would never allow it."

"Gotta ask."

"Look, I know I have a short temper. You know that from back when I was too short to get up on the stool by myself."

"That I do."

"I feel awful, Trooper. I liked Oliver, appreciated his talent, even though we didn't always see eye to eye."

"Like yesterday."

"Like yesterday," I echoed.

TROOPER HADN'T QUITE SAID I WAS IN THE CLEAR, BUT I felt a lot better about my situation than before he'd eaten about two days' worth of my food. And he hadn't cuffed me and taken me away with him. He'd offered to stay around while I called my parents, but I was ready to be alone, which meant with just Benny.

I sat with Benny for a few more minutes, acknowledged to him and me that I was stalling needlessly, and that I owed it to my mom especially to be the one to deliver the bad news.

I kept Benny on my lap—as if I could send him off if I wanted to—and rehearsed for a bit what I would say. Slipping my hands around in Benny's fur, in rhythm with his purring, had the calming effect it always did. I put my chin on top of his head for a while, and then I called Mom's cell.

"Hi, kid. How are you?" My dad's voice.

"Is this a good time to talk for a few minutes?" I asked.

"We're in the middle of lunch with the Russells and some other people. Can you call back in a half hour or so?"

"Sure. This can wait."

"Okay."

I was about to end the call when I heard my mom in the background. "I'll take that." Then, "Sweetie, it's the middle of the night there. Is something wrong?"

It was all I needed. I tore through the story, complete with sobs, hardly stopping for a breath. I told her the few facts I knew, leaving out the part where Trooper had asked for my alibi and whether I owned a gun. When my mom ended up comforting me, I figured I was doing something wrong. Oliver had been her friend for many years. I should have been comforting her.

"I'm so sorry, Mom."

"You have to help him, Charlie."

"What? Who?"

"Cody. Trooper Graham. You have to help him. He has no staff to speak of, as you know, and you know how much help he's likely to get from Anchorage, or even Talkeetna, for a crime in Elkview."

I let her go on for a while about the low ratio of law enforcement officers to citizens in our state and how our town was safer than only three percent of the cities in the United States. I made it a practice never to argue about statistics, especially with my mom. I resorted to helplessness as a strategy.

"There's nothing I can do. I'm not a detective."

"You went to law school."

"For a year, Mom. Remember?"

"That's a year more than anyone else I can think of right

now. And you're smart. You can pay Trooper back for all those math lessons he gave you."

"But—"

"Charlie, there's nothing I can do now for my friend. And in all those mystery books I read, the detectives always say that you have to get going on solving a murder right away or the trail goes cold."

I had to laugh. I knew my mom read a lot, but I didn't realize that crime novels were featured, or that she'd adopted the jargon of the crime buffs of the world.

"Who are you and what have you done with my mother?"

"A girl, even an old one, has to keep her secrets."

"Mom—"

"Just say you'll try, sweetie. Promise me you'll try."

Of course, I agreed, emphasizing "try." I explained it to Benny, back on my lap and determined to challenge me for the mug of hot chocolate I'd brought to the rocker, attempting to hit it out of my hand with his soft paw.

What kind of help could I give Trooper? Mom didn't seem to know the difference between a criminal investigator and someone who had spent a harrowing year touching on civil procedure, contracts, property law. A whole class on constitutional law, another on legal methods. We covered a lot of ground, but I didn't remember hearing the word "homicide." Ever.

In the end, I'd decided the law was not for me. Whether the decision had anything to do with being dumped by my lawyer fiancé for his adorable young paralegal, I couldn't say without a lot of therapy I wasn't willing to invest in. If Benny couldn't figure it out, who could?

As usual, Benny turned his furry body around and around on my dark blue bathrobe. I heard myself entertaining counterarguments meant to bolster my confidence. Certainly finding

Oliver's killer swiftly would also bring a swift close to the notion that I had anything to do with it. I could only guess that others might suspect me, especially anyone who'd ever seen me have it out with Oliver, not just yesterday, but on and off through the last months.

Victor, his sister Nina, and many regular patrons were on the list of those who knew of our contentious relationship. I'd once heard Manny, of Manny, Moe, and Jack, arguing with Oliver about his arguing with me. I'd had no idea he'd been paying attention to what went on in the kitchen. If anything, I considered him Oliver's friend, since the two of them often ate lunch together when their schedules coincided.

Those I knew very well, like Annie, were off the list, but all the others might well be labeled suspicious, even in some small way. I desperately wanted to take Chris and his journalistic pen off the list, but I couldn't bring myself to do that yet.

Mom had said she'd text me any auxiliary contact information she had for Oliver. Now that I knew of her hitherto secret reading habit, I made a note to ask her for a bibliography to jump-start my investigation.

But the first order of business was to let Trooper know he had a willing partner in the job ahead. As soon as I had a few hours of sleep, I'd be ready to help him solve our friend's murder.

FIVE

"ABSOLUTELY NOT."

Trooper's voice came across the phone line louder than the industrial-strength blender I'd bought for the diner's ice cream shakes.

I could have blamed my mom for urging me to insert myself into the investigation. *She made me do it, Trooper.* Or simply bowed out, grateful I had an excuse to give Mom for keeping my distance. A mandate from law enforcement, in fact.

Some might have called it stubbornness, some determination, still others foolishness. But whatever it was, I'd spent a good deal of energy talking myself into accepting Mom's assignment, and I wasn't going to let it go so easily.

"Can we talk about it over rhubarb pie?" I asked Trooper. "I still have some of Mom's preserves from last summer."

"Not fair, Charlie. I'll eat your pie, but I still won't let you interfere with this case."

"It will be ready after the breakfast rush." *And it's not interfering, it's helping,* I added to myself.

Besides, I'd already begun, in a way, by looking through Mom's files. As I expected, her records were impeccable. But it seemed that Mom had hired Oliver on something other than a completed application. Oliver had written his name, address, and Parisian credentials, with one reference from a professor. I had to applaud her good instincts, but wished there were useful information. This would never have passed muster if he had been applying for a government security clearance.

Annie's crowd was due any minute, agitating for coffee and bear claws at a minimum, but I found time to dig out one pie's worth of strawberry-rhubarb preserves from the canning closet. Then I pulled out another jar, in case someone else needed motivation today.

Victor had come in early, happy to help while I figured out how to replace Oliver. Or replace Victor, if he moved into Oliver's post.

Elkview didn't have the attraction of Anchorage or Fairbanks, though it had become a second gathering place, after the larger Talkeetna, for climbers on their way to and from Denali. There were not a lot of chefs clamoring to work in an Elkview diner. It had been different at my old job in San Francisco. With no effort on the manager's part, the news of an opening would spread around the city's major restaurants. When I gave my notice, a steady stream of hopefuls made its way into the manager's office within a few days.

Here in my hometown, I might start with a CHEF WANTED sign in the window and move up to an ad in Chris's paper, the *Elkview Bugle*, as well as papers in Anchorage. Neither seemed the right thing to do when Oliver hadn't been laid to rest yet.

I'd received the text from Mom with the name of Oliver's older sister, Kendra Burke, whom he'd never mentioned to me. Mom had added the tag "administrator," though she hadn't said what exactly Kendra administered. The latest address Mom had was in Anchorage, Alaska's largest city and, most tourists were surprised to know, the fourth-largest city in the US, by land area. There would be a great many job opportunities for administrators in all fields. She could be anywhere.

In Mom's text was also the name of an ex-girlfriend of Oliver's, Lana. Oliver had never married, but apparently always had a girlfriend. When I asked about the tall, thin, presumptive relative who'd visited Oliver in the diner a month or two ago, Mom said he had no brother that she knew of.

Annie called while I was gearing up to help Victor in the kitchen, and Nina, who'd also clocked in early, at the tables.

"I heard," Annie said. "I'm so sorry, Charlie. It's awful."

"Is it in the paper?"

"My paper hasn't come. You know my second cousin—"

"Is Doc's receptionist, nurse, and answering machine. I know. And Doc is also—"

"The medical examiner, yes. Flo wouldn't have said anything to anyone else. You should have called me last night."

"It wasn't until after midnight that I heard, Annie, and I didn't know if—"

"If Pierre and I—?"

"Well, yes, Pierre and you."

"Not yet," was all she'd say.

Wasn't I lucky to have a friend I could speak with in shorthand?

THE BUS WITH ANNIE'S GUESTS PULLED UP AND BEHIND it Annie herself, with Pierre, in her pickup. I figured Annie would tell me more about their evening whether or not I asked.

I didn't have an exact count from last night, but there seemed to be more people climbing down the bus's steps today. Maybe due to rave reviews for last night's mooseloaf? I could only hope. In any case, I was glad Tammy and Bert had made enough bear claws and crepe batter for a small army.

In minutes, the diner was almost at capacity, with only one booth free when a climbing foursome came in, all in worn and nicked parkas that had seen their share of ice and mud—a sharp contrast to the clean and shiny parkas of the tour group.

We'd had word that the weather and road conditions to the north were not good enough for traveling. Instead, today would be a day of hiking locally. It was bound to happen: one of the tourists exclaimed, "But it's snowing."

"It's Alaska," said another, thus sparing a native from reminding the travelers where they were.

Another tourist was smart enough to recognize the four pros, three men and one woman, when she saw them. She talked the four into giving informal advice on the nearby trails. I noticed that Beth, the tour guide, seemed miffed when one of the climbers took over, planting himself on a stool in the center of the diner, rippling through the pluses and minuses of all the nearby tracks, trails, and loops. He included the skill level needed, the elevation, and the total mileage commitment, and even the types of trees found at different heights. He described birch, spruce, cottonwood, in ascending order. There was an outburst of laughter when he designated one trail as having a "low avalanche hazard." He took a final round of applause with aplomb. I hoped Beth would get her fair share of gratitude before the trip was over.

I snapped to attention when the *Bugle* truck pulled up. Its driver unceremoniously tossed a bundle of newspapers in front of the diner. I threw on my jacket and slipped outside through the back door, eager to see what, if any, coverage there was of Oliver's murder. I dragged the bundle inside and extracted the top paper. I took a seat on a stool at the freezer end of the kitchen and scanned the headlines.

News from Anchorage about their tripod watch: the ice on the Tanana River was due to break up soon and tip over the tripod standing on it. The lower forty-eight has its Groundhog Day; Alaska has its tripod weather beacon and its Marmot Day. I skimmed a heartwarming tale of a grocery clerk who adopted a child about to age out of the foster care system. I barely noticed that the governor's budget was rejected a second time. Finally, I caught a glimpse of the word "murder" in a heading, directing me to page four. I rustled the paper to that page, not caring whether the folds stayed neat. The story was about a killing in Palmer, the hometown of the couple my parents were traveling with. A man was stabbed to death over an undisclosed incident that had taken place twenty-five years ago in Utqiagvik, the northernmost city in the United States.

Who waits a quarter of a century to exact revenge? For that matter, why do *Elkview Bugle* subscribers need to read about it in column space that could have been devoted to the slaying of one of its own? I crumpled the paper into a messy ball and tossed it into the recycle bin just outside the back door.

"Hey, that's my livelihood you're trashing."

Chris's voice, teasing as it was, surprised me. He'd parked his beat-up pickup, crossed the parking lot, and arrived at the trash bins before I saw him. If I hadn't been so annoyed with the lack of meaningful coverage in our local paper, his paper, I might have been embarrassed.

"What's the story?" he asked, pointing to the blue container where the *Bugle* had landed.

"My question exactly. Technically, *where's* the story?"

"You mean about Oliver." His face turned somber.

He followed me into the diner and we took seats at yesterday's ad hoc dining area. With a pang of sorrow, I realized we didn't have to worry what Oliver would think of the arrangement. Or of the ketchup.

"Trooper says you've got some rhubarb pie," Chris said. I could tell he was doing his best to keep me stable, whatever that meant.

"Not yet. And are you two joined at the hip or what? Did he send you to talk me out of wanting to help with the investigation? I want you to know, I've already got some notes. I have phone numbers, and also I looked up some stats on crime in the state and in this area, as well as the rate of solving them. Trooper's foolish if he doesn't recognize that he needs help."

"I agree."

"He's in over his head. He needs us." I paused, cocked my head. "You what?"

"I agree with you. I'm on your side."

"Oh."

"That's what I want to talk to you about. I have resources at the paper; you have the personal knowledge—and, well, you're smart."

It might not have been the nicest thing anyone ever said, or at all true, but in my current state, I needed to believe any compliment that came my way.

"We need to convince Trooper," I said.

"That's easier said."

"It shouldn't be hard for you. You've been buddy-buddy lately." Not that I was peeved or anything about the way Trooper and Chris seemed to have some important secrets.

"It was just a coincidence that Trooper and I were working on a story about how all the law enforcement agencies work together in the state, and then Oliver went missing and I happened to be there when he found out."

I tried not to show my embarrassment at jumping to conclusions. I put my energy elsewhere and came up with an idea.

"We need to devise an investigative plan before he tells us we can't."

"I'm in," he said.

I looked out at the tables. People were chatting and eating. A good sign. It seemed Annie had already taken over management duties. She caught my eye and gave me a thumbs-up that said everything was under control. I realized we needed an IOU signal and made a mental note to do something special for her when this energy drain was over.

I returned my attention to Chris and my mug of coffee. He had positioned his tablet back to back with my laptop and had begun to make notes. A quick study.

"We need to list all the possibles," he said. "If you don't mind, I'm leaving you and me off the list."

"Did he ask for your alibi, too?"

"Only for the thirty minutes we were out of each other's sight yesterday. He's part of that feature I'm writing on law enforcement. He has many years of service and has been involved in all kinds of incidents. I'm on sort of a protracted ride-along."

"It's unnerving, isn't it, when he views you as a suspect?"

He mimicked a shudder passing through his shoulders. "Imagine how a guilty person would feel."

"I don't know, maybe nothing," I said. "If they're cold enough to kill another human being, do they even have feelings?"

"Good point."

We abandoned the heavy talk and got to work, filling in a chart with the names and contact information that we had. Chris had access to databases available only to members of the press. "And other privileged groups, like law enforcement," he said.

"Trooper might already have all this," I said.

His phone pinged. A text message came in at the same time that my phone rang. Chris stepped away to check his message while I accepted my call. It dawned on me that we had different motives for pouring ourselves into Oliver's case. For Chris, it meant being on the front lines, able to report minute-by-minute progress and, ultimately, have a scoop on the result. Was he hoping that the *Elkview Bugle* would get its name on the map with a Pulitzer? Would it be disqualified if the Pulitzer committee found out that the *Bugle* was named for the bugle, the cry of the elk, a high-pitched screech made by the male elk during mating season?

Why was *I* suddenly so keen on participating in a murder investigation? How presumptuous of me to assume I knew Chris's motive when I was unsure of my own.

My call was a quick one. While I waited for Chris to finish his, I snuck a visit with Benny via my cell phone. I decided to lay off the laser dot game for another block of time. I'd bought him a robotic mouse that I could operate remotely. I wasn't surprised that it didn't hold his attention.

"You're smart enough to know it's not a real mouse, aren't you?" I asked Benny. "And therefore it's not as tasty."

Benny shot a look of disgust at the robot and marched away across the kitchen floor. Poor Benny. I was terrible company. A neglectful pet companion.

I remembered that a couple of weeks ago, a diner customer told me her cat loved to fetch.

"I thought that was a dog thing," I'd said.

"Yes, but cats like it, too."

She told me she discovered it when her cat was pestering her while she was on the phone. She tossed a hard candy wrapped in cellophane into the next room and the cat brought it back to her. She threw it farther away; the cat fetched again. It was worth a try with Benny as soon as I got home. For now, I signed off with him, promising I'd be home at a decent hour tonight.

"You look like you have news, too," Chris said, when he'd hung up.

"You first," I said.

He wiggled his cell phone in the air, showing me the source of his information. "We don't have to worry that Trooper is getting way ahead of our chart. Major snowmobile accident near Girdwood, involving broken ice and a couple of passenger vehicles."

"Is that Trooper's jurisdiction?"

"It's not completely clear, but it's all hands on deck, no matter what. Even Josh, Trooper's deputy who looks like a teenager, is being pressed into service. So Trooper won't be giving much attention to a homicide in Elkview. On my to-do list is a piece on the state's law enforcement program. Especially on the paucity of personnel in the small villages. Something like one in three communities have no cops closer than a half-hour flight away."

"It's a good thing we're on the job."

Chris pointed to my cell phone, now resting on the table

between us. "How about your call? Something pertinent to Oliver's case?"

I smiled. "My mom's on her way home."

OUR CONNECTION HADN'T BEEN THE BEST, BUT FROM what I gathered, my mom would be arriving in Anchorage sometime tomorrow evening by way of Seattle, by way of Amsterdam, and starting out in Vienna. I assumed she'd call from Seattle, where the connection was sure to be better. Part of me wondered if she'd faked the bad connection, the first unclear one of their trip, so I wouldn't have a chance to try to dissuade her from cutting her vacation short. I did hear "I" a lot, rather than "we." Dad hadn't interacted much with Oliver over the years, except to withstand Mom's periodic rants about him. Knowing her, she'd convinced him to stay on and finish his business with Barney Russell.

For another twenty-four hours or so, the coast was clear for Chris and me to fill in the details of our investigation. I'd talked things over with my full-time staff and decided that we would operate the Bear Claw as normally as possible for the next few days, using our usual cadre of reinforcements that we brought in when entire buses unloaded on us, a phenomenon that was on the upswing ever since Annie had reopened her parents' inn. When we knew the details of Oliver's service, which might in fact be up to Mom and me, we'd close the diner for the day to walk-in patrons and arrange for a gathering of family, friends, and regulars who knew and cared about Oliver.

At Chris's prodding, I set Nina up with the rhubarb pie ingredients and recipe, in case Trooper did drop in. And in case Chris had a craving. It boggled my mind the way Chris stayed so fit, given the number of calories he consumed in front of me, let alone the rest of his day. Today he was wearing a long-sleeved polo shirt that strained around his biceps. Not that I was paying particular attention.

We spent another hour—long enough for the pie to be prepared and come out of the oven—dividing up our suspect list and working out a strategy.

I volunteered to talk to Doc Sherman, our local physician and, when necessary, medical examiner. "Annie's cousin works for the Doc," I reminded Chris. "He might be willing to tell us more about the condition of, you know." *When did I become squeamish?* When I knew the person who had the condition, I guessed.

"That works," Chris said, not forcing me to finish the sentence. "I was thinking I could make contact with Kendra, Oliver's sister, with the idea that I'm interviewing her for the paper."

We carried on, filling my laptop and Chris's tablet with notes and ideas for lines of inquiry, doing searches for addresses and social media profiles. *What a team,* I thought, wondering if Chris had any idea of following up sometime later, much later, with a date. I decided I'd give him a month, then broach the subject myself.

We'd been friends on and off since high school, though we'd never dated. Chris had hung with the jock crowd; I'd been on the debate team. Not that I was smarter; sometimes what we did in high school had little to do with later choices or what we'd learn about our talents and real interests. It was certainly true of me—short-term law student followed by chef and restaurant manager. If I thought about his future at all, I pictured Chris marrying Kelleyanne, the head cheerleader, and coaching Little League. Wasn't that how it usually turned out? I couldn't remember how I had pictured myself.

One thing for sure: now was not the time to think about that.

I caught a glimpse of Annie now and then and, aside from feeling guilty that she was doing my job, I was impressed that she gave equal time to all the tables, not lingering at the captivating Pierre's.

Just before nine a.m., Beth called an end to breakfast and the tables cleared. Nina took the pie out of the oven, and at the same time Trooper Graham strode through the back door.

Chris and I scrambled to close the covers on our devices, stuff the sticky notes into our pockets, and paint on innocuous smiles. So much for confronting him with our plan.

Trooper chuckled. "Thought so."

We hemmed and hawed—"We were just catching up on the news"—then the three of us had a laugh that cleared the air.

SIX

IT DIDN'T TAKE LONG FOR THE SIX OF US IN THE DINER
to demolish a whole pie.

In deference to the fact that we were an investigative
team at a business meeting, though Trooper hadn't quite
bought into the idea yet, Victor, Nina, and Annie took their
half of the pie to a booth at the other end of the diner. I
figured Annie was disappointed that Pierre had joined the
tour group, bound for a day of hiking, instead of hanging
out with her, but she seemed in okay spirits.

Trooper gave us an update on the situation in Girdwood,
which seemed a complicated traffic accident, an amalgam of
an impaired automobile driver and allegedly faulty snowmobile equipment.

"On top of that, some hikers wandered off onto a mush-
ing trail."

Uh-oh. Our knowledgeable patrons had earlier warned
Beth's hiking group, as I thought of my recent breakfasters,
that the rule was strictly enforced: hikers were to yield the

right-of-way to dog teams. I hoped the group had paid attention.

"One fatality from the traffic accident," he reported, "and he was an elected official from Anchorage. Can't release the name yet, but there's a mountain of paperwork and the political fallout to deal with."

Trooper pointed out that more resources might be poured into a district assemblyman—"Oops," he said—than an Elkview diner chef.

Whether it was the delicious, warm rhubarb pie and excellent coffee or a simple acknowledgment of the enormous tasks before him, Trooper seemed amenable to having some help with Oliver's case.

"Nothing dangerous, you understand?"

We nodded. We wouldn't dream of it.

"I'm serious. For instance, neither one of you goes anywhere alone if it involves the case."

Chris and I looked at each other and, though we couldn't see through the covers of our devices, looked down at the spots where our plans lay, our gazes seeming to burn through metal.

"I was planning to see the Doc by myself," I said, with somewhat of a pleading tone.

"Doc is not going to tell you anything without a badge."

I mentally scratched Doc Sherman off my list. This was not going as well as I'd hoped. I thought of piggybacking on my mom's opinion of my investigative skills and reminding Trooper that I'd had a course in depositions in law school. On second thought, I decided, I should leave it to my mom herself to convince her old friend the trooper that her daughter had extraordinary talents as an interviewer.

"Oliver's sister should be okay seeing me," Chris said. "I'd talk to her as a reporter."

"Kendra?" Trooper shook his head. "Is she on your list of suspects? You *have* made a list of suspects, I assume."

"We have," we both said, like two middle schoolers, excited to have the right answer for the teacher.

"We thought of her more as a source of information," Chris said.

"You never heard of siblings taking a shot at each other?" Trooper paused while I silently acknowledged that I had. Chris tapped his fingers on the table as if counting the number of sibling murders he could think of. "Well?" Trooper continued. "She's a suspect until she's not, and you don't go there alone."

I didn't know about Chris, but I wished we hadn't waited for the pie. We would have been on the road by now, carrying out our plan, without Trooper's nonnegotiable admonishments. Sitting across from him now, with three witnesses close by, it would be hard to claim ignorance of his rules. As it was, we promised to stay together, and to let Trooper know ASAP of any information that was newer than what we might hear on the radio or read in the paper.

"Or on your phones," Trooper added, with an air of coolness, as if proud that an old guy like him knew about smartphone news apps.

Trooper stood, stepping out from the table. "Okay. Now stand up."

We did.

"I'm going to deputize you. Raise your right hands."

We did.

"Repeat after me: I solemnly swear to uphold the laws of Matanuska-Susitna Borough in the State of Alaska, so help me God."

We repeated it.

"Wow, I didn't know that was a thing," Chris said.

"It isn't," Trooper said. "But it felt good, didn't it?"

He donned his hat and left.

WE'D BEEN TRICKED BY THE WEATHER GODS INTO thinking the snow was over for the season. Lately, temperatures had been in the forties—practically flip-flop weather. But today the Department of Transportation issued an extensive list of warnings. Even though only light snow was predicted, we heard reminders of frosted surfaces, frozen slush, icy patches, and black ice.

"Stay back two hundred feet from snowplows and other snow removal equipment on the roadways," warned a weatherman, in the happy tones of someone who finally had something exciting to report.

With all of that in mind, Chris and I headed for the *Bugle* office.

Chris and I agreed we'd start with an easy one, the recorded history of familial murder aside. The *Bugle* had all the databases it was legal to download, and we expected to find Kendra Burke's current address and place of employment without a problem. While Chris did that, I wandered the modest-sized newsroom. Not abuzz as I'd imagined from TV dramas. A mere half dozen people, each working solo, seated at desks with laptops and a mess of peripherals, and the occasional blooming plant.

The walls were covered with articles someone had thought worthy of framing. Maybe each newsperson got to pick her or his proudest moment. I checked them out. A profile of a local stand-up comic, signed by said comic; a successful effort, spearheaded by *Bugle* staff, to save a his-

toric house in town; a photograph of a winning kids' baseball team, with a trophy proclaiming them the best in the
borough. An article and a set of images featuring Sitka's
famed onion-domed St. Michael's Cathedral, a remnant of
early Russian control of Alaska.

I was mesmerized by a set of photos documenting a
group of climbers starting out in Talkeetna, the town where
climbers came to stage their expeditions to Denali. Photos
showed them eating a hearty breakfast, then boarding a
plane that would take them to the base of the Kahiltna Glacier at around seven thousand feet, and then climbing another thirteen thousand feet to the summit.

I was shivering from my intense scrutiny of icy mountains and waterfalls, as if I'd been scaling the peak myself,
when I heard Chris call out.

"South Anchorage Realty. A small branch of a major
player that's based downtown, it seems. I'll take her home
address also."

"It's a little scary how you can get all that so quickly."

"It's a good thing I'm trustworthy," he said, pulling his
knit cap down over his eyebrows.

"A sinister look if I ever saw one."

"Truthfully, it took a little longer than it should have to
find Kendra. I figured Kendra Burke might be too common,
so I added 'Whitestone' as a middle or maiden name.
That's Oliver's last name, right?"

"Right."

"I got nothing. 'Kendra Burke' worked, however."

"Interesting."

It was time to embark on our first official interview. Too
bad Trooper hadn't really made us official. Maybe if there
had been a Bible in the diner? And a couple of badges in the
cutlery drawer?

* * *

IT MIGHT HAVE MADE SENSE TO COMBINE THE TWO UP-coming reasons for heading to Anchorage—to interview Kendra, and to pick up my mom at the airport tomorrow evening. But we were both eager to put Oliver's killer away and to do our part in making sure that happened. Besides, there was no telling when Mom would arrive, what with all the connections necessary to complete her trip.

The next strategic question was whether to call ahead to Kendra.

"It makes sense. It's a two-hour ride," Chris said. "What if she's on vacation?"

"What if it spooks her?"

"That would be assuming she has something to hide."

"It's not as easy as I thought it would be. Being depu-tized," I said.

Chris laughed. "Let's go. It's only a two-hour ride."

We settled on heading for the real estate office at ten, giv-ing us time to pack our standard traveling-in-Alaska emer-gency bags. My auto parts duffel lived in the trunk of my car permanently. One could never tell where the next service sta-tion would be, whether it would be open, or if it would have fuel if it was open. Every native I knew carried spare parts—hoses, tires, pumps, gas can, spark plugs among them—and knew how to use them. My duffel wasn't quite as large and high-tech as the famed Gamow bag that fit an entire person who needed a change in altitude to treat mountain sickness, but I wasn't planning on scaling Denali today.

My second duffel was for the day's trip. Crackers, cheese, chocolate, and of course two carefully wrapped bear claws. I threw in a couple of less-than-perfect tangerines. Fresh fruit was scarce at this time of year. Vacationers to the lower forty-eight were known to smuggle in a pear or a mango as souvenirs. Summer was our produce season, when we could expect zucchini the size of Benny, thanks to all-night sunshine.

I checked the first-aid kit and declared the bags ready to go.

I felt confident leaving the Bear Claw in the hands of my staff. Victor was in an especially good mood, high-fiving Nina when she ordered Adam and Eve on a raft.

"Two eggs on toast," Victor explained to a small boy on a stool, who sat mesmerized at the whole kitchen scene. Victor and Nina had a running contest to see who could out-jargon whom when it came to retro expressions for diner food.

Lurking in my mind was the inescapable awareness that Victor's life was so much easier with Oliver gone. Even the simple pleasure of kicking around expressions for butter—like the unappetizing term "axle grease"—wouldn't have been allowed with Oliver present.

"This is not a schoolyard," he might have said. Or maybe an even more cutting blow: "No wonder you're a cook and not a chef. This is serious business."

I pushed away the thought that Victor was angry, ambitious, or vengeful enough to take drastic steps. After all, I reminded myself, Victor could simply have quit and found employment elsewhere. Alaska wasn't the easiest state in which to find work, but the corridor between Anchorage and Fairbanks certainly had enough diners and restaurants to accommodate one more cook. He must have known that I'd give him an excellent reference.

Once packed, I took a few more minutes at home to say a proper goodbye to Benny. I knew he'd have a special treat tomorrow when his first love returned. I considered taking him to the airport with me, but couldn't count on his understanding the reason for the trip and, therefore, behaving well in his carrier—not his favorite venue, so I usually used it only for going to the vet. I could wait to make the airport decision. For now, I made sure his feeder was full and that the Bennycam was pointed in a good location for maximum viewing area while I was on the road.

Chris's vehicle had seen better days, and it didn't take much persuading for him to agree to make the trip to Anchorage in my Outback. Especially since I offered to let him drive.

"I have to get me some new wheels," he said, sounding like a whiny fifth grader. I was relieved to see a smile that indicated he wasn't serious. I'd been back in town for less than a year, and this journey south would be the longest number of consecutive minutes I'd spend with him, and we'd be confined to a vehicle. It would be a bummer if he turned out to be unpleasant company.

Chris settled into the driver's seat without adjustment, his legs apparently matching mine in length. He slipped his hands into heavy gloves but removed them when he realized I had a heated steering wheel.

"I think I'm in love," he said. I had no doubt he meant with my Outback.

We took the quickest route, the multilane George Parks Highway, Alaska Route 3. We cruised past more than one saloon by the side of the road, rumbled across a bridge over a gulch, and noted many signposts pointing to random locations, including the North Pole, which was far from where we were headed.

I'd made this trip often enough, sometimes just for a fresher bit of produce than what reached us in Elkview, but I seldom took the time to go off the beaten path. Today, though our mission was not a pleasant one, I was in the passenger seat and it was impossible not to focus on the landscape. Willows, cottonwood, elm trees seemed to float by without a break. And for a short time, we stopped to observe an enormous moose walk—plod—down the grassy median strip, baying as if he were not having a good time. Unlike the almost musical elk's cry, the cry of the moose was a low, grunting sound, more of a growl. I hit the app on my phone to alert the animal control people. I figured I wasn't the only one doing so, but better too many calls than none at all when the poor moose was probably just looking for help getting home.

I looked beyond the trees to the mountains. I hadn't been west of AK-3, the Parks Highway, since I was in high school. Maybe it was the photos on the *Bugle* wall that got me thinking. Maybe it was the fact that Oliver never traveled much for pleasure either. He'd taken a brief European vacation just before I returned home. I remembered my mom telling me he'd had to cut the trip short for some reason and had never gone back to Europe. Or to anywhere outside of Elkview. Now it was too late. I wasn't planning on dying soon, but I resolved right then to do more touring. A life not just feeding tourists, but joining them, being one.

It was easier than ever, wasn't it, to plan a tour in our grand state? One search could bring up tour after tour. Chris paid attention to the road, I hoped, and drummed his fingers to a Vanessa Carlton album—his self-confessed teenage crush—while I imagined myself fishing, kayaking, hiking. I'd probably stop short of scaling Denali, but I used to love to hike and ride my bike. When I lived in San Francisco, there was always a group of friends willing to walk or ride in Marin Headlands, enjoying the peculiar wildlife.

Or tackle one of the more than two dozen trails through the Presidio, the national park at the Golden Gate Bridge. I still had friends in the Bay Area who'd been nagging me to fly down for a visit. As soon as we found Oliver's killer, I told myself, there'd be no stopping me.

"We're here," Chris said, pulling into the office parking lot. "I think you fell asleep."

"Actually, I took a trip, from the Seward Peninsula all the way down to San Francisco."

"You must be exhausted."

"Invigorated." I spied a café right next door to the real estate office and steered us toward it once we got out of the car. "But I do need coffee. And thanks for doing all the driving, by the way, Chris."

"My pleasure. I'd even be glad to drive you around the Seward peninsula if you like."

What? How am I supposed to take that? As a joke, or the world's sweetest pickup line?

Luckily a server greeted us with menus before I needed to respond with anything other than my best smile.

OUR COFFEE STOP INCLUDED BEAR CLAWS, IN KEEPING with my goal of testing them everywhere and comparing them to mine.

"No comparison," Chris said, tapping into my thoughts.

"We should have a plan," I said. I pointed toward Kendra's place of business.

"You mean like 'good cop, bad cop'?"

"More like a list of questions."

Chris smiled, a little crooked, the cutest kind. "We really are amateurs, aren't we, Charlie? And I call myself a journalist. If this were an interview with a baseball coach or a town representative about a new housing bill or the recall of a blender or—"

"I get it. This is new to me, too. For one thing, there's more at stake in this situation than whether Elkview beats Palmer."

"And it's a lot more personal."

"It certainly is."

KENDRA WAS NOT ON VACATION. I FOUND MYSELF wishing she were. Yes, I'd ridden two-plus hours, left my diner and my cat, only to hope that it all turned out to be for nothing. Some investigator.

Kendra fit my stereotypical image of an office worker. Mid-to-late fifties, I guessed, graying hair neatly pulled back into a French twist, modest skirt and mint green sweater set.

Kendra was more subdued than her brother, informing us immediately upon introductions that she was a supervising administrator and had been in the real estate business for almost thirty years. Older than she looked.

We offered our sincere condolences on the death of her brother. She mumbled a thank-you, without further comment. I was mildly surprised that we didn't hear something like "He was a good brother" or "I'll miss him," which would have been on my list of expected responses.

"Is the business good in this part of town?" Chris asked, skipping ahead.

"I suppose so. I don't really participate in that part of the business. My job is support—phones, distribution of correspondence, expense reporting, calendar and scheduling, meeting coordination, and maintaining tenant, vendor and property files, including insurance certificates, lease abstracts, and so on, in accordance with prescribed standards."

Kendra couldn't have explained it better if she'd been reading from a job posting, which I'd have bet she was in charge of preparing.

Chris and I had managed to put together a presentation of sorts. We hand waved a vague sentence about how we were here to help with the investigation into her brother's murder. For a moment, I wished I could have shown her a badge, if not a gun. We sat across from Kendra at a table in the staff break room. The smell from the large metal coffeepot was overpowering, and not in a good way. Also lingering in the air were the remnants of lunches. Chili? Salad dressing? Tuna? An everything bagel? Again, not in a good way.

We launched into our questions, many of which sounded like those in every crime drama we'd ever watched. People, presumably staff, wandered in and out of the small room, some heating items in the microwave oven, others lingering over choosing a snack from the vending machine. Trying to decide who we were and why we were there? I thought so. Mildly intimidating, but Kendra paid no attention to them. She let us ask our questions.

"When was the last time you had contact with Oliver?"

"Can you think of anyone who might have wanted to hurt Oliver?"

Here, a young man, with a head as completely shaved as Chris's was, stood peeling his orange. At last, a pleasant odor. He shifted his body closer to our table and resumed his task, removing the bright orange rind and sacs more carefully than the task warranted. I was glad neither he nor anyone else took a seat at the only other table in the room. Perhaps it was an unwritten protocol for the break room.

"No, and no" was all the young man got for his attempts to tune in.

"Had Oliver seemed different in any way lately?"

"Did he seem anxious or worried?"

"Was he on good terms with his neighbors?"

We were getting nowhere with Kendra's perfunctory responses.

We did learn that Oliver didn't like to make the drive to the highly trafficked (his words, she said) Anchorage, so she went north to visit him on holidays. She hadn't seen him since just after Christmas. He seemed the same as always, worked his regular hours while she was there, didn't introduce her to anyone new. She couldn't keep up with Oliver's girlfriends, some of whom were bad news.

"Can you say which ones were bad news?" I asked.

"And what kind of bad news?" Chris added.

Kendra twisted her lips to the side and waved her hand, as if to say, "Never mind," which she did ultimately say out loud.

Finally, before burgeoning nausea from the lunch odors took over, I decided to break away from our list.

"Would you mind telling us a little bit about your brother, Kendra? Maybe how he was as a kid or other things you remember?"

"He's not actually my real brother."

Way to bury the lede, Kendra.

SEVEN

BOTH CHRIS AND I LEANED FORWARD IN OUR CHAIRS, in one stunned, choreographed movement.

To her credit, Kendra admitted, "Oliver was adopted. I guess I should have told you that already."

To my credit, I did not respond, *Ya think?*

Kendra stood abruptly. "I haven't even offered you a drink. Coffee? Soda?"

We said we'd love some water. And a lot more information, now that we had plastic cups of water from a cooler that looked like it had barely survived the last century.

Chris recovered from the surprising news faster than I did. "Did Oliver ever find or want to find his birth parents?"

"My parents adopted Oliver when he was about eight. I was a teenager, so I can't say I was overly nice to him, if you know what I mean. I mean, I was wrapped up in my own things. High school stuff. And here was this little kid encroaching on my perfectly fine life. I remember I used to get peeved when I had to babysit him."

Kendra sat back and pushed her hands up through the

sleeves of her sweater. Maybe protecting herself from how we might judge her. My mind turned over and over with, *Does Mom know this?* I felt sure she would have mentioned it.

"It wasn't something we talked about," Kendra continued, circling back to Chris's question. "It wasn't like now with open adoption and how everyone knows everything, or you can find it on the Internet. I have friends who adopted an infant last year, and the birth mother is a regular visitor to the baby. She'll be part of that child's life as if she's a favorite aunt or something, and the child will know everything from the start. It wasn't like that with Oliver. Or anybody else who adopted back then. Privacy meant something."

There was no doubt in my mind that Kendra preferred the old model of adoption. I wasn't about to offer an opinion and derail the track we were on. Chris and I had a long way to go before we left Kendra. I was glad the room had quieted down. No more coming and going. No more whirring microwave oven or slamming of the vending machine when it didn't deliver the goods smoothly. Lunch hour was over, it seemed.

The next questions in my mind were of such a personal nature, I didn't know how to start. Questions like *Why didn't her parents have more children?*; *Why would they adopt an eight-year-old?*; and, of course, *Does any of this matter in terms of who killed Oliver?*

Then it was too late. Kendra announced that she, too, had to get back to her desk.

"We do have more questions," Chris said.

"Only a few more," I added, hoping my pleading voice would keep her in the room.

Kendra took a deep, audible breath, most likely mulling

over whether she wanted to deal with us another minute. Surely, she knew the next questions would be tougher.

"If you can, come back around three thirty. A student intern will be coming in then, so I'll be able to leave my desk."

We'd spent less than a half hour with Kendra. Now we'd have a two-and-a-half-hour wait for the next session. And there was a good chance we'd be driving home after sunset. We looked at each other. Chris gave a slight nod.

"We'll be back," I said.

IN THE END, IT SEEMED LIKE A NO-BRAINER.

"We're here with our devices and a café nearby, no distractions, and we have research to do," I said.

"My thoughts exactly. But this time we need a real lunch."

It was true, the pre-packaged peanut butter crackers and trail mix on the road and the experimental bear claw were not going carry us through the day. We went back to the café next door, which had a much more appetizing aroma than the break room, and ordered fish chowder and sandwiches.

"Wow," Chris said. I knew he wasn't referring to the food but to the newfound information that Oliver had been adopted.

"Ya think?" I was finally able to say.

"We need to find out where Oliver came from."

We'd been told as we were leaving Kendra's office building that we were welcome to stay in a conference room, but we'd agreed it was better not to risk Kendra's walking by and getting a look at our searches. In a good faith gesture toward the coffee shop staff, we ordered more coffee and fresh cookies to go, and promised a big tip.

We took turns manning the table and going for brief walks around the block. I texted my mom—who knew where she was? I'd lost track of the time zones she'd be passing through. If she'd even left the ship by now. Besides wishing her bon voyage and sending her a photo of Benny looking like he knew she was on her way, I asked a couple of questions.

Oliver adopted?

Lana and Gert. last names? addresses? emails?

They were long shots, but who better than girlfriends or ex-girlfriends for the inside scoop on any man? And weren't intimate partners always the prime suspects in a murder? And bosses, I reminded myself. I remembered reading an article claiming that fifty-nine percent of male victims were killed by an acquaintance. It was a pretty broad-brush statistic meant to play down random violence—everyone's worst fear—as a major factor in murders. My cynical side said this was a tactic used in the tourist trade.

When Chris returned from a trek to stretch his legs, he logged in to the *Bugle*'s archives, then used his credentials to dig into those of surrounding local papers.

"We don't know where he and/or Kendra grew up," I said.

"Shall I run next door and ask her?" Chris asked.

"I don't think . . . oh, you're kidding," I said.

"Eventually you'll pick up on it faster."

"It? On what?"

"When I'm kidding." He lowered his head to his keyboard as if he, too, felt awkward about how the conversation had veered toward the personal once again. One might even have said toward the *flirty*.

I checked my phone for a text from my mom. Nothing. There was a voicemail from Victor, however, asking what he should do about the new design for the menu. The printer needed an answer ASAP. It had been Oliver's idea, redoing the menu with a retro drawing on the cover. A lineup of people sitting on stools, their backs to the viewer, wearing fifties-style clothing. Other clues about the era were the hairdos sported by the figures and, perhaps the biggest giveaway, the fact that everyone was reading paper copies of a book or a newspaper. I told Victor he should have Nina proof the text, then give it his seal of approval if he was happy with it.

"I already see they spelled 'hollandaise' wrong for the eggs Benedict. I fixed it right away. We have to keep Benny happy," he said.

Victor knew the way to my heart. "Yes, we do."

"I'm wondering if we should put that cherry cheesecake mousse back on the menu?"

The item that Oliver had wanted removed for some unknown reason.

While I was thinking about what to do, Victor continued. "It's a big favorite, Charlie."

"Put it back on," I said.

It made me sad that Oliver wouldn't be able to complain about my decision. But I couldn't dwell over whether it was the right one. It was just a dessert, wasn't it? On the menu or not on the menu. What did it matter? I was going to have to deal with things like this for the near future.

Chris had been productive while I was mentally back in Elkview before things got turned upside down. Before Oliver was murdered. Before I was in Anchorage, practically deputized and trying to find his killer.

"Get a load of this." I moved my chair around, and he turned his computer so I could read the screen. "I'm checking out the Anchorage papers for children in 1977. I found this in the *Gazette* archives."

I read the headline—FIRE LEVELS LOCAL GROUP HOME—and the sub-headline—All but three children perish in middle-of-the-night blaze.

"Awful," I said, wondering why he sounded so excited.

"Last year, before you came home, we had a big celebration for Oliver's fiftieth birthday. So I went back to 1977, when he would have been eight years old. I kept asking myself, why an eight-year-old? I wanted to see if anything came up. Check this out."

We read the article together, sitting side by side, mumbling key phrases at each other. The home had been in operation for decades. Not maintained very well. Faulty wiring was believed to be the cause, but inspectors hadn't made a final determination. The facility sheltered children who were older or otherwise hard to place. The surviving children's names were not released, but their ages ranged from five to eight. We tossed about what-ifs and it-could-bes as we learned that the state administrators made arrangements to place the surviving children in temporary housing.

It was impossible to be sure we'd found the beginning of one phase of Oliver's life. It was also impossible to ignore.

When the bell over the door rang, for perhaps the tenth time, we both looked up. Was this Kendra coming in to check on us? What would her reaction be if she caught us looking into her personal history? We laughed together at our shared anxiety.

"We should check a couple of other things, like when Kendra's parents were married," I said.

"You're thinking that if they married late, had only the one child, they might have been good candidates for taking in an eight-year-old."

This time, both our keyboards were assaulted as we clacked away. Chris started with Burke, Kendra's last name; I went for Whitestone, Oliver's last name, which might have been a maiden name for Kendra.

"No wedding photo, but I found a twenty-year anniversary photo and announcement for a couple named Burke. A dinner was held at the church where they were long-time members, and"—he raised his fist in a victory salute—"they're pictured with their daughter, Kendra, age sixteen."

"Thus, possibly Good Samaritans. When that home burned down, they'd be likely to help."

"Way to stereotype churchgoers," Chris said. This time I knew immediately that he was kidding.

"Only in the FBI-profiling sense. Nothing wrong with that."

"I suppose we could have gotten all this from Kendra. But now she'll know what good researchers we are and maybe she'll open up about other, less obvious things."

"Hopefully things that will actually help find her brother's killer," I added.

We did a few more searches. If Oliver had a criminal record, it was sealed. The group home, the original article said, was no longer for juvenile delinquents, its original intent, but for children who had no homes for other reasons. Their parents were deceased or otherwise unable to care for them. *Perhaps their parents were delinquents,* I mused.

"I have an idea," Chris said, as if it were the first we had all day. "What do journalists love?"

"Is that a trick question?"

"Follow-up stories. The 'Whatever happened to' kind of feature story. I don't know if readers like them, but news writers certainly do."

"The three children who survived the terrible fire that took everyone else. 'Where are they now?'" I put quotes around the last phrase to indicate I, too, knew some journalese.

"Uh-huh. Let's start with nine or ten years later, when that eight-year-old might be finishing high school."

With me back on my own side of the table, we each took an archive of a local paper and searched ahead to when Oliver would have come of age. It seemed likely that he'd stayed with Kendra's family all the while up to then, since she did still keep up with him. I hit pay dirt with a *Gazette* feature.

"Here it is." My eureka moment, thanks to Chris's newsman's sense. I sent him the link. "Good thinking," I said.

"We make a good team."

I liked hearing that.

We each scanned the article on our separate devices. The three children, all boys, had attended a school associated with the church where the Burkes had been members. They'd been on an overnight field trip, the winners of a contest sponsored by a service organization in town, when the fire broke out. The oldest was about to graduate.

Chris expressed embarrassment at the reporter's questions.

"This is the worst one," he said. "'Do you feel guilty that you survived when so many of your friends did not?' What kind of sensitivity training did people not have back then?"

I pointed out that we still heard similar questions these

days, whether it was after a fire or a fatal accident or any other disaster. "You might be the only sensitive reporter there is," I told him.

I spied the blush I had hoped for.

We skipped ahead to the grainy photos, almost as bad as the photos in our old family albums.

"It's the middle guy," Chris said. "The caption says his name is Oliver Quinlan."

I strained my neck and squinted. "Yes, that could definitely be Oliver. Quinlan is a common name, but it sounds familiar to me."

"In any case, Oliver seems to have changed it to Whitestone at some point, for some reason."

"It's hard to believe all our wild guesses got us to this point."

"This point" was three fifteen. Almost time to meet Kendra. We packed up to head back to the real estate office. I was impressed that Chris grabbed some napkins and wiped off our table. After Ryan What's-His-Name, who lived as if he was used to a crew of servants, I was easily impressed.

"What do you mean by wild guesses?" Chris asked. "I call it following a careful trail. Besides, do you know what I sacrificed for the sake of this research?"

"Do tell."

"A restored 1952 Hudson Hornet patrol car. It's downtown in the Alaska Law Enforcement Museum."

"If I'd only known."

"Actually, I've been there a number of times. Great exhibits of old uniforms and an entire history of the state troopers."

"To which we almost belong."

A text from my mom interrupted the banter.

Nooooooooo.

Lana in old addy bk. Bad news Gert by email.

Will call tomorrow morning.

I showed my phone to Chris and walked him through the messages. "I'm guessing the extra-long 'no' is in reference to whether she knew Oliver was adopted. She's probably wondering why not, since she's known him for years and years."

"Death is like that. It exposes all kinds of secrets," Chris said, too somber for me at the moment.

"I guess I'm lucky I haven't had a lot of that in my life." I went back to my mom's text. "In case you don't know these particular secrets—Lana and Gert are old and new girlfriends of Oliver's. Bad news could mean anything, I guess. Lana is bad news or Gert is bad news or there's bad news about Lana, or . . . I wish I could reach her by phone, but no luck."

"I wonder also what your mom means by 'tomorrow morning,' since she'll be traveling through a few time zones."

We walked quickly, almost in step thanks to our long legs, an advantage on a thirty-degree day like today. Alaskans are among the few people who know enough to bundle up even to walk the length of a city block. I was glad I had a few layers on as the wind whipped around, the frigid air attacking the few inches of my cheeks that were exposed.

"What do we want to know from Kendra?" Chris asked, holding his scarf tight around his neck. "She would have graduated high school before Oliver was even a freshman.

Though she might know when and why he switched to Whitestone. Maybe it's his birth name."

"But he's Quinlan at eight and eighteen."

Chris agreed that was a mystery Kendra might be able to help with, besides telling us what she knew about the latest two girlfriends.

"There's also what she plans to do about a service for Oliver. Maybe she'd like our help with that, assuming she'd have it in Elkview. I know my mom would want to be involved." As we approached the office, I could have sworn I smelled stale leftovers with onions, though I knew it was unlikely the odors could waft this far. "We should have invited Kendra to join us at the café, instead of going back to that awful lunchroom."

"You're spoiled by that special diner you live in."

"True that."

I NEEDN'T HAVE WORRIED ABOUT THAT AWFUL lunchroom.

"I'm so sorry, folks." The young woman behind the desk made a special effort to appear sorry, raising her very blond eyebrows and tilting her very blond head. "Kendra was called to a last-minute meeting over at city hall. Something she couldn't get out of."

I felt Chris's hand on my arm, just in time to stop me from ranting about how we'd waited two and a half hours. How we could have been home by now, before it got dark. How she had our cell phone numbers and could have called or texted us to let us know.

"Maybe we can continue another time," Chris said.

"I'll let her know." The young woman turned away in time to avoid my scowl.

* * *

CHRIS LET ME GRIPE ALL THE WAY TO MY CAR.

"I'll bet she's hiding in that lunchroom. She knows we'd never go back there if we didn't have to."

"I wonder what she has to hide?"

"I'll bet I know."

"You don't think—" Chris sounded incredulous.

"Remember Trooper's warning," I said. "'She's a suspect until she's not,' and now that she's fled from us—"

"That's a little dramatic, but not too far off base."

"She's officially 'not not,' if you know what I mean."

"It kind of scares me that I do." He paused. "Know what you mean."

We gave each other a mutual nudge, bumping shoulders, which felt strangely pleasant.

Eight

CHRIS HAD DRIVEN THE WHOLE WAY FROM THE DINER in Elkview to Anchorage. I wanted to take my turn at driving duties and ferry us home, but Chris insisted otherwise.

"I never get a chance to drive a new car like this." He laughed. "A heated steering wheel? Come on, Charlie."

"I guess it's a little over-the-top."

"Not for me. And I haven't checked out all the other features. I might want one of these. Think of this as you letting me test-drive."

I agreed, mostly because I was feeling guilty for leaving Benny home all day. If Chris were driving, I could pay some attention to my cat. Maybe I could finally interest him in the new robot mouse I bought him.

Worst of all, though, I was afraid Benny would find a way to rat on me, so to speak, and let my mom know I'd been neglecting him. He had his ways, and I was sure I didn't know all of them.

I warned Chris that if he drove, I'd be talking to Benny more than to him.

"No problem. I'd like to meet him sometime."

Points for Chris.

I checked in with Benny via the camera and hit the laser dot app first. I'd read that it was a good idea to let the laser dot fall on something solid now and then, so the cat feels like he's been successful in catching his prey. To that end, I'd left a few toys around on my living room floor. A bright green spindly ball. An old-fashioned stuffed-animal-type mouse. A fish-shaped crinkle-sound toy. A catnip yellow banana toy. If Chris thought it was strange that I laughed and cheered each time Benny's paws landed on a toy via the laser dot, he kept quiet about it.

"Do you have a pet?" I asked Chris after engineering a particularly fun wrestling match between Benny and a fleece-wrapped upright ring.

He shook his head. "I always did as a kid. Hamsters, dogs, frogs. Whatever my mom would let me take in the house. But now I live alone and I don't spend much time there, so . . . to answer your question, no, but you're sure making it look like fun."

More points for Chris.

We hadn't driven far when Chris asked, "Do you need to get back to the Bear Claw right away?"

"What do you have in mind?"

"A little side trip. It won't take long."

"I'm game."

"I can almost guarantee there'll be game."

I liked his sense of humor.

We detoured west and ended up at a place I hadn't visited since I was a kid on field trips. A few miles of twisting, turning roads that ran along the Eklutna River brought us to the beautiful, glacial Eklutna Lake. The late-afternoon sunlight seemed to skim the surface of the water. It was

Alaska, so of course we saw game, represented by more than one moose and a pair of mountain goats. Mosquitoes, the stuff of legend in the state, weren't due in full force for about three months, in mid-June.

I enjoyed watching an old guy kayaking across the lake in a bright yellow vest to match his one-man ship, a few backpacking hikers, and—nearly overgrown by tree limbs—the carcass of an old Buick.

We took the ends of a wide log and placed it in position to serve as a bench, at least as comfortable as the metal chairs in the café in town, with the added advantage of facing the lake. A sobering moment, thinking of the origin of this lake, from glacial activity, now the source of drinking water for Anchorage and a little-known ice-skating rink in winter.

Still, it was just a body of water, and therefore fair game for skipping stones. I couldn't wait to take my dad on when he came back. He thought I was hopeless at it, and I was, until now, under Chris's tutelage.

The cove shielded us enough from a cold wind to allow time and space to talk and solve all the world's problems, as well as a few of our own. I learned a lot about Chris, the man beyond the jock I thought I knew in high school. His parents were gone now, his siblings spread over the lower forty-eight. He'd joined the army shortly after high school and had been stationed at the Fort Wainwright base in Fairbanks, now one of the largest training camps in the U.S., he explained.

"It was Mr. Dudley's history class that inspired me," Chris said. "Learning about our country, how people died defending what we take for granted." He turned to face me. "Not that I wanted to die. But, you know, it was post nine-eleven, and I wanted to do my part."

"You were so much more noble and patriotic than I was. What I remember of Mr. Dudley's class was the day he brought in MREs."

Chris laughed. "Meals Ready to Eat. I remember that, too."

"When I heard that a water-activated flameless ration heater was included with each entree, I knew my mom's diner could do better."

"I ate my share of MREs, and believe me, you were right."

The conversation turned to the tragedy that had brought us together, wondering when to brief Trooper, whether we should make a follow-up phone call to Kendra or let her make the next move, how we'd go about dealing with Lana and Gert.

"My mom will be here in the next twenty-four hours, hopefully," I said. "She has a lot of history with Oliver, and I'm sure she'll be eager to help."

"It's really important to you, solving this case, isn't it? You seem determined."

"I'm not happy being considered a suspect, for one thing."

"You don't seriously think Trooper pegs you for a killer? If he does, why is he letting you be part of the investigation?"

"I'm not sure. Maybe it's some kind of trap, where he figures this way he can watch me and maybe I'll slip up and incriminate myself."

"That's a stretch. Not that you asked my opinion."

"Not that I asked, but I'm happy to have it. Whatever helps. And it's not something I can talk to my mom about."

"Speaking of that, I'll be glad to take you to the airport to pick her up."

"Thanks, but I don't even know the flight she's on or when she'll arrive."

He shrugged. "I'm not going anywhere."

"Great, then. I'll let you know the time."

It was a nice end to a very nice detour. Also a welcome offer to have company to the airport, especially if it turned out to be in the middle of the night. It didn't even matter if the offer was due to me or to my well-heated Outback.

W E RETURNED TO THE BEAR CLAW FEELING PRODUC-tive from our time doing research in the café and refreshed from time spent with our state's natural beauty. An enviable and rare combination.

Chris pointed to his battered pickup and grimaced. I hoped at least the heater was working, even if neither seats nor steering wheel were heated. "You sure you don't want to trade down?" he asked. Then a hug, more or less pla-tonic, as my mom would say, and he was gone.

I'd just missed the rushed dinner hour, lucky me, and walked in on Victor cleaning up. Nina was in the front booth with her laptop, the table strewn with books. I presumed she'd already done her share of the work for the day. She gave me a wave, but since she didn't remove her earbuds, I assumed she didn't need to hear anything from me.

"Yo, boss," Victor said. "Great day."

He had the music turned to such a high volume—another Oliver no-no, and no wonder Nina needed her own music source—that I couldn't tell whether he was telling me he'd had a great day or asking if I had one.

"Great," I said, covering both options.

"A nice crowd, mostly Annie's inn people. They sure love that cherry cheesecake mousse. There's not a portion left. I want to try the chocolate version next time if that's okay with you."

"Sure. Just add cocoa powder to the shopping list."

"Annie just left. She kept trying to reach you. I told her I got through earlier, so I didn't know what was wrong."

I wasn't up for sharing with Victor my by-the-lake-and-out-of-touch time with Chris, notwithstanding the fact that I was his boss, not the other way around. "I might be out of juice," I said, and fiddled with the charging station at the back of the kitchen for effect. "Do you know what she wanted?"

Victor shrugged. "Something about the Swiss guy. He's MIA, I think. And you have a ton of other messages, too. I left them up front."

Nina was ready for her turn with me. She reached under her textbooks and pulled out an arty sign she'd created from markers we kept on hand for patrons under ten.

"What do you think?" she asked me.

I read her careful script, which said there'd been a death of a staff member and our hours would be sporadic for the next few days. Our telephone number was listed below and people were encouraged to call to be sure we were open before returning.

"Thanks, Nina. This is just what we need," I said, willing myself not to release the tears I felt welling up.

The ever-sensitive Nina put her arm around my shoulders. "I know this hard for you. I want you to know I'm here for you. I can work extra hours, whatever."

I thanked her and turned to the sounds from the kitchen: Victor hanging up saucepans and utensils. He slapped his hands together in an I'm-done gesture. He came around to the customer side of the diner. "Oh, I brought in a friend, Charlie. A great cook who's between jobs right now. I didn't think you'd mind. You can even take it out of my pay if—"

"Of course not. That was good thinking, Victor. Maybe I can meet her tomorrow?"

"How did you know it was a her?"

"Just hoping," I said, earning a chuckle from Nina.

I knew that eventually I'd have to get serious about finding a full-time replacement for Oliver. I'd made some notes on a job description but didn't have the energy it took to finish and post it. Too soon to acknowledge that Oliver was never coming back. Too real.

"I'll see you tomorrow," I told Victor and Nina. "At some point tomorrow evening I'm going to have to pick up my mom at the airport in Anchorage, and I'd appreciate if you could cover here."

"No prob."

After Victor and Nina departed, the diner was empty except for one scruffy-looking guy with a mug of coffee and a newspaper in front of him. Many walk-ins used the Bear Claw as a warm refuge. Usually fine by me, except that this evening I entertained far-reaching thoughts about whether he or someone like him might be Oliver's killer. A random guy instead of the people on the list Chris and I had been working on. That would be easier to take, more reassuring than believing that someone we all knew, considered a friend, could be a murderer.

I checked in with Benny—"It won't be long now. Go get yourself a treat, because when I get home, I'm going to dump a lot of anxiety on you." I couldn't be sure he heard me, since he was out of camera range, but I knew he hadn't run out of food or water and could paw himself a treat whenever it pleased him.

It didn't take long to go through my messages, all from suppliers checking on inventory, and thankfully not the "ton" Victor had referred to.

When Random Guy left, sending me a friendly goodbye wave from a distance, I took a turn around my place, filling the sugar canister from a fifty-pound bag in the back room, wiping spots here and there on the Formica counter. I settled up at the register and left messages of my own to my suppliers. A down jacket had been left on a coat hook attached to a booth. I crumpled the slippery lavender garment into a box under the register at the front. Our version of a lost-and-found department. I couldn't imagine anyone forgetting a jacket once she opened the door to the freezing weather, but maybe our delicious, hot moose stew took the place of a layer of clothing. I'd have to remember that line the next time I needed to write up a new ad.

All in all, the siblings had done a better-than-usual job of tidying up. They'd tied up the garbage and disposed of it in the dumpster, I assumed, but there was still paper trash in a medium-sized container by the back door. I bent to lift the liner and its contents and noticed a stack of envelopes of different sizes, all opened, some bound together with a rubber band. The correspondence with a visible front were addressed to Oliver Whitestone. There were also notepads with Oliver's name printed along the top. I recognized the pads as having been among the gifts I'd given each employee at Christmas.

I straightened up, took a deep breath. This was Victor's doing. He'd taken it upon himself to clean out the middle drawer of the old desk in the staff area, the drawer everyone knew was Oliver's. Oliver kept it locked, but everyone knew the old-time skeleton key that we kept in the small filing cabinet could open anything that was equally old-time.

Since the container held clean paper waste only, I was able to sort through the contents and scoop out the envelopes and papers that were from Oliver's drawer. I carried them to my briefcase, holding them with a clenched fist, as if they might float back to the trash. I was glad Victor had left. I needed time to relax my jaw, to balance this with the good work he'd done for me, especially in the last couple of days.

It bothered me that a person as intense, full of life, and dedicated to his job as Oliver could be dismissed so quickly in death. Trooper Graham had no time to try and find his killer; his sister couldn't spare another hour to talk about his life; Victor couldn't wait to clear out his things and take over. None of the three had said they'd miss him; none had expressed any emotion at his violent death.

I knew I had no right to judge how others responded to death or to any traumatic event. When it came down to it, I was the one whose last words to Oliver had sent him storming out the door of the diner. I hadn't killed him, but had I in any way contributed to his murder? If he hadn't felt the need to get away from me, would he still be alive? If I'd suggested we sit down for a cup of coffee and talk over our differences, would he be at home watching TV right now, or out with Gert, instead of on a cold table in Doc Sherman's basement lab?

I needed to get home to Benny. I needed perspective, forgiveness. I needed motivation to find Oliver's murderer, for myself as well as for justice for him. It was a big job for an orange tabby, but I knew he was up to the task.

My CAR WAS STILL WARM WHEN I STEPPED INTO IT, REminding me of the peaceful time by Lake Eklutna. Sunlight was long gone and the roads were slippery. More than once I swerved and had to pull over to find traction. Most of the shops along Main Street were shut tight for the night. Only old Lucas was still at the ready, on his porch, hoping to snatch his last tourist sale.

I was glad to pull into my driveway, and really glad to open the door to a waiting Benny, who immediately wrapped himself around my ankles.

I tossed my briefcase in the front hall, then leaned forward and lifted Benny onto my shoulder, one of his favorite positions (as I could tell by his lilting *meow*), and carried him to the chair by his feeder.

"I hope you're in a good mood, Mr. Eggs Benedict, because I have long list of things to throw at you."

Benny never refused me. He nestled on my lap and perked up his ears. I let loose.

What a difference, talking to Benny about all the things that were bothering me about the last day and a half. I organized my thoughts and managed to suspect everyone of being Oliver's killer, from his sister to the guy who claimed to be his brother to his well-built girlfriend. Only Chris escaped the list. And me, but I couldn't let go of the fact that I might still be on Trooper's list. The sooner we knew who had killed Oliver, the sooner I'd be able to sleep well.

Except that I seemed to have fallen asleep while constructing my suspect list, because the next thing I heard after my cat's purring was the ring of my cell phone. I'd left the volume on, anticipating a call from my mom or Trooper. I was treated to a few bars of generic guitar strumming. I was never happy with my ringtone and changed it up every week or so. Chimes, waves, keys, popcorn, ripples. I'd cycled through them all. The old-fashioned dial tone seemed the least startling of them.

"Charlie!"

An excited Annie on my speakerphone. I'd forgotten all about needing to call her. I patted my thigh, which always summoned Benny, ready for a scratch on his cheeks or a tickle under his chin. How convenient that cell phones allowed for hands-free conversation.

"I'm so sorry I was out of reach for a while today, Annie. Is everything okay?"

"Victor didn't tell you?"

"Not much. He thought there was something the matter with Pierre?"

"There is. I mean, there was, and I thought Victor would have told you and you'd be worried, but he didn't, so you weren't, and you don't have to be."

Typical Annie talk, especially when she was, or had been, or was about to be in a frenzy.

"I'm glad. I think."

"Yes, we're all relieved. He didn't come back from the hike with the rest of the group from the bus. I was worried sick. But he just wandered off to get some different kind of photos and got lost."

As much as I was aware that Annie had a soft spot, or whatever it was called these days, for Pierre, I also knew that she'd have been equally concerned about anyone who didn't return from a day of touring. She was an all-purpose good guy, the ultimate sympathizer and empathizer.

She continued her recounting of Pierre's adventure. "You know how those trails can quickly become impassable or just so confusing. So, by the time he figured out he was lost, the bus was gone. Though I don't know why Beth wouldn't have done a head count? Except, of course, technically he's not part of her group, and he ended up hitchhiking all the way back and it took more than one ride to get him here, but now he's safe and sound."

I was having a hard time mustering sympathy for Pierre— he hadn't been murdered, after all, or even injured, as far as

I could tell—but I wanted to sound interested, for Annie's sake. "Did he get them?"

"Did he get what?"

"The photos."

"Oh, yes. He showed me some incredible shots that we will be seeing in the magazine. They're on his phone. We can show you tomorrow."

A sign of the times that Pierre used his phone for photographs commissioned for a magazine. No more two-pounder strapped around the neck, plus a load of supplies and peripherals. I remembered how my ex—what was his name?—had outfitted himself when we were on vacation. I shook away that memory.

"I'm glad it all worked out." I started to give Annie a review of my day in Anchorage, but it was clear that she hadn't yet come down from the up, or up from the down, of her own day. "I'll see you tomorrow. Will you be needing breakfast for everyone?"

"We will. We all understand that you might not have everything you usually have. No problem."

"Thanks, Annie. Have a good evening."

"Oh, I will."

We giggled as we might have in the sixth grade. I didn't mind revisiting that memory at all.

Nine

VICTOR'S FRIEND RACHEL CAME IN TO THE BEAR CLAW with him and Nina early on Wednesday morning. Women like Rachel made me feel old, beyond my thirty-three years, in wardrobe years anyway. She was wearing a top with cutouts everywhere, as if she'd been mugged on the way in, the villain snipping off parts of the sleeves, elbows, and back of her shirt, and then shortening the garment to within an inch of her navel.

She'd met Victor in culinary classes in Los Angeles, she said, and admitted that neither of them had the desire to complete the program.

"I'm thinking I might relocate here. Victor's really glad he came back home, and I know a couple of other people down around Anchorage."

"How long have you been here?" I asked.

"I just flew up from LA yesterday, so not long, but Victor said you all could use some help, so I thought, might as well make myself useful."

"I appreciate that."

She looked around the diner, at the walls, the light fixtures, the old jukebox, seeming to take in the decor. "It's a nice place you have here."

In my current mental state, once I thanked her, I immediately registered that Rachel had a solid alibi for the time of Oliver's murder. She was still in LA.

I wondered if Trooper and all the other real police officers in the world carried this burden, unable to separate themselves from whatever case they were working. I hoped not, but I had a sudden desire to send them all thank-you notes. I was all the more grateful when I considered statistics I'd read recently that our state had fewer than two hundred officers for every one hundred thousand people. It was almost enough to make me want to run for office and try to improve those odds. Almost, but not enough. I felt I could do more good helping to feed those officers.

In timely fashion, Trooper Cody Graham stopped in for his coffee and bear claw. Generally, it was left up to the particular law enforcement agency—there were more than fifty in the state—whether its personnel were permitted to accept free food or other gifts. It was clear to me that they deserved it, so Trooper and I had an agreement, instituted by my mom, that we would run up a tab for him, to be paid in full at some later date. Those receipts were kept in a box that apparently had a false bottom, such that paper fell through to the center of the earth. Today Trooper ended up wrapping half the pastry in a napkin and taking it with him. I figured he came in just to make sure I was still alive, not killed by the same person who'd shot Oliver. He was probably on his way to check on Chris.

Victor and Rachel seemed to be reliving good old days of working together as they tossed diner jargon back and forth. Nina had quickly picked up the language when Victor first introduced her to it.

"Blonde with sand," Nina said.

"Coffee with cream, that's the 'blonde' part," Rachel explained to the customer who ordered it.

"I get it. And sand is sugar," said the young boy with the customer. He kicked his legs under the table to emphasize his delight. I got the idea that his schoolyard, wherever it was, would hear the line soon. "Tell me another one," the boy said.

"In the alley," Rachel said. "What do you think that means?"

The family all screwed up their noses, thinking.

"The food fell on the floor and it's dirty," from the boy.

"Never!" Rachel said.

"Leave off something. Like onions or mayo or something," from the dad. "Like throwing it out the door into the alley."

"Close. Sort of," Rachel said.

"Serve it on the side," from the mom, her hand raised, waving excitedly, leaving me to wonder if she was a grade school teacher.

"Right," Rachel said, high-fiving everyone.

Part of me was annoyed that my staff-of-the-day could be spreading laughter and cheer while Oliver was not around to enjoy it; the other part was grateful my patrons were spared a downer of an experience at the Bear Claw.

Nina, ever the sensitive one in any group, came back to where I was sitting in a booth with my laptop. "Don't worry, Charlie, we'll be more sober once the sign goes up and people know that we lost one of our team."

"Thanks, Nina," I said, meaning *for everything*, grateful to hear her call Oliver part of our team.

Other than banter and jokes from the kitchen help, there wasn't a lot of good news this morning. The weather up north was still too bad for the tour bus to continue on to Fairbanks. Many were clamoring for the Arctic Circle Tour, as promised, and as paid for. Beth did her best to appease them with more food on the house—her house, not mine.

"How about a Bear Claw Diner mug for everyone?" she offered in a cheery voice, to a mixed reaction. My feelings were only slightly hurt at the few boos I heard.

It wasn't the first time a tour guide had had to make an adjustment to the schedule because of inclement weather. There were warnings in every brochure I'd ever seen. It was Alaska, after all.

The roads were still okay and the weather a little milder near Talkeetna than they were closer to Fairbanks. I wondered if Beth had listed a zip line ride, a Talkeetna favorite, among the options. I couldn't imagine a better way to immerse oneself in the beauty of Alaska than cruising in the treetops with zips, suspension bridges, rappels, and platforms set up for the most breathtaking views. But some tour guides were themselves fearful of heights and demanding physical maneuvers in the three-hour excursion and were just as happy not bringing it up.

Another piece of bad news came from the mechanic, the only one in Elkview, who was having trouble getting the part for Pierre's rental car.

"Poor Pierre," Annie said, making her way to my booth. "If Max had been honest to begin with, he probably would have just abandoned the car and taken a flight up to the northern lights. But he's making the best of it, hiking around here, even though yesterday must have been harrowing. Getting lost and all."

"Do I hear my name?" Pierre himself had arrived, this

time not having waited for the bus group but having taken a ride over from the inn with Annie.

"I may do a kayak trip today," he said. "These travel magazines will take anything from Alaska. It's so different from, what do you call them, the lower forty-eight?"

"I offered to go on a short hike with him," Annie said. "I think he'd like the Byers Lake area, so we'll see."

I tried not to imagine Annie's hoping Max would withhold the needed automotive part, keeping Pierre around longer. I was happy to notice an increase in the level of his interest in her. Maybe she'd be booking a European flight after all.

Things started to look up when my phone rang and I checked the screen.

"Mom! Are you in our time zone?"

She laughed. "I think so, sweetie. Everything's in English, so that's a good sign. I'm in LA and I'm booked on a flight with a stop in Seattle. I get into Anchorage a little after ten o'clock tonight."

"I can hardly wait. I'll hold up a sign." I was finally in a cheerful mood.

"It'll be so late, though. I thought I could get a hotel in Anchorage and you can pick me up in the morning."

"What? No way. First, Benny won't stand for it."

"I hate to think of you making that drive so late."

I thought it best not to tell her I'd already made the drive yesterday. "I'll be there tonight, Mom. Just give me your flight number."

"Well, okay. I guess it's either late tonight or we'll be driving up there at an ungodly hour tomorrow morning. I want to be sure to be on time for Oliver's service. I'm not sure when it starts? Otherwise I'd try harder to talk you out of it."

I sat up straighter. "What service?

"Kendra sent me a message this morning. I thought she would have sent you one, but I guess since she doesn't know you, she figured I'd pass it on."

It was all I could do not to tell my mom that Kendra did know me, well enough to skip out on me.

"I'm going to sign off, sweetie. We can talk more about it on the way home. Maybe you have an email with the details of the service. Right now, I'm starving for some real food, and a nap if I can find a comfortable chair. I'll see you tonight, then? Maybe we can go to your place so—"

"So you can see Benny. Of course. He'd claw me to death if I kept you apart."

I must have set a record for the world's fastest turn-around time between hanging up on one call and making another. Then another.

First, I clicked on Trooper's number. "Isn't there some kind of law about when you can bury a person who's been murdered? Don't you have to wait until all the evidence is collected and someone identifies—?"

"Slow down, Charlie. What's up?"

Since there were still a few stragglers who'd begged out of the kayak trip—in the end, to Annie's chagrin, Pierre had left with the bus group—I did my best to keep my voice down. I told Trooper my mom's news. "Isn't this kind of fast? Did you know about it? Did you have to approve it?"

"Let's see if I have all your answers straight. That would be yes, yes, yes, and yes. Though I may have missed one."

"Very funny." I blew out a breath. "Here are a couple more. Have you solved Oliver's murder? Is the killer in jail right now?" I used my best whisper for these last two questions. *Take that, Troop!*

"Are you upset that you weren't included in the arrangements?"

"I wasn't even included in the announcement. I had to hear it from my mom, who's about four thousand miles away."

"But you can still go to the service. It's not till tomorrow morning."

"That's not the point. Whose side are you on? It would have been nice if our staff here could have participated. We could have ordered flowers."

Even I knew that was pretty weak. It was all I could do not to hang up on Trooper. But he didn't need to see the often ill-tempered teen he'd nursed through adolescence. And whom he'd recently come within inches of treating as a murder suspect, probably for that very reason.

"Are you going to be at the Bear Claw for the next hour or so?"

"Yes and yes, to quote you."

"Why don't I come by?"

Now I really felt silly, blowing a slight from a veritable stranger out of proportion. Nothing says "grown-up" like keeping a state trooper from two serious investigations over a minor affront. "That's okay. I'll be okay. I'm going to pick my mom up tonight."

Trooper would know what I meant: that Mom would make everything all right.

"I'll get over to you as soon as I can, I promise."

My "thanks" was tentative and loaded with guilt. I checked my email in case Kendra had contacted me in the last five minutes. Nothing.

It was now close to ten o'clock in the morning, and time for the second phone call. Maybe I could transfer a load of that shame onto someone else.

"Hi, Charlie." Chris's voice. Hesitant. Sheepish. As if he'd neglected to warn me about an impending ice breakup on Talkeetna Lake. "I was picking up the phone to call you."

"Did you know?"

"Too late, huh? I found out a few minutes ago, when I got in. The obit was in my in-box."

My email provider checked for new input every ten minutes, but I clicked on GET MAIL again manually anyway. Still nothing. I took a breath. No one was to blame for this turn of events except me. I was overreacting to an oversight.

"The important thing is to make sure everyone who mattered to Oliver knows about the service," I told Chris. "Can you tell me when and where? My mom is coming in tonight, and I'd like to be able to tell her right away."

"Is she coming into ANC? I can drive you."

"It's late. Ten something. I have to check the flight number."

"I'd like to take you."

While I considered my response, an uproar rose from the kitchen. A hose from the faucet had gotten loose and was spraying anyone and anything around it. Items on the open wire shelving were the most vulnerable—jugs of oil, loaves of bread, packages of beans and rice. The narrow, forceful beam of water traveled high and low and side to side. It was a sitcom writer's dream scene.

Typically, Victor was doubled over with laughter, helpless, while the women wrestled the hose until, finally, its nozzle ended in the sink where it belonged and Victor started on the cleanup. The stragglers had all left, so no diners were on hand to enjoy the incident, and no employees were injured. And no thanks to me. It was over before I realized what was happening.

"It's nice to hear you laugh," Chris said as I did my best to describe the scene.

I felt it was my duty to assist with the cleanup. I hung up with Chris, after accepting his offer to drive me to Anchorage. It turned out that a small kitchen disaster was a nice stalling technique when you were otherwise ambivalent about life's choices. And besides, it served him right for not telling me the particulars of Oliver's service immediately.

No diner owner, let alone a restaurateur, wants to be caught mopping up the place where food is handled. The activity could be interpreted as a sloppy sanitary practice. So I was relieved when the tinkling of the bell over the door was from the entrance of two friendlies, as we faux cops liked to say.

I saw both a patrol car and a semitruck with a blue cab hauling a railroad container car parked close to the diner. Trooper Graham and trucker Manny walked in together. Both men looked somber, and both were huddled in their jackets. I hoped it didn't mean that their vehicle heaters were out of order. The men waved to Victor and Nina and, by extension, to Rachel, and walked toward the booths.

"If you don't mind," Trooper said, indicating that he was going to take a booth at the back. "Charlie and I have some business to attend to."

"No problem," Manny said, giving Trooper a salute. He slid into a front booth and, unless I was mistaken, seemed glad to be alone. Of the three truckers—Manny, Moe, and Jack—Manny was the only one who lived close by, and it was never a surprise when he dropped in alone.

"Just coffee today, Vic," he said. That *was* a surprise.

Manny pulled out a magazine that seemed to be about cars, then folded it up again and stuffed it in his jacket pocket. I decided to go up and talk to him once Trooper and I finished our business.

For now, I was feeling equal parts shame and relief that Trooper had stopped by.

"As to your original question," he began, in typical

waste-no-time fashion, "there wasn't much for Doc Sherman to do. It was a very simple autopsy. There was no other family, and his sister, Kendra, wanted to take care of things as quickly possible."

Trooper moved toward the edge of the seat, as if he'd come to say that and leave.

"I appreciate your stopping by," I said. "I'm sorry I ragged on you. I feel like such a—"

"I'm sure you want to know where and when the service is?" He patted his pockets. "I wrote it down, but I can't seem to find it." How nice of him not to let me finish my self-recrimination. "I know it's at the Chapel of Atonement, right outside of Petersville."

Another petty thought crept into my mind: how appropriate for Kendra to choose a negative-leaning aspect of a religion, albeit a nondenominational one. Not a chapel for joy, or hope, or resurrection, or life. One might almost think she was atoning for something.

Trooper continued to pat himself down before finally giving up and easing his body closer to the aisle of the Bear Claw so it was half off the bench.

"Don't worry about that," I said. "I'm sure I can find out what time. I'll see you there?"

"Sure enough."

I walked with Trooper to the front of the diner, where Manny was still twisting his mug of coffee, staring into space. I'd noticed that now and then he'd looked toward the through window, either remembering Oliver or trying to decide which of the menu items looked good today. He himself did not look good, but I didn't want to pry too much. The other guys, Moe and Jack, often teased him about his age and how it was about time he retired.

"Everything okay?" I asked him.

"I heard about Oliver and thought I'd stop by. The other guys were wondering if there was any kind of funeral. Me, too. We'd all like to go."

I pointed to the seat opposite him. He nodded that it was okay for me to join him. "I was just talking about that with the trooper."

And in the spirit of overlapping company, the over-the-door bell rang and Chris walked in.

I moved over to make room on my bench. "Sorry I was so—"

But Chris wouldn't let me apologize any more than Trooper had.

"I don't blame you, Charlie. She must know you were Oliver's boss, that you made the trip all the way to Anchorage. You should have been on her list of invitees."

"You talking about Kendra?" Manny asked. "She's something else."

I was startled. "You know Kendra?"

Manny looked like a guy who wished he could swallow his last remark. "Not really. I guess Oliver mentioned her."

Oliver mentioned his sister to Manny but not to me?

What else did I not know about my murdered chef?

TEN

CHRIS HAD ALL THE INFORMATION WE NEEDED ABOUT Oliver's service, which was at eleven the next morning. He'd made copies of the obituary as printed in the *Bugle*, along with directions to the chapel, and piled them at the register.

Manny took a couple of copies—"For the guys"—and left the diner.

"Curious," Chris said, "that Manny knew more than you did about Oliver's personal life."

"No kidding."

He handed me a copy of the *Bugle* announcement. I read out loud, summarizing parts of it.

Oliver Whitestone, 51, chef at the Bear Claw Diner in Elkview.

"He'd like that," I told Chris. "He coveted the title 'Chef' as opposed to 'Cook.' He thought his Parisian credential earned him that, and my mom agreed. She always called him 'Chef.'" I ran my finger down the page. "And that's about all that's here as far as educational or other background information."

"Kendra must have written it, and in a hurry, too."

Whitestone leaves behind his sister, Kendra Burke, of Anchorage.

"Interesting mishmash. She calls him her brother, but doesn't use the name he had in her household, Quinlan."

Few details were included about Oliver's career path between Paris and Elkview. However, a photo of Oliver's class at culinary school was attached. Three long rows of newly minted chefs, about fifty graduates in all, roughly equal numbers of men and women. They were dressed uniformly in dark pants, white jackets, and the tall white cylindrical hats they'd never wear again.

"Long caption," I said. "No names of the students, just kind of an ad for the school."

The largest network of culinary schools in the world, in twenty countries with tens of thousands of students.

"And on and on, and then the photo credit."

Photo courtesy of Kendra Burke.

"Funny that she would choose a class picture. But I guess it fits with Oliver's pride in his alma mater," Chris said.

"Oliver never liked having his picture taken."

"Who does?" Chris said, running his hand over his shaved head.

I set the sheet on the table next to the staples of Oliver's trade. Some of them, Oliver shunned: the ketchup and mustard containers (good for nothing); the salt and pepper shakers (food on his platters was already perfectly salted and peppered). One item in particular that he did like: the menu he had designed, with his name at the bottom. OLIVER WHITESTONE, CHEF.

Oh, no. His name at the bottom.

I slid out of the booth. "Victor!"

"What's up, boss?"

I held up a copy of the old menu and pointed to Oliver's name. "The new menu. Has it already gone to the printer?"

"I took his name off," Victor said. "I figured, leave that space empty for now."

I relaxed my shoulders and took a breath, thanked Victor for his alertness, and returned to the booth.

"Close call," Chris said.

"I'm sure there'll be many more."

"I know you're busy, but we do have a few more connections to track down. Lana, for one. Oliver's ex. Did your mom have anything to offer on her? Last name?"

"Are you looking for Lana Bickford?" A voice from the kitchen. Nina. "I couldn't help overhearing you."

"Yes, we thought she might like to come to the service tomorrow," said quick-thinking Chris, thus preserving the secrecy of our investigative work, such as it was.

"Was Oliver still in touch with her?" I asked, there no longer being any reason to pretend that I, Oliver's boss, knew squat about his personal life. Maybe if I spent more time in the kitchen? Did Victor and Nina have significant others? Most likely, although they did both seem to be available to work anytime I needed them. What was Nina studying? I knew vaguely that she majored in business, but what in particular? Did she have any math courses? What were her favorite classes? What kind of music did she or Victor like?

I was giving myself a headache. I'd have to deal with this later.

"Well there was a thing a couple of months ago," Nina said, when I'd almost forgotten my question. "Because Gert found out that Oliver sent Lana a birthday card. I think Lana left a thank-you message on his machine and Gert heard it."

"Gert got it all wrong," Victor said. "That's all it was.

Just a card. Gert made a big deal out of nothing." He slammed a cleaver into sausage links in a way that said he might be having similar problems himself.

Who knew what went on in the kitchen? Not me. I was just the boss.

LUNCH HOUR WAS PLEASANTLY BUSY. SOME DINERS had taken the obituary notices from the register counter as they came in and expressed condolences to whoever was serving them. Nina had also hung her sign on the front door so regulars would have warning about the erratic hours. She'd also posted a notice that the Bear Claw would be closed all day tomorrow and that everyone was welcome to join us at the Chapel of Atonement.

A climbing group whose plans had been thwarted due to weather conditions was engaged in trying to make other arrangements. Though most climbers used Talkeetna as a jumping-off point (so to speak), Elkview got its share of teams coming from or going to Denali or the iconic Moose's Tooth formation, a nearly mile-long, low-angle, east-to-west summit ridge resembling that part of a moose's anatomy.

I remembered as a kid studying the large photo of the range that my dad had hung behind the cash register. I would try to compare the photo of Moose's Tooth with ones I found in a book, of a real moose's tooth. I'd pester my dad with questions about how they were alike, or not, every week or so, with a different argument.

Those sessions came back to me.

"Why isn't the mountain range called Moose's Teeth?"

"I don't know, honey."

I'd shove a book under his nose. "See, there are lots of peaks, just like there are lots of teeth in the moose's jaw."

"I see what you mean, honey." He'd then point out the main tooth.

"Still, maybe it should be called Moose's Jaw."

"Maybe so, honey."

"Why couldn't it be Elk's Tooth? That sticks up, too."

"I guess it could be, honey."

"Who named it, anyway?"

Then would follow the history of the name from Mount Hubbard to Moose's Tooth, which was the translation of the indigenous Athabaskan name for "peak."

"Where's the apostrophe?" I asked, once I looked it up in the encyclopedia and saw the official name from the United States Geological Survey. No apostrophe. "Mrs. Milbury says there should always be an apostrophe if it belongs to someone or something."

My dad was a very patient man, but now and then he'd threaten to remove the photo if I didn't stop asking questions.

Today, I learned the special reason that we were entertaining a group of three climbers—it seems they were only half of a six-person team. This half was no longer on speaking terms with the other half. I'd seen it before. People got stressed and touchy or even nasty, with fatigue, horrible weather, changes in elevation, being confined to a tent, and the uncertainties of success in reaching the summit, or in getting down from it.

As I served them, I heard this group congratulating itself on getting a flight out of the base camp during a short window of decent flying weather. The weather soon went lousy, to quote one of the diners, most likely stranding the other three in the base camp for a week or so.

Back in the kitchen, decidedly determined non-climbers Victor, Nina, and Rachel were whispering about how they wouldn't in a million years head up a mountain in any weather, and in this case, they really didn't know which half of the team to root for.

I snuck in a recommendation to the three diners for Annie's inn, but they snickered and assured me that their SUVs were perfectly comfortable. And much warmer than a tent on the side of an icy mountain, I guessed.

A few stragglers I recognized from Beth's tour group came in, still complaining about being stuck in Elkview when they should have been arriving at the arctic circle by now. I tried not to take offense.

I took a turn at working the counter, typically filled by singles who ended up talking to each other across three or four stools. Sometimes they were already friends or neighbors who happened to wander in at the same hour; other times strangers who struck up a conversation about a sporting event or when spring might finally arrive. Still others engaged me by sharing the reason they had ended up in an Elkview diner or where they were headed next.

I got all the advantages of human interaction from behind a counter without the worry that one of them might end the day with a DUI.

Chris had hung around, working on his laptop, nibbling at his BLT, which Nina knew exactly how to construct: with more B than L or T. He called me over at one point and turned his screen toward me.

"Lana Bickford has a blog," he said.

I checked out the full website where Lana sold her handknit goods. Photos of custom-knitted socks, scarves, hats, and gloves with and without fingertips filled the pages. Another section was dedicated to her blog, with patterns, supplies, and instructions, plus the usual blogger's take on life, doled out in weekly morsels. Apparently she was good at it: she'd won a blue ribbon at the state fair two years in a row, once for a re-versible bargello jacket in blue tones, and again for a silvery beaded shawl with stitches so fine I'd have thought it was tatted lace.

There was no physical address, of course, but there was an email address. Chris and I composed an email giving her the details of Oliver's service, "in case you haven't seen the notice." We went back and forth about whether to tell her we'd like to talk to her, and decided against it. If she showed up, we could approach her then; if not, we'd look further into getting an address.

The rush was over, and Chris and I packed up to go our separate ways. Except that Chris announced his nonnego-tiable plan to pick me up at my house at six thirty this eve-ning for the trip to the airport in Anchorage. Mom's flight was due at nine fifty. Roads to the south were clear and we'd have plenty of time to get there and possibly pick up a bouquet of flowers, which were in short supply in town, but would most likely be available at the airport. I didn't argue.

We'd make a good climbing team, I thought, but kept it to myself.

BENNY WAS WAITING AT THE DOOR WHEN I ARRIVED home around three o'clock. I picked him up as soon as my hands were free and pressed him to my shoulder. I hated to tell him that I'd be leaving again in a few hours, but the good news was that I'd be bringing Mom back.

I'd decided that I'd fix up my guest bedroom, which doubled as an everything room, for her so she would be taken care of for the evening, could play with Benny all she wanted, and could have a nice breakfast made for her in the morning. I'd brought home bear claws in case she preferred to stay home before heading to the chapel for Oliver's service.

I kept myself engaged, preparing a cheese omelet for Benny—was he the only cat in the world who loved brunch? I chalked it up to the fact that he was very familiar with the diner menu. I made a batch of Mom's new favorite cookie, salted caramel squares with chocolate chips. I straightened up the guest room, arranged a few magazines on the bedside table, and fluffed the pillows three times. Once Benny had eaten and groomed himself, he joined me in testing the mattress and walking over the magazines, making his favorite crinkling sound. Benny's tail stood straight up, the end twitching. It was as though he knew his true love would be sleeping here soon.

It seemed forever since I'd seen my mom, though it was only a little more than two weeks. But so much had happened. Well, maybe only one thing had happened, but it was a huge thing. A violent thing that had shaken me.

The obituary in the *Bugle* brought many thoughts of Oliver. Good things that I hoped would eventually overshadow the petty disagreements we'd had recently. I was inspired by the pride he took in his work—I'd seen him dump an entire platter of food because of a pinch too much salt. I was impressed by the generosity he showed whenever I needed an errand run or an extra hour from him. And when Victor broke his ankle skiing, it was Oliver who set up a schedule of volunteers to get him to and from work, signing himself up for a large share of the rides.

Was anyone ever happy with how she'd treated someone who died suddenly? I wasn't, and it was not Oliver's fault.

I prepped Benny for Mom's visit in case he hadn't intuited it. I was pretty sure Mom would have some elaborate toy for him. She thought of him every time she made a trip to Anchorage, where there was a shop, Purrfect, that catered to felines. But she'd also do things I seldom thought of doing, like wadding up tissue paper and leaving it around for Benny to play with or sleep on. I couldn't wait for the reunion.

As much as I enjoyed Benny, I was having difficulty filling the time this afternoon. Eager for my mom. Maybe it was Benny who gave me the idea by climbing onto a large shipping box in my hallway that Oliver had helped me carry in. Or maybe it was seeing Oliver's paycheck on my desk. He'd never warmed up to automatic deposit. In fact, Victor would tease him about not having a bank account, and Oliver never denied the allegation.

I called Chris. "Are you busy?"

"Nothing I can't walk away from. What do you have in mind?" He paused. "Am I always asking you that?"

"What would you think of visiting Oliver's house?"

"Whoa. Is that legal?" Another pause. "Wait. I'm a journalist. I can't believe I'm asking that."

"Funny."

"It's probably unlocked."

"Unless Troop locked it up. I assume he's been there."

"Did Trooper tell us not to go there?" Chris asked.

"No. He said to stay safe. Not to do anything alone."

"What could be safer than Oliver's house? The killer's probably not going back there," he said.

"Good point. And we wouldn't be going alone."

"Nope. We'd be together."

Yes, we'd be together.

CHRIS RANG MY DOORBELL AT FIVE O'CLOCK. I'D BEEN sitting on my mom's glider rocker in the guest room, my coat on my lap, Benny on my coat.

"Wish us luck," I told Benny, taking his face in my hands, nuzzling the top of his head, patting between his ears. "We're going to be taking a bit of a risk."

Benny wiggled out of my hands and scooted under the bed. I tried not to take it as a bad omen as I brushed his fur from my dark coat.

Chris had parked his truck off to one side so we'd have a clear path getting my Outback onto the street. I noticed that he'd changed into better pants than the old jeans he was wearing earlier. I'd dressed better for the airport also, with wool pants and a new turtleneck. One might think we were flying out instead of destined for the arrivals lot.

We had two hours before we'd have to head for the airport. Two hours in which to change our minds about stopping at Oliver's house. We could stop instead for a leisurely dinner at one of Anchorage's many fine restaurants. We could drive straight to the fifth Avenue Mall, which housed both national chain stores and boutiques, plus a post office and live jazz at certain times of the day. It would be a good opportunity to replace the worn, dated aprons in the Bear Claw with something new and fun from their housewares stores.

"Are we doing this?" Chris asked as I buckled in. He looked over at me and smiled as he positioned his hands at three and nine for optimum warmth from the steering wheel.

I couldn't quite acknowledge that, yes, we were doing this. I nodded, the most I was able to commit. Chris whispered an "okay," apparently his best confirmation.

"What if the house is locked up?" Chris asked.

"No one locks their door in a remote place like this."

Chris seemed to accept that and backed out of my garage. I punched in the address I had for Oliver's home: American Eagle Avenue.

"We won't need a number," I said. "It's the only house on the street."

"You've been there before?"

"Twice. Once to drop off his check when he wasn't feeling well, and a second time to deliver a container of soup for the same reason. Now that I think of it, I wasn't invited in either time. He said he didn't want me to catch his cold."

As we drove the rough road off Parks Highway, I was surprised to see the familiar dull red single-engine air taxi flying north, toward Talkeetna. If the passengers were climbers expecting to scale Denali today, they might be unhappy, grounded at the base camp, unless weather conditions had changed significantly. If they were tourists looking for a luxurious lodge and browsing the many shops along the main drag, they'd be satisfied. It was a little-known fact that air taxi pilots were the most flexible people in the transportation business. Whether it was a single person or a group looking for a trip to an odd location at an odd time, as long as there was a landing strip nearby, it could be arranged. Fares negotiable. Trade-offs welcome.

It was a short commute between Oliver's home and the Bear Claw, under a half hour, but that was enough time to place his home in a remote location, even by Elkview standards. The GPS directed us down a road with a sign that read AMERICAN EAGLE AVE., as if a one-home gravel pathway needed a wooden arrow on a post.

We reached the end of the path and stopped in front of the steps leading to the first-floor porch. I removed my sunglasses for a better view, and to be sure of what I was seeing ahead of me.

Uh-oh.

ELEVEN

WE'RE NOT GOING TO LET A LITTLE YELLOW AND BLACK tape stop us, are we?"

"We've come too far," I said, thinking I might be quoting from a movie or a top-selling album, but not sure what it might be.

"I'll bet Trooper or Deputy Josh What's-His-Name came out here, stuck the tape up, and didn't even go in," Chris said.

"Josh Peters. Why don't we move the car around to the back?" I said. "Just in case."

"Right."

In case what? I wondered if Chris knew any more than I did.

"Home" might have been too lofty a word for Oliver's abode, which was more like a two-story log cabin. We walked around to the front and up six steps to a massively cluttered porch. Smashed gasoline cans, car and bicycle parts, light bulbs, broken folding chairs, soda cans and bottles, buckets and jars, unidentifiable pieces of metal and glass.

"I remember all this junk from when I was here. It didn't

seem at all like Oliver, considering what a spotless kitchen he runs." I closed my eyes and took a breath. "He ran."

Chris put his hand on my shoulder and squeezed. "I'm sorry. I know this is hard for you."

I nodded my thanks.

"This is the sign of a military man," Chris said. "It's so no one can sneak up on him. This place is like a fortress." He swept his arms to include the whole building. "Did you notice how few windows there are, and all small? A security camera every few feet. No trees or bushes for cover. Clear line of sight to the lake."

"Fascinating." I hadn't noticed. Clearly Chris was better suited for detective work than I was.

"And look at the tiny deck above us," he continued. "It's a gun post. I'll bet there's a gun rack up there and an arsenal in the room that it's attached to."

"Oliver wasn't in the military. I'm pretty sure of that. Was he paranoid?"

Chris shrugged. "Maybe. Or maybe someone was out to get him."

We drew in a collective breath and fell silent.

THE CRIME SCENE TAPE HAD BEEN TACKED ACROSS THE front doorway, loosely, in the shape of an X. We approached it gingerly, trying to see under and over it, assessing whether the door behind it was locked.

"If he went to all that trouble with cameras and barriers, creating the perfect lookout, surely he locked his door," I said.

"Trooper might have left it open."

"If he went in," from me.

"If he went in," from Chris.

One of us was going to have to make a move. My chef, my responsibility, I decided. Besides, it was way too cold to stand around debating. The thermometer hanging by the door read two degrees Fahrenheit. I slid my hand under the crossover of the X and pushed my palm against a wooden side panel.

The door creaked open. We both took a step back and to the side. Expecting someone to rush at us from inside? Or worse, a gunshot? I tripped backward, falling into an old snow-filled wheelbarrow. As if I weren't cold enough.

Silence. No sound from inside. On the outside, only the weird guttural call of the winter-white willow ptarmigan, our stately state bird.

This time Chris took the lead, bent down, and crab-walked under the tape. He opened the door wider, and I followed, shaking off as much of the icy wheelbarrow snow as I could. We were hit with a musty smell, but in a kitchen with the level of neatness we'd expect of Oliver. Inside the house wasn't much warmer than the outside, but at least there was no wind. I removed my knitted cap and stuffed it in my tote.

"Look at that," I said. A shiny black espresso machine sat on a kitchen counter. "No wonder Oliver never drank Bear Claw coffee. Which is pretty good, I might add."

The rest of the first floor was more like Oliver than the messy porch. A row of coat hooks on the wall of the entryway held winter coats, jackets, and scarves piled on one another. Nestled among the down and fleece clothing was a rifle, leaning upright against the wall. A sentinel. Or a last-minute accessory when Oliver headed out?

In the kitchen, a large rack of pots and pans hung from the ceiling. Another rack, circular this time, hung above the stove, laden with skillets of various sizes.

"Why would he have all this cooking equipment? He

lived alone. You'd think he'd want to do anything but cook after all the hours cooking at the Bear Claw," Chris said.

"Busman's holiday, I guess."

"Did he come home and cook himself a six-course meal? Me, I have three saucepans. Small, medium, and large. And one skillet. Takes care of everything."

I chose not to remind Chris of the many meals he ate at the diner.

"I'm sure he tested recipes here," I said. "Or cooked something for himself that wouldn't translate well into mass production for the diner."

"Do you do that?"

"Now, that's getting really personal. Are you interviewing me?"

"Shall I?" He gave me one of those broad smiles I'd come to appreciate.

"I can see the *Bugle* headline now." I waved my hand, marquee style. "DINER OWNER DINES ON TAKEOUT."

Chris laughed. "What a good idea. I'll do a feature on the Bear Claw Diner. How climbers love the atmosphere. Truckers, too. The bear claws, of course. The cherry mousse. The great photos on the walls. What do you think?"

"Let's do this first," I said, not intending to follow through on an interview, ever. I cast my eyes around the sitting room that adjoined the kitchen. Using my own place as a reference, I estimated the total area of the first floor was not more than five or six hundred square feet.

We started up the stairs, each one creaking so loudly I thought it would break and we'd be plunged onto the kitchen stove. It made for a creepy feeling in the otherwise silent, empty house.

"Is this a military thing, too?" I asked the ex-army guy, who confirmed my thought.

The top landing led directly to an exercise room. Among smaller items was a contraption with ropes and levers and gears that resembled an entire gym-in-one.

"Again, I have to wonder," Chris said. "Why spend money on expensive equipment like this when you can run around the lake right outside your door?"

I was embarrassed to admit that I did neither, though I had resolved on New Year's Day to join a gym. I renewed that resolve now, almost three months later.

"If Oliver had a computer, it's not in here," Chris said. "That's what we'd need to see. But I doubt that he had one. He was pretty low-tech. No smartphone. No texting."

"And he never mentioned buying things online, the way Nina talks about getting her toothpaste online," I said.

In what was probably billed as bedroom number two of a two-bedroom house, we had to take back our judgment.

"Here it was," Chris said.

In a corner of the room was an old-fashioned rolltop desk with multiple slots above the writing surface. Its surface was dusty, but with a clear, undusty patch that was coincidentally the size of a laptop. The slots of the desk were empty, as were the side drawers.

"So Trooper was here," I said.

"Or someone was."

I snapped my fingers to a sudden memory. "I remember now that Oliver brought the computer into the diner when he first got it, months ago. He wanted Victor to help him set up software so he could write down recipes. I recall Victor wanted to show him a database program to go with it, but Oliver said something like, "Maybe later. Let me learn this first."

"So whoever took this"—Chris pointed to the telltale outline—"will be disappointed in what he finds."

"Or doesn't find."

We looked around the sparsely furnished room, Chris heading for a stack of sturdy storage trunks by the glass door to the small porch, I to a beautiful antique chest of drawers with a marble top that also had a dust pattern, though not as clear as that of the rolltop.

I expected the drawers of the chest to be as empty as those in the rolltop, and they were. Ditto for the closet. No clothes. No luggage either. Was it Oliver who'd stripped his bedroom, or the cops? Something to ask Trooper, as soon as we were ready to admit we'd-not-broken-into Oliver's home.

Chris opened the storage lockers and had the same lack of success. "Whoever was here carried off a large collection of guns," he said. He pointed to empty weapon-shaped gray molds of different sizes and shapes.

I was not sorry to hear that they were empty. My dad was never into hunting, preferring spectator sports and the occasional game of indoor tennis with his business partners. For a brief period, my parents decided the Bear Claw should have a gun on the premises. But it took only one news story of a child who'd accidentally shot himself at home with an allegedly secure pistol and the diner gun was history.

Now whenever hunters entered the Bear Claw we'd respectfully ask them to leave all weapons in their vehicles.

Surrounded by empty drawers and containers, we threw up our hands, if only figuratively. We'd started toward the stairs when I had another thought.

"That chest of drawers," I said, pointing back into the room. "It's a lot like one in old Lucas's shop."

"Beautiful carving. And the locks and keys on each drawer are pretty special. It looks like a pirate's chest."

"Funny you should say that. The one in Lucas's shop is supposed to have belonged to a pirate. Or maybe that's his way of justifying the four-figure price."

"But this one's empty, right?"

"Maybe not." I walked over to the long, elaborate piece of furniture. I bent low and felt around the edges of the bottom panel, below the last of the three drawers that had brass rings for opening them.

"You think that's another drawer?"

"On the one in Lucas's shop it is. It holds a sword with a fancy metal scabbard, supposedly from the War of 1812."

Chris chuckled. "I might have to check that out."

I continued running my fingers around the edges of the panel and managed to get the right leverage to pull it open from an overhang at the bottom. It was not a smooth ride for the drawer, with no spring loading to help. Chris squatted, and together we pulled out a long drawer.

The hidden drawer held paper, in the form of envelopes of different sizes, some bound together with rubber bands, some loose in the drawer.

"Pay dirt," Chris said. "It's Oliver's version of a safe-deposit box. No financial institution involved."

"Maybe it all belongs to a pirate."

We got comfortable in cross-legged positions on the floor and each reached for an envelope.

Thud.

The sound of a door slamming. We stopped short, our hands in midair.

I recovered quickly and hurried to clear the secret drawer of its contents and stuffed everything into my tote.

Chris tiptoed to the window that overlooked the front of the house. I looked at him, waiting for information. He shook his head and mouthed *I don't know.* He came back close to me and whispered, "Not a cop car. Regular sedan. Blue Toyota."

I gestured that I didn't know anyone who owned such a vehicle. I didn't know whether to be glad or sorry that it wasn't law enforcement, back for a forensics run. I did know that the shiver I felt was from fear, not cold.

The intruder, a different intruder from us, made a considerable amount of noise on the first floor. Someone ripping off the espresso machine?

Chris, probably sensing my fear, seeing the restlessness in my arms and feet, put his arm around my shoulder. The gesture had the calming effect it was meant to, but I wasn't sure for how long.

"Who's up there?" A voice from below. Deep, but most likely a woman's. "You dripped in enough snow for an army, but I'm guessing there's only one or two of you, or you would have stormed down here. I'm warning you, I am armed." I heard a loud click. Or it might have come from my brain, picturing the rifle I'd seen leaning against the wall in the entryway. "Come down the steps, slowly, with your arms in the air."

Not a wild and crazy voice, at least. It didn't take long for us to obey. Chris cut in front of me and started down the stairs. He unzipped his jacket and held his arms high and wide. I sensed that his intention was to provide a shield for me. *How nice,* I thought. And then I hoped we'd both be alive long enough for me to introduce him to Benny.

I risked a glance over Chris's shoulder to the bottom of the steps.

Kendra? Yes, Kendra, though she was so bundled up with thick jacket, hat, and scarf that I didn't recognize her immediately. She looked not wild and crazy, but not welcoming, either.

Oliver's sister did seem relieved to see us, however. Or was it a you-idiots-again look? In any case, she stared at us, put the rifle down by her side, and leaned on it. I wondered if I should be hurt that we seemed to pose no threat to her.

I started in on a little speech that I constructed as soon as I saw her. "We're here looking for things we might use for Oliver's memorial service or a little shrine in the diner. And I wanted to say something for a eulogy, or put together some photos. I—"

"Just leave," she said, her voice gruff. She waved the rifle as if it were a broom, sweeping us out the door.

"I don't want you to think we—"

"Sorry to bother you, Kendra," Chris said, ushering me out the door. Kendra had pulled the crime scene tape off the door and dragged it inside. We stepped over it. Chris gave me a gentle but firm shove in front of him and marched me down the steps. He didn't put his hand over my mouth, but his behavior had the same effect: *Let's quit while we're ahead, Charlie.*

I got the message. But I wished I could have made double espressos for us all. I pictured us sitting at the kitchen table sharing stories of Oliver's life. Instead, before I knew it, I was buckled into my Outback and on the road.

TWELVE

FOR THE NEXT HALF HOUR, ON THE WAY TO ANCHOR-age, our conversation was restricted to statements that required no comment and questions that required no answers.

"So scary."

"Kendra, huh?"

"I thought we were goners."

"Why is she avoiding us?"

"I wonder if she's staying in Oliver's house now."

"Did she take his computer?"

And finally, from me, "Thanks for shutting me up. I couldn't stop myself."

"I saw that. Pretty quick thinking, though. Coming up with that story."

"Thanks. It was kind of true, though."

"Meaning?"

I indicated the tote bag between my feet. "I stuffed some of the papers in here on the way out. They might contain something useful for the eulogy. Or the investigation."

"Let's hope. Nice going, by the way."

"Thanks."

"Now I know why women always carry purses."

"So we're always ready to raid a crime scene?"

"Something like that."

"We can look at it all when we're at the airport."

"You mean when we're sitting down to eat? I'm starving."

Chris was always starving, but that was a good thing for a woman who owned a diner.

We arrived at Ted Stevens International Airport, named for a World War II pilot who later represented Alaska as a US senator for four decades. I stopped to read a poster with salient FAQs about the airport. My childhood obsession with trivia, like why Moose's Tooth wasn't Moose's Jaw, was understandably reinforced during my days working at visitors' centers in various state parks. Who knew when I'd be asked to answer a question like "Where does ANC rank as a cargo hub?" (Answer: ANC is among the top five cargo hubs in the world.) Or "How many jets land at ANC on any given day?" (Answer: around seventy-five big ones, for an estimated three million tons of freight.) And, a fun fact to tell people you meet at a cocktail party: Anchorage is nearly equidistant by air from New York and Tokyo, and less than ten hours from ninety percent of the industrialized world.

While I immersed myself in ANC trivia, Chris had checked out the list of restaurants in the terminal and picked up a bouquet of flowers for my mom. More points for Chris. If he even cared about that.

We were early enough—eight twenty for my mom's nine fifty arrival time—to have a meal where there were tablecloths. But my eyes landed on a poster ad for Wright's Classic Diner.

"No, really?" Chris asked.

"I have to check out the competition."

Agreeable as usual, Chris joined me in following the signs to the diner. Wright's was nestled between a coffee chain and a dimly lit bar, all of which were sparsely populated at this hour. The image of Oliver's kitchen fresh in my mind, I had an urge for an espresso. I upgraded to a large macchiato, taking the risk of being turned away if I attempted to carry the green and white cup from the coffee shop into the diner.

Not a problem. The greeter hardly glanced at my cup. I'd never had that problem at the Bear Claw, since there was no coffee shop close enough, but I wondered if I'd be so lenient about other people's brands coming into my domain.

Once seated, I whipped out my notebook and, in spite of Chris's indulgent grin, listed the subjects of the photos along the wall, many of which celebrated Wilbur and Orville Wright and Kitty Hawk, of course. It occurred to me that the Bear Claw should have more photos of people, not only scenery. No question, our mountains, lakes, and photogenic wild life were spectacular, but why not also feature native Alaskans, or people who wrote about Alaska, like Jack London and John Muir?

Wright's Classic Diner was exactly the distraction I needed after the harrowing end to our time at Oliver's home. If you could call having a rifle trained on you harrowing—and I certainly did.

Today, before we even opened our menus, I heard "Burn one" for ordering a hamburger and "Bloodhound in the hay" for a hot dog with sauerkraut.

I thought about ordering hash just to hear the waitress say, "Clean up the kitchen." Instead I told Fran, our waitress, who looked old enough to have invented some of the jargon, to please bring me a splash of red noise. She let out a hearty laugh and yelled into the kitchen, "Bowl of tomato soup."

"Show-off," Chris said.

But it had been worth it to bond with Fran and tell her a little about the Bear Claw. Chris and I had taken a back booth with windows that looked out onto the airport's shopping mall.

I pulled my tote onto my lap and looked at the jumble of papers and envelopes I'd taken from Oliver's desk. I wrestled with whether to think of them as stolen or not, since I'd be using them for Oliver's benefit, not my own. I decided not to empty the tote onto the table but to extract only a few items at a time, to minimize the risk of dropping a piece of paper or an envelope and inadvertently leaving it behind. As paranoid and private as I now knew Oliver to be, I wouldn't have been able to live with myself if something personal had fallen out of my tote and been left on the floor at the airport.

I took out one of the larger envelopes, a standard brown color, nine by twelve inches with a brad closure. I saw the label for the first time. In Oliver's neat printing across the front: KENDRA BURKE.

I felt a wave of light-headedness. "Oh, no."

"What is it?" Chris asked.

I showed him the envelope meant for Kendra. "I never would have taken this. It's very personal." I took a breath. As if the other items in my tote were impersonal. "And what if she's looking for it right now? What if that's why she came to the house in the first place? To find these papers?" I made a move to stuff the envelope back into my tote.

"Well, there's no going back, Charlie."

I knew he didn't mean simply to American Eagle Avenue.

* * *

I TOOK CHRIS'S ADVICE: "NEVER MAKE AN IMPORTANT decision on an empty stomach."

After we finished our soup and bread dinner, Chris left the diner to check the sign for arrivals and found everything on time. The flight from Seattle was still listed as due at nine fifty. I asked Fran if she'd mind if we used her table as a work space for about half an hour.

She waved away any problem. "Anything for you, hon. And let me bring you some cookies right out of the oven. On the house." She winked. "Professional courtesy."

Chris rolled his eyes. "Diner love," I told him. He rolled them again.

I braced myself and retrieved the Kendra envelope, this time holding it with my thumb and index finger, as if to leave as small a set of prints as possible. *I hardly touched it,* I told the judge sitting on my shoulder, wagging his finger at me. Chris leaned over, took the envelope from me, and pulled out the sheets of paper. Three or four of them, it seemed. I figured he acted quickly lest I take them back and run off and give them to the police. Or turn myself in to the TSA, or whatever law enforcement was handy.

"Legal papers," Chris said, scanning them. "Sort of. Not a formal will. No letterhead. A simple statement that Kendra should get his house. It is notarized. Then there's a list of places where there's cash. Doesn't say how much."

"Places in his house?" Inexplicably, I whispered that question. A few more people, bearing shopping bags, had entered, and one woman took a seat at a table next to our booth. What if she were a cat burglar? She was, after all, wearing black leggings. I telepathically sent my apology to Benny for using that awful term.

"Some locations are in his house. Some in a storage unit. There's an address for that." He shuffled the pages. "This last one has to do with his vehicle, also going to Kendra. When it was last maintained and so on. All together, it amounts to a simple will."

Irrational as it was, I felt better not handling the pages, instead having Chris read them to me. I was pretty sure Chris knew that. He tapped the pages neatly and inserted them into the envelope.

"Are you getting the impression that Oliver was hiding something? Hiding himself, in fact?"

I knew what he meant, but I asked him to explain anyway. I needed time to think.

"A name change. A more or less cash existence," Chris said. "Working in a diner in Alaska when his credentials could have gotten him into a four-star restaurant in any big city." He paused. "No offense."

I smiled, pointing to the generous plate of cookies Fran had brought us. "None taken. I get your point. Living remotely with all that security and means of protecting himself seems to be another clue."

"It's like Witness Protection without the government."

"Not that it did him any good."

"It did for a while," Chris said. "Twenty-plus years at the Bear Claw, right? That's more than going to ground ever gets you unless you move around a lot. And for some reason, he didn't. It's a wonder he didn't just pack up that new extra-large vehicle and move."

I snapped to attention. "His vehicle. Oliver's new SUV. Where is it?"

"Wasn't there a detached garage? In fact, I thought we were headed there next, until Kendra arrived."

"Yes, but this new monster SUV, longer than my Outback, wouldn't fit in his garage. Oliver was bummed about it, but he really wanted the larger-model vehicle, so he'd made plans to extend the garage or build a new one. He was getting bids."

"Maybe he was planning to make a run for it and that garage remodel was a cover story so we'd think he'd be living here indefinitely," Chris said. "We need to ask Trooper where Oliver's vehicle is. Or was."

"Do you think it was at the crime scene? Like, maybe Oliver drove there, where he was—" I couldn't finish the sentence. I wondered if I'd ever be able to.

"It could be." Chris didn't need me to finish right now.

"Trooper wouldn't necessarily have told us that. He was short on details," I said.

Chris stretched his arms across the table and held his hands palms up. "Let's see what else we have in that tote."

"First, how do we get that envelope to Kendra?" I pointed to where the pilfered pages were covered up once more, invisible in the run-of-the-mill office supply envelope.

"We could mail it to her from here. It would have an Anchorage postmark, if any."

"Adding one infraction on top of another? Couldn't that be considered mail fraud?" I couldn't remember a time when I had to worry so much about bending—or outright breaking—the law. It all started with that little white lie to my mom on Monday when I denied that Oliver and I had almost come to blows over a change in a recipe. There was something to that slippery slope argument I'd learned in logic class.

"I think you're making more of this than we need to," Chris said. "Chances are there's no other family, right? So Kendra would get the house and car by default. She wouldn't need a piece of paper that doesn't even have a lawyer's letter-head."

"But she'd have to go through probate, which is a hassle."

"With that informal so-called document, she probably would, anyway."

You'd have thought I'd have been the one to acknowledge that, what with my property law creds and all.

"And the cash?" I wasn't about to give in so quickly. "How would she know where it is?"

"Some is in the house, which she'd clean out, and therefore find it. There must also be some kind of receipt for a storage rental in there"—he pointed to my tote, filled with useless papers in his mind, apparently—"and she'd go and claim whatever is in there."

"It sounds like you've done this before."

He laughed, but didn't deny it. Was this a one-off for Chris? Or a glimpse into how journalists got their stories?

Much of the rest of the loot was innocuous. Receipts for gas in one small envelope, groceries in another, clothing in another, and so on, for all the categories of items a typical adult will buy over the course of several months. It was hard to understand why he'd felt it necessary to put these ordinary receipts in a secure place. Well, almost secure. I felt awful, disloyal, and sneaky, browsing through Oliver's personal purchases. I had to remind myself I was doing it for him.

The final bundle was the thickest, barely squeezed into an extra-large brown clasp envelope. Two volumes were bound with plastic combs that gave them the look of a home crafts project.

The cover pages read: FRENCH RECIPES BY OLI-VER BLANCHARD, VOLUME ONE, and the same title with VOLUME TWO. I handed Volume One to Chris and kept the other.

"Why another name?" I asked myself, as well as Chris.

Chris scratched his head. "This guy has some weird stuff going on. I can't remember if our photo of the French culinary school had a caption with names."

I shook my head. "I'm pretty sure there were no names in the *Bugle* obituary photo, just info about the school. The earliest surname we had for him was Quinlan, when he graduated from high school. Then Whitestone. In between, I guess, was Blanchard."

We flipped through the pages, which were filled with recipes in the typical format: ingredients followed by instructions. Almost every one included a short anecdote, about a family's using the recipe for a holiday, or a description of the origin of the recipe, or variations that would also work. Some of the notes were handwritten. I was ninety-nine percent sure it was Oliver's handwriting. Oliver Blanchard was Oliver Whitestone was Oliver Quinlan, not necessarily in that order.

"So Oliver was writing a cookbook," I said. "And using a pen name."

"If he was, he was taking his time. This volume is dated almost thirty years ago."

"Same with Volume Two," I said.

I riffled through, and the would-be book fell open to the cherry cheesecake mousse that we'd almost taken off the Bear Claw menu. I remembered that Oliver had been adamant about getting rid of it, even though it had great reviews from our regular customers and on social media.

"I had it once or twice myself," Chris said. "This volume has no desserts. But there are a lot of fancy entrées, some in French with no translation. I think I can figure out *soupe à l'oignon,* but what's *confit de canard*?"

"It's essentially marinated duck, cured and slow cooked, but takes about a day and a half to prepare properly."

"Never mind."

"You prefer the Bear Claw's moose stew?"

"Well, I'd have to go to France and try that duck dish to really make an informed decision. Want to come?"

"Sure. Let's check the departures to Paris." I picked up my phone and noted the time. "Oops, we'd better get to the arrivals from Seattle first."

I started packing my tote, retrieving the potential cook-book from Chris, in case he had designs on publishing it himself. As it was, I felt pangs of guilt every time we strayed from the task at hand, like joking about French food or trips to France, instead of focusing on helping Trooper determine who had murdered Oliver.

"I wonder how all this fits together. The names, the se-curity, life pretty nearly off the grid. I guess that's how it is with death a lot of times," Chris said.

I nodded. "Someone looks at your connections, positive and negative, and tries to make sense of it all."

"You think one of those connections is related to Oli-ver's murder?" he asked.

"It's hard to say, isn't it?"

THIRTEEN

CHRIS AND I WALKED A FEW MILES, IT SEEMED, TO GET to the correct elevators, all the way remarking what a good thing it was that we were inside and on level ground. We arrived at the baggage claim carousel for my mom's flight before my mom and before her luggage reached it. Chris took a seat nearby but I was too excited to sit still. I used the restroom, where I brushed my hair and straightened out my turtleneck and sweater. As if my mom might send me to my room, which she might have done before I reached the preteen excessive grooming phase, when I'd started spending an hour in the bathroom getting ready for school.

Eventually, a crowd of late-night travelers headed our way, creating an avalanche of noise. The area was taken over by bouncing roll-ons; tired, cranky children; happy, screechy reunions; a blaring PA system with unintelligible messages. We could only hope they weren't warning us about an imminent disaster.

It was at times like this that I wished Mom were taller. I knew she was buried somewhere within the mob of tall and even medium-sized passengers who had deplaned the flight from Seattle. I remembered the days when I was glad she was so short, especially when I first shot up past her. It was always hard to reprimand a person you couldn't make easy eye contact with, even if that person was your daughter. It was embarrassing to point a scolding finger at someone several inches taller, and with broader shoulders. Mom's trick was to have me sit whenever she was about to issue an order. She wasn't about to deliver a "Clean your room, young lady" command while looking up at me.

Not that she delivered many edicts. Her strategy was to let me learn from my mistakes. When I was in middle school, I tripped and fell over the dirty laundry and odds and ends of tchotchkes on the floor of my room. The incident resulted in a sprained ankle, and caused me to miss a Saturday of ice skating on the lake with my friends. I'd kept the tidiest of tidy rooms from then on. I smiled thinking of that and became more eager to see her.

And there she was, peeking between two basketball-player-size guys who were helping her with her carry-on and her VIE-logo shopping bag from the airport in Vienna. I expected that they might swoop her up any minute and deliver her to me by air. She'd obviously made new friends, as usual. She seemed reluctant to leave them but managed to hurry toward me for a hug. A true Alaskan, she'd known enough to pack a windbreaker, scarf, hat, and gloves into her carry-on for easy access for the trip to the car and any other potential outdoor jaunt. She wore some of those items now.

During the long embrace, Mom whispered "Sweetie" and "How sad," over and over, rubbing my back. Always the consoler, no matter what.

When we broke, she noticed my companion, who handed her the flowers I'd completely forgotten about.

"From Charlie," he said.

"Thank you, Chris. How nice to see you."

Only then did I realize I hadn't told Mom that Chris would be with me. From the looks she gave me now, I knew she thought Chris and I were on a date. I mentally banged my palm on my forehead, as punishment for being so dumb. I knew I was in for some serious questioning once we got home.

"Sorry you had to cut your trip short," Chris said. He'd overseen the transfer of Mom's carry-ons to an airport cart while we waited for her major pieces of luggage.

"There'll be plenty more opportunities to see the rest of Austria. I want to hear about the investigation. Was Kendra any help? Are you at all close to finding out who did this to my friend?"

We did our best to fill her in on all the progress we'd made. Unfortunately, it didn't take long.

ONCE WE'D FOUND OUR WAY BACK TO SHORT-TERM parking and had Mom settled in the back seat with a baggie of the salted caramel cookies I'd made, she announced that she was going to nap. Right after she gave us the highlights of her first cruise, that is.

"Charlie, when all this is over, you have to go on a cruise. I highly recommend this line. Have you ever taken one, Chris?"

"I had all the cruising I could stand in the army, thank you."

"Oh, that's different. Did you have bathrooms with heated floors?"

"No, but Charlie has a heated steering wheel." He caressed the wheel at the two and ten positions for emphasis.

"My steering wheel is his new best friend."

"How about gorgeous views from the ship's deck, right on your veranda? Oh, never mind, you're going to tell me you can see Denali from your porch."

"Close," Chris said.

"I've got it. How about a putting green on the deck?" Chris gave her a "Me, golf?" look he made sure she could see in the rearview.

"Dad was happy with the green," she continued. "He also loved having Internet access most of the time, plus a comfortable lounge right in our suite, with a television and newspapers from around the world. And snacks. Lots of snacks. You probably don't want to see all the photos on my phone, so I'll spare you, you Alaska snobs."

"I'm glad you had a good time, Mom."

"Uh-huh. I have to admit, I'm an Alaska snob, too, and I love our state. I think a lot of my enjoyment was just having all that free time with so many options. Movies, card games, a library, live music, dancing. Not that we did much beyond a token turn around the floor, but everything was right at our fingertips. And one stop was at a small town in Germany where there was a magnificent cathedral, St. Stephen's, with an organ that has almost eighteen thousand pipes. Can you imagine?"

It was clear that Mom didn't need an answer since she dozed off immediately after asking the question.

MOM WAS REJUVENATED FROM HER NAP, WHICH TOOK the rest of the ride home, and Benny was the beneficiary of her newfound energy.

Benny had an excellent long-term memory. He remembered people he loved as well as people who irritated him.

Trooper and Annie were among his good friends, but Mom was at the top of the list. For causes unknown to me, the woman who delivered our mail was Benny's least favorite person. He made himself scarce whenever she rang the bell and handed me a package. I was sure he had his reasons.

Benny was more than ready for Mom. It was as if he'd known she'd be coming and took a nap at the same time as she did so they could play together. Unlike me, they were both chipper at one thirty in the morning.

After a sufficient amount of chin scratching, back rubbing, and eye contact with his old friend, he walked around the living room floor, his tail held high, its tip twitching in contentment. I heard the soft trilling he used in greeting.

Mom had brought Benny an elaborate wand toy with feathers and bells from a shop in Passau, a small German town where the ship had docked. A piece of colorful fabric cut in a circle with a stiffened edge, the toy was equipped with a battery-operated motor that propelled the feather around the edge at selected speeds. Benny chased it dutifully, meowing in gratitude.

Mom had more stories about people she'd met, plus two presents for me. One of them a tall hand-cut dinner bell made of western German crystal. I picked it out of its gift box by its exceptionally long handle.

"This is beautiful, Mom," I said, running my hand over its intricate design. "But it's so heavy. And long. This handle alone must be eight inches. How did you manage to carry it?"

"You know me. I can't be discouraged by details like that. Dad calls me the most impractical shopper."

"Let's see if Benny likes it."

I unwrapped the ringing device, a chain of glass beads with a crystal bead at the end. Benny, who usually bolted at loud noises, responded well to its lovely sound, adding his own purring to the chorus.

I needed to place the bell where Benny wouldn't knock it over. Wonderful cat and companion that he was, he didn't always respect the boundaries between my toys and his. For now, I put the bell back in its box and left it at ground level, under the coffee table.

The second present was a box of Belgian chocolates. For Benny's protection, that one would be safe neither low nor high, but in a cabinet inaccessible to even the most agile of felines.

It would have been a grand celebratory homecoming if it weren't marred by the reason Mom had returned early.

I THOUGHT I MIGHT HAVE TO SHAKE MOM AWAKE ON Thursday morning, but Benny took care of that, walking all over her bed and settling on her stomach with a giant purr. Too bad he didn't understand that not only had she just survived nearly twenty hours in airports and in the air, but her body thought it was still in Vienna, ten hours later. Or maybe he understood but didn't care.

Breakfast was "a stack of Vermont," Mom's long-standing phrase, from an informal diner dictionary, for pancakes with maple syrup. I seldom made breakfast at home. Why would I, when I had a staff at the diner to feed me? But it was fun to cook for my mom, Mrs. Evelyn Cooke herself.

"Excellent," she said, pointing her fork at me while holding it close to her breast at the same time. Of course, I was pleased.

YOU NEVER OUTGROW YOUR NEED FOR PARENTAL APPROVAL wasn't just a bumper sticker.

Benny was happy to have his daily dental treat without

syrup. Benny's taste in food was unusual for a cat, since he'd grown up with carefully selected leftovers from the Bear Claw. He ate quickly and slipped onto Mom's lap, too full to even sniff at her plate.

We took a call from my dad, who was heading down to the ship's dining room. He missed us but there was no question that he was looking forward to a steak dinner. "Beef, not moose," he clarified.

Mom was ready with further thoughts on the investigation into Oliver's murder. And I was eager to hear her take on Oliver's beginning, wondering if she was surprised that he'd been adopted. At the same time I remembered that I hadn't told her about his three names. That we knew of. What a job it was to keep track of everything in a murder investigation. Not the least of our problems was remembering who knew what information when. I decided to start a special notebook to keep track of things—or maybe I would ask Trooper for a sit-down and a summary of everything he had learned at Trooper School. I supposed my mom could give me the same kind of training from her crime-fiction habit.

Mom began with the adoption issue.

"Strangely, I never gave it much thought, how he had no family except Kendra. And no friends, it seemed, except girlfriends, and the occasional vendor or regular patron that he'd chat with, sometimes eat his lunch with. Like Manny, of Manny, Moe, and Jack. We were close when it came to the diner, both working hard and wanting it to succeed. But we didn't socialize together. Heck, your dad and I didn't socialize, period, except for the occasional dinner out when he had a client to impress. A few times on a holiday, if Kendra didn't come up from Anchorage, Oliver would join us. Or maybe they both would, but that was rare."

I never gave much thought to how hard my parents worked. Neither of them had a nine-to-five, no-homework kind of job. They didn't take weekends off, or even a day, unless you could count my middle school piano recitals and the parent-teacher conferences they were subjected to. Funny that it took a death to bring that home.

"As you saw," my mom continued, "I couldn't even remember what Kendra's job was."

"Real estate, as you now know."

"I'm sorry that trip didn't get you much information. But you did get a nice long ride with Chris."

I reached down and held out a tuna treat for Benny, thus putting that thread of conversation to rest. Benny gave me a knowing look, as if to say he knew I was using him as a distraction, not giving him a treat out of the goodness of my heart.

I moved on to Oliver's names, how Chris and I had tracked him from Quinlan to Blanchard to Whitestone. I described our visit to his home, leaving out the inauspicious, nearly smoking gun ending. I promised to show her the two volumes that had all the earmarks of a cookbook he was writing.

"Remind me later this afternoon," I said, aware of the approaching chapel time.

"I feel awful that I didn't know all this. What kind of employer, mentor, friend was I? Not the caring kind, that's becoming obvious."

It was my turn to help absolve my mom. "How could you have known? Did you hear what I told you about the way he secured his environment? Cameras, guns, noise-makers so you couldn't sneak in? For all we know, even the name changes were designed to keep anyone from getting too close."

Benny had gone off somewhere and now crept back in. My guess was that he heard my mom's sobs, as soft as they were, and came back to comfort her. I moved my chair closer, and the three of us shared a few moments of despondency and hope together.

THE USUAL WARDROBE PANIC SET IN, AS IT DID WHENever women were expected to show up at a special event. It didn't matter whether the event was a high school prom, a movie date, or a funeral service. Today, Mom and I helped each other pick out outfits that were serious, but not morbid; cheery, but not too cheery.

We decided purple was a go-either-way sort of color, and we layered accordingly, with lavender underpinnings and black winter coats with floral scarves. Not identical twins, exactly, but close.

I'd half expected Chris to call with an offer to drive us. I had a mixed reaction when he didn't. On the one hand, his absence would get me out of a discussion about him with my mom; on the other hand, I wanted to see him again.

"Would you like to stop at the Bear Claw before the service?" I asked.

She shook her head no. "I thought it would be good for us to get to the chapel a little early, while people are milling in the lobby, and see what we can find out. We don't have nearly enough clues to suggest who might want Oliver dead."

"You mean interview people in church?"

"It's not exactly church, sweetie. It's a nondenominational chapel for weddings, funerals, other services, I'm sure. Where to sit?" she said. "We should leave the front pew for Kendra, naturally, and maybe Gert? I believe she's Oliver's most recent girlfriend?"

"As far as I know. We haven't been able to contact Lana." Reporting to my mom added a different dimension to my project. Through no fault of hers, I felt like a failure, as if I should have made a citizen's arrest by now, perpwalking Oliver's killer into Elkview's two-trooper station.

"I'll probably recognize Lana. I met her a couple of times." Mom tapped her fingers next to the mug holding her second cup of coffee. "It might look strange if we're not up front, but I'd like to be far enough back to be able to see the other guests, to catch their expressions and so on."

First Chris, and now my mom. Did everyone in Elkview know more about detective work than I did? I guess a journalist and an addicted crime-fiction reader trumped a manager of a diner in that regard, even one with a year of law school under her belt.

It must have been thinking of my year of law school that triggered a decision. While Mom stepped away for a moment, I made a call to Chris.

"Hey, what's up?"

"I only have a minute while Mom is out of the room, but there's something I have to do."

"You want to give Kendra the papers."

"How do you know?" I asked.

"I do, too."

What I'd hoped to hear.

"I can hand them off at the service. It might be the last time I see her. I can say I found them in his Bear Claw desk," I said.

"She'll never believe you."

"So what?"

"I like the way you think," he said.

"But not the cookbook," I said.

"No, not the cookbook. It's practically part of the investigation."

"I like the way you think," I said.

MOM CAME BACK, AND SEEMINGLY OUT OF THE BLUE came the question she'd had probably been waiting all morning to ask.

"So. Chris?" She smiled, cocked her head, and raised her eyebrows. "Huh?"

"What about him? He offered to drive me to the airport."

"Uh-huh. And you went to visit Kendra yesterday. Together."

"Remember when I told you he's interested in helping Trooper? Trooper deputized both of us." We laughed at my retelling of the ceremony involved. "Chris knows the sorry state of law enforcement resources. And, you know, he is a journalist. I'm sure eventually he'll get a story out of all this."

"So that wasn't a date last night?"

"Not at all. Just an airport pickup."

There was one more unresolved issue in my mind. I hadn't told my mom about my run-in with Oliver the day he disappeared. I needed to confess how I'd kept the truth of our argument from her. I'd wanted to wait until Oliver waltzed into the Bear Claw, ready to go back to work as usual after one of our spats, and my parents had returned from their cruise, to tell her about it. If at all. But with Oliver never coming back, it was impossible for me to keep this from my mom.

I spilled it all, right up to Oliver's storming out and her

phone call a couple of hours later. "I just wanted to add a little chocolate," I said, trying to keep the whine out of my voice.

I shouldn't have been surprised at her response.

"Sweetie, I've known Oliver since he was younger than you are now. I knew he wouldn't take a recipe change lightly. And, most of all, I knew you wouldn't want to spoil our trip by telling me. Thank you for that."

Like the days when she applied bandages to my scrapes, she never failed as Healer in Chief.

Fourteen

I'D BEEN WRONG IN MY ASSUMPTIONS ABOUT THE Chapel of Atonement. Far from giving off a negative vibe, the property featured a lovely courtyard with strips of garden on either side of a large fountain and arched entryway.

Flowers bloomed everywhere—not easy to do in Alaska. If I hadn't been so intimidated by the formality of the setting, I'd have reached out to verify that the shrubbery and flowery arrangements were organic and not plastic. In fact, I suspected there might be small heaters, since the courtyard was so much more comfortable than the twenty-ish degrees outside.

The main altar was visible from the foyer, illuminated by light coming through a beautiful stained-glass window. Biblical quotations adorned the walls; a large panel offered the entire twenty-third psalm, "The Lord Is My Shepherd," meant to soothe the hearts and minds of mourners.

Eventually, maybe.

I'd followed my mom as she entered the foyer and joined the group that had gathered around Kendra. The man next to Kendra, whom I assumed to be her husband, looked familiar to me, but I couldn't say why. I wondered about the marriage I'd just arranged in my head, since Kendra's surname was the same as her parents'. I remembered that from the anniversary picture and article Chris and I had found in an Anchorage newspaper. It was still possibly her husband next to her. Many women kept their own names. I was embarrassed to think how I'd once envisioned myself as Mrs. Charlotte Jamison.

Had it only been yesterday that I'd seen Oliver's sister brandishing a rifle, with Chris and me at the wrong end? Here was another instance of my mom's failing me: I couldn't hide behind her. The fact that she'd worn flat-soled boots and mine had a wedge heel didn't help. I felt exposed to Kendra and as nervous as though she still had a gun trained on me.

Kendra accepted my mom's hand when she offered condolences, but managed to avoid taking mine.

"Oliver loved working with you," she told my mom. "Thank you for coming."

It was now or never. I moved my mom aside as gently as I could and approached Kendra, one hand already deep in my tote, grasping the two envelopes, ready to whip them out.

"Kendra," I said. "These appear to belong to you. I found them while going through Oliver's things at work." I managed to whisper the phrase "at work."

She gave me a withering look and asked, "You found them where?"

Another guest was nearby and seemed surprised when I moved out of the way to give him access to Kendra.

I cut my losses and drifted over to Gert.

"It's awful," I told Gert. "We really miss him at the Bear Claw."

"He was a big man," Gert said, surely referring to his personality and not his physical size. She was wearing a navy blue peacoat that might have been the most formal item in her closet. It was possible that I was envious of Gert's physique, since my ratio of gym sign-ups to gym appearances was embarrassingly high.

"What a strange coincidence," I said, "that he died the day you came into the diner looking for him."

"Yes, we were supposed to go to my friend's fiftieth birthday party that night. She was very disappointed, but"—she shrugged—"of course, we didn't know."

"Of course not. But I thought you were going to the movies?"

"Oh, right. I was thinking of another night."

"Did you go without him?"

"Huh? Oh, no. I stayed in."

"On birthday party night or movie night?"

Gert's back stiffened, like Benny's when he feels trapped. "Both. But why do you care? Why all the questions?"

A black-suited gentleman took center stage, sparing me the need to account for my not-so-subtle interrogation. Gert took the opportunity to walk away. With an appropriately soothing voice, the man in charge suggested that we all make ourselves comfortable in the main chapel.

I caught up with my mom, who leaned in to me and whispered, "Let's split up."

I assumed this was a tactic she'd learned from Agatha Christie, so that we could each survey a different part of the chapel. I gave her a barely perceptible nod, CIA-like, and took a seat in one of the middle rows of highly polished benches. In the spirit of good detection, I didn't watch where she ended up.

I'd seen smaller side chapels on my trek down the long,

wide center aisle. One of them had an enshrined Bible that
was larger than the lectern. I wondered why Kendra hadn't
opted for one of the less massive chapels, given the small
number of guests. I counted a dozen people in front of me.
When I cast a furtive glance behind me, I saw about the same
number, including Trooper, who was slinking into the back
row. We were too far away from each other in the cavernous
chapel to connect, but I felt his gaze nevertheless. I noticed
he was in his dress blues and hat, not the logo windbreaker I
usually saw him in.

I looked in vain for Chris, thinking he might see me and
join me in my otherwise empty pew. Maybe he was following the same rule as my mom, distributing resources for the
investigation. I opted for that interpretation.

Kendra had planned an extensive program of musical
selections. I had the thought that she was making up for the
dearth of speakers by filling in with hymns. It was to be
expected that not too many of Kendra's circle would make
the drive from Anchorage to the Chapel of Atonement,
more than two hours' drive on a good day. And some late-
season precipitation was predicted for today, which could
mean anything from sprinkles to icy rain. Besides that,
there had been virtually no time to gather Oliver's loyal
customers.

I used the musical interlude to assess those present vis-à-
vis viability as a suspect.

Gert was directly across the aisle from me, her hands in
the pockets of her thick coat. She'd already made the suspect list when I considered how she'd dashed into the diner
asking for Oliver on the day he was murdered. My newly
suspicious mind had decided she was motivated by the
need to be remembered as wondering where he was, even
though by then he was dead. Today she went up a notch on

the list when she told me a different story about that aborted date. A simple misrecollection? But it had been only three days, and while a movie date might be easy to forget, missing a friend's fiftieth birthday party wasn't. I considered whether to pursue that line of questioning at the reception following the service. In the end, it depended on whether there was enough of a crowd around me, in case she was a killer.

Victor had always been high on my list, since, other than Kendra, he was probably the only one who benefited from Oliver's absence. He now sat in front of me and to the right with Nina. He'd texted me earlier that Rachel, who'd never met Oliver, would stay behind and do some cleanup and be available in case a vendor showed up. We'd also need her if any guests took us up on our offer of dessert at the Bear Claw.

I had the idea that the minister of the chapel could announce the invitation, after the wine and cheese reception following the service. Rachel would get a text with an alert to start the coffee, the ovens, and the cherry cheesecake mousse if we had any takers. The graveyard-shift team of Tammy and Bert were also on call for the possible memorial crowd.

Annie, who was a few benches ahead of me, was always willing to step in. She'd texted me earlier that Pierre's car part had come in and he'd be leaving soon. A sad-face emoticon followed.

It took me a minute to identify the man sitting next to Annie. Not Pierre. Neither he nor any of Annie's tourists had ever met Oliver, so I didn't expect them to attend. A closer look told me that Annie's seatmate was Manny, the local-resident third of the Manny, Moe, and Jack trio, looking dapper in a suit. No wonder I hadn't recognized him right away. I wasn't surprised to see him, since I remembered that he and Oliver sometimes had lunch together when their schedules allowed, even if Moe and Jack were not around.

Still no Chris.

So what?

Back to my focus on the suspect list for Oliver's case.

I wondered if one of the women I couldn't identify in the ad hoc congregation was Lana, Oliver's ex-girlfriend. My mom had said she'd recognize her, and maybe Mom was even now assessing Lana's behavior. Why hadn't I thought to quiz my mom about what to look for when sizing up a potential suspect? Despondency? Sly smiles? Engaging in cheery conversation or withdrawn and stoic? Was there a way to tell crocodile tears from genuine ones? Was there a class I could take in case I found myself in this situation again?

It wasn't pleasant, but I had to think of my next in command after Oliver. Victor's candidacy as a suspect was awkward to consider, as was that of anyone I thought I knew well. Who wants to suspect someone with whom she has daily contact, trusts with her business and her patrons? Victor was very thoughtful and supportive of his sister, helping her with college funds. Did real cops consider sibling bonds when dealing with the profile of a murderer?

In a struggle, if it came to that, it was hard to say who'd have the advantage. Oliver was heavier than Victor by a lot, but Victor was more fit and more agile.

Another big factor leading me away from Victor as the killer was his age. Oliver was fifty-one years old, Victor barely thirty, in a position to wait his turn to take charge of the kitchen. But the speed with which he took Oliver's name off the new menu and emptied Oliver's desk drawer was suspect in itself.

Come to think of it, I hadn't sorted through the envelopes I'd retrieved from the wastebasket that day. My head hurt from having to remember so many details. I needed a spreadsheet. Or a secretary. Or to give up trying to play detective.

But with all the players surrounding me in the chapel, I couldn't resist.

Kendra was front and center, with the man I assumed to be her husband. Why had she rushed to have this service? So no new evidence would surface that might incriminate her? I wondered about her financial situation. Had she been counting on her inheritance from Oliver? It would be useful to know what her husband did for a living. Were they in debt?

Most nagging question: how did a badgeless temporary deputy find out the answers to these queries?

Second most nagging question: What if the killer was no one I knew? Not in the Elkview community. A friend or colleague of Kendra's. One of several people scattered in the pews who I couldn't identify. A Mr. or Ms. X, who might also be the real reason for Oliver's reclusive life?

Worse, what if the villain was a random killer? Someone passing through town who didn't even know Oliver.

In all these cases, I'd never find them. Isolating a few people from the population of a state with more than seven hundred thousand people seemed an exercise in futility.

While I pondered these heavy questions, Kendra stood and walked to the podium. Burgundy was definitely her go-to color. She could have been a television weather lady in a dark long-sleeved dress with a cowl neck and narrow belt. The look was more contemporary than the fifties-style mint sweater set we'd seen her in at her office.

I could barely hear Kendra's eulogy, only catching words like "devoted brother" and "generous friend" and "sorely missed."

When she returned to her seat, the man with her took her place. His outfit was like that of all the other men in the assembly: a dark suit, light shirt, and tie. *How easy for men,* I thought, not for the first time.

"Good morning," he said. With the light focused on him, standing there, tall and thin, I knew a split second before he said it. "I'm Stanley Burke, Oliver's brother."

I remembered the two occasions when he'd come to the Bear Claw, months ago. One time looking for Oliver, the other time finding him there and fighting with him. And a third, when I saw him in the lobby this morning, thinking he looked familiar. I wished I'd paid more attention during his brief visits.

A wave of irritation hit me—yet more questions in a case with nothing but. *Kendra, Kendra. Did you forget that one small detail when we met? And why wasn't he mentioned in the obituary? What else are you keeping from us? Why are you so not transparent? Don't you want your brother's killer brought to justice?*

Stanley Burke was most likely Kendra Burke's real brother, assuming either she was not married or she'd kept her name if she was. In any case, it would make sense that she'd protect her blood brother if he'd murdered her adopted brother.

Although his voice boomed, I could hardly pay attention to Stanley. I concentrated instead on checking out my mom's reaction, but she'd been dwarfed once more by those around her. I looked for Chris and saw him sitting where Trooper had been, apparently having arrived late. And

Trooper—it seemed he had sneaked out early and missed this little addition to the suspect list. Besides that, Moe and Jack had arrived when I wasn't looking, and I saw them now in one of the last rows. While not as formal as Manny in his suit today, they both looked considerably more cleaned up than when they swung themselves down from their rigs for lunch.

I did what any millennial would do. I buried my smartphone in the folds of my coat, with only part of the screen and keyboard visible, and sent a text to Trooper.

Oliver had brother Stanley Burke.

Will find out where he lives.

After closing hymns, the next step in Oliver's final day was to carry his ashes to the columbarium. A covered walkway led to an enormous area lined with separate niches for storing and displaying urns. Nothing was small-scale in the Chapel of Atonement, including the final resting place for the ashes of its clients.

A plaque at the entrance advised that there was accommodation for more than eight thousand urns of cremated remains in nearly five hundred feet of wall with curves and turns in several places. Some of the niches had room for more than one urn or a vase of flowers, at the pleasure of the deceased's family. The documentation also listed notables whose remains were held here. Alaska city mayors, sports figures, educators, and more than a few explorers were listed, with the corresponding location in the maze of stone.

The family—who actually knew for sure how many members there were?—of Oliver Whitestone, born Quinlan, aka Blanchard, had chosen a one-urn corner cube with what seemed to be a plexiglass door. A small chorus of young people sang a hymn, and the gathering moved once more, this time to an elaborate hall where wine and cheese and plates of canapés were offered.

It was not an orderly procession from the pews through the walkway to the columbarium proper. I noticed people siphoning off to visit the more compact chapels and gardens on the way, perhaps to meditate, perhaps to find a rest area. As for me, I wormed my way to the side of Stanley Burke. Not a difficult feat, since we were both taller than the average mourner present today.

"My condolences on the loss of your brother," I said, mimicking my mom's sentiment to Kendra. "It must have come as a shock."

"You were his boss, right?"

I nodded. "For the last year, yes. I'm Evelyn Cooke's daughter, Charlotte." I held out my hand and, unlike his sister, he accepted it graciously. "Oliver worked with my mom for many years."

"Well, you probably both know that Oliver could be difficult."

I thought it an odd comment on a recently deceased family member. But, of course, Oliver was not Stanley's blood relative. "Was he in any particular trouble that you know of?"

Way to be subtle, Charlie.

"You mean other than putting everyone else in danger?"

"I didn't know. I wonder if the police are aware of this? As you know, they're investigating his death. Maybe you should—"

We'd reached a fork in the road, in more ways than one. Stanley veered to the right and gave me what might be considered a tiny salute. "Excuse me. I'm going to find my sister."

And, I supposed, find people who genuinely wanted to offer condolences and didn't just want to interrogate him.

For the moment, the only thing I could do, stranded as I was in a tangled web of columbarium nooks and crannies, was test a canapé.

Servers in black-and-white uniforms had been weaving among the guests carrying trays of decorative canapés that would have done Oliver and his French cuisine training proud. I spotted mascarpone with sprouts and onion on a cracker, smoked salmon mousse with mustard and dill on toast, herbed biscuit bites with ricotta and seeded jam. Recipes and aromas reminiscent of my own culinary training came back to me. This was not diner fare, and it forced me to question issuing an invitation to the Bear Claw.

I slipped a miniature deviled egg into my mouth and closed my eyes for a moment to analyze the ingredients.

"Pretty fancy, huh?" Chris was next to me.

I put my hand to my mouth to prevent unpleasant spraying and nodded. "I'm rethinking my idea to have a little gathering at the diner."

"Don't be silly. The Bear Claw was Oliver's place, not this setup." He reached out to a passing tray and nabbed a canapé with chopped Greek olives over something white. "Mmm." He smiled. "You should get the recipe for this one."

Without warning, he leaned in to me. "Did you make the drop?"

I laughed. "The pigeon has landed."

It was the best I could do on short notice.

I let Mom follow through on what we'd initially decided. She handed the man in charge a slip of paper. He tapped on a piece of wood that was part of the wall, and once he had our attention he read from the note.

"Everyone is welcome to share a final goodbye to Oliver at the Bear Claw Diner in Elkview, where he plied his craft for twenty years." The address followed; then he nodded toward me and my mom. "Thank you, Ms. Cooke and Mrs. Cooke."

The modest crowd headed for the Chapel of Atonement exit.

Though I couldn't be sure what the count would be, I texted Rachel:

crowd on the way. approx 30 min.

cherry cheesecake mousse, limited menu in case, lots of coffee.

Mom and I convened in the parking lot and headed for the diner in my Outback.

"That was nice," Mom said. "And I'm glad we're going to do this at the Bear Claw. I doubt Kendra and Stanley will come, but they may be shamed into it if, for example, friends of theirs from Anchorage want to come. They can't very well say they're not interested. And they—by 'they' here I mean cops—say that the killer almost always shows up at funerals, and the Bear Claw now is part of the memorial celebration, so let's be on the lookout."

"For what?"

"For anyone who doesn't belong, for one. Someone we can't account for as a friend or a relative. Also, anyone who asks about the investigation. Sometimes that means they're really interested because they care about the victim; sometimes they're just voyeurs; but other times they are the

killer and want to know if the cops are close to finding
them out."

"It sounds tricky."

"It is. But you're good with people."

I was tempted to remind her of my failed engagement to
a particular "people," Ryan What's-His-Name.

"You've been in customer service in a way for many
years," she continued. "You'll know, sweetie. Just keep
your eyes and ears open. I'll be doing the same. We're going to find Oliver's killer."

It seemed that roughly half of a cruise ship existence
was enough for my mom. I no longer wondered what she
was going to do in retirement. I couldn't wait to see how
Trooper, her old friend, would react to her vision of her next
career as an amateur sleuth. I surprised myself by picturing
me, her only child, as a willing partner.

FIFTEEN

FOR THE LAST COUPLE OF MILES BETWEEN THE CHAPEL of Atonement and the Bear Claw Diner, my mom used my phone to play with Benny and the laser. She also accessed the remote robotic mouse and found more features than I had been aware of.

"These apps will never replace hand-to-paw contact," she said, "but it's more fun than I thought it would be. I don't know about talking to him, though. He might have been a little freaked out, wondering where the human behind the voice is."

"We have a very high-tech cat. I'm sure he knows what's happening."

"Here we are," she said, pivoting. "Remember our mission. To root out Oliver's killer."

"Assuming he's here. He could be anywhere."

"Don't be discouraged, sweetie. We just have to keep at it."

I pulled around to the back lot of our diner. Today the jolly bright neon sign over the front windows seemed inappropriate. But I was ready to cook, to serve, and to be on the lookout, using my eyes and ears as Mom had counseled. It occurred to me that she'd given me more detective training than Trooper had.

Once again, I was proud of my Bear Claw staff. I'd seen Victor and Nina make a beeline for the exit at the chapel once the invitation was issued for a final tribute to Oliver. I'd counted at least three, if not four, "final" steps to the memorial day already, but Oliver deserved every one of them.

He would have been pleased at how many turned out to acknowledge his great contribution to Elkview's diner, especially given the short notice Kendra had given us. I looked around as recommended by Detective Mom and saw almost everyone who'd been at the chapel.

It seemed easier to let people order from the menu than to try to put together something fancier.

"They've already had 'fancy' at the chapel. Let's give them a real lunch," said Victor, who was all fired up for the task. I did my best to keep from judging him for being so cheerful. His attitude as well as mine was fodder for tonight's debriefing with my mom and Benny.

Nina had put her own spin on things when she asked if it would be okay to close off the booths that lined one side of the Bear Claw. I agreed that booths were restrictive, and it would be better for mingling if only the tables were available for today's guests. The stools would also be handy for the overflow.

"I unplugged the jukebox," she said. "The queue was full of rockabilly, which I thought might be too upbeat. I brought some classical music on my tablet. Okay if I play it?"

"Good thinking, Nina. Thanks."

Sometimes I wondered if the Bear Claw needed me at

all. Then a voice in my head—Benny's?—reminded me of the behind-the-scenes work I spent a significant fraction of every day taking care of. Budgeting, inventory control, ordering supplies, paying the utility bills, and—not my favorite—ensuring our compliance with licenses and health-and-safety legislation and guidelines. The last item seemed to change on the whim of our elected officials. I remembered my mom's anti-stress advice when she'd symbolically handed me the keys:

"Just keep the lights on and you'll be fine."

It had taken a little more than that, but for the most part, I was enjoying the learning curve. One of the responsibilities I knew I'd neglected was that of any kind of marketing. Mom told me she hated that, too. The one time she'd managed to get something going along those lines was shortly before I came back. She'd gotten the Bear Claw's name included on a list of what were deemed "Good Old-Fashioned American Diners." Maybe that could be my particular contribution to the growth of the business. Chris might be able to help. Hadn't he said we made a good team? Once we cleared up this police investigation, who knew what else might be in store?

I pushed all that to the back of my mind and focused on today. With soft piano music and the aroma of melting cheese in the background, I tried to talk my mom into sitting on a high chair in front of the register and handing people menus, telling them what on the menu was available this afternoon.

"You mean you want me to be a greeter? I don't think so." She'd pointed to her flat-soled leather boots. "I'm ready to work."

She lived up to her promise, working the kitchen and the dining area. And working the room. Now and then, she'd find me and ask how I was doing. I wished there were more to tell, some clue I'd uncovered, an aha moment when the killer slipped up right in front of my eyes.

Not surprisingly, Oliver's siblings didn't show up. Chris told me he'd overheard Kendra tell a couple she couldn't join them at the diner because she had to be at work early tomorrow morning.

Trooper was also among the missing, but I expected him to stop in when he had a break in his exacting schedule. That was my hope, that he would consider Oliver's case as important as any other he might be called to.

On the plus side, Annie picked up Pierre and two other members of Beth's tour group who'd offered to help us out. The three of them made decent servers despite their lack of training. Pierre failed miserably, however, when it came to American diner jargon. He didn't buy the usual rationale—that the lingo was a shorthand means of communication between the waitstaff and the kitchen staff.

"How is 'keep off the grass' shorter than 'no lettuce'?" he asked.

He had a point. Victor's justification was reduced to "It's more fun."

Chris spent some time talking to a woman who seemed to be alone otherwise, both at the service and now in the diner. They each maintained a somewhat serious expression, except for the occasional smile. It was hard to tell her age since she kept bundled up the whole time in a winter coat with a spectacular hat and matching scarf, though the diner was at its usual comfortable temperature. I noticed Chris making two trips to their table, with coffees and two plates of cherry cheesecake mousse.

My mom came up to me as they started in on the dessert. "Don't worry, sweetie. He's with Lana Bickford, Oliver's ex-girlfriend. Getting some intel."

I'd never admit it to Mom, but I was relieved. A little. At the same time, I remembered that Lana was a first-class knitter and sold her craft through her blog. Thus the amazing red bargello hat-and-scarf set she wore today. "Why would I worry?" I asked my mom.

"No reason," she said, as she danced off with a tray of water glasses to serve the row of tables.

Lana stood as soon as Gert Marcus entered the diner. Lana shook Chris's hand and approached me.

"Thank you for inviting me," she said. "It was all very nice."

"I'd love to talk to you some—"

"Have a good day." She turned so quickly that her scarf almost hit me. She left without looking back.

Lana and Gert were following a time-honored rule: only one girlfriend or ex-girlfriend at a time in any confined space.

Mom and I took a turn at loading the dishwasher. We decided not to run it lest it drown out the lovely music Nina had chosen, this time from a chamber orchestra. If she ever wanted to quit the diner, she could apply for a position at the Chapel of Atonement, running their piped-in music department.

"I assume you planned to absorb the cost of this?" Mom asked when the sink was ready for another round from the cooks.

"Of course. You might want to mention that in your toast."

"Are you sure you don't want to make the toast yourself?"

"It's just math, Mom. My one year versus your twenty with Oliver. I'll stand next to you, how's that?"

"Okay." She cleared her throat. "Just so you know, I moved the tip jar a little, so they'll see it as they pass." She cocked her head toward the ovens and stove. "The staff really came through, didn't they?"

I couldn't have agreed more.

A few minutes later, Chris cornered me in the back hallway.

"That was Lana, Oliver's ex, I was talking to. I have a lead on why they broke up, and it fits with what we're thinking."

It was a lively day for information flow in the Bear Claw. Chris related what I already knew about Lana's crafts and the Alaska State Fair. But the rest was enlightening.

"There are competitive food exhibits at the fair—I've covered them, actually—and Lana was always after Oliver to participate. There were ribbons and pretty sweet cash prizes, but Oliver never wanted any part of it. She apparently oversold it, pushed him too far. He claimed she talked about it all the time since she won prizes every year. One day he just called it off, said she was obsessed with exhibits and prizes, and he didn't need that kind of approval, et cetera." Chris threw his shoulders back. "How about that?"

"Another check mark in the 'Stay out of the Limelight' column," I said.

"Hey, have you ever thought of entering your bear claws at the state fair?" he asked me. "Or anything else from your kitchen? That incredible cherry cheesecake mousse, for example?" Here he rubbed his stomach.

"What? No. I have enough to do." I waved my hand around my diner, now being managed beautifully without me. "I could never compete with the sixty-five-pound cantaloupe that won last year." It was the best excuse I could come up with for not showing off at the fair.

He laughed. "Or the thirty-five-pound broccoli the year before?"

Something that had been bothering me finally surfaced. "Why here? Why come back here if he wanted to hide? It doesn't make sense."

"Okay, I won't nag you like Lana did to Oliver. Are we back to the theory that he was hiding?"

"He was born here, or close to here. He grew up in Anchorage, at least from when he was eight years old or younger in the group home. He graduated from high school in Anchorage. If he wanted to disappear, why wouldn't he go to Florida?"

Chris shrugged. "He likes the cold?"

I snickered. "Someplace in Maine, then. Or North Dakota. There are plenty of cold cities, if he wanted to remain in the States. One of my college roommates lives in Minnesota, about ten miles north of the Twin Cities. She told me it was minus forty-eight degrees there on New Year's Eve."

"Okay, I hear you. We need to figure out why he came back. It wasn't for a woman, that's for sure."

"What's not for a woman?" Annie came to the back of the diner looking for my mom, to tell her that people were making moves to leave and she might want to make her toast soon. She shook her finger at Chris and me, smiling all the while. No one would ever believe that Annie had a strict and scolding bone in her body. "While you're enjoying yourselves, I've been trying to gather intel like your mom told me to, Charlie."

"We're all ears," Chris said, while I cupped my hands to mine.

"Don't get excited. I found Oliver's girlfriend, Gert Marcus, and bombed. I tried the 'Where were you when you heard that Oliver had been found dead?' trick, but she was onto me and said she went shopping in Palmer with a friend all day, then they had dinner together."

I told Annie that what she'd reported actually was exciting, since it was the third alibi Gert had offered. Two alibis might be blamed on poor memory. Three alibis means you're out.

"I ended up just talking to her about the new theater since she worked for the construction company," Annie said. "I asked her when it might be open, because we have a plan for a movie a week. Right, Charlie?"

"Right." Something like that.

"Well, much to my dismay, Gert said she didn't know. She'd quit last week, thinking she might be moving out of the area, maybe to the lower forty-eight, but now she's up in the air and doesn't know what she's going to do. So we'll have to find another contact at that construction company."

"Oliver and Gert were planning a getaway," I said.

"How do you know that?" said the small group, in one form or another.

I opened my mouth to explain, then realized I had no proof. It had been a random thought that wouldn't have left my mouth if I'd given it any thought. I was glad when the back door opened and Alaska State Trooper Cody Graham entered the already crowded hallway. We all fell silent, as if the teacher had caught us talking during quiet hour.

When my mom joined the group, it was time to make a move. I broke the silence.

"It's time for the toast, Mom."

AFTER A LITTLE SCRAMBLING TO FILL EVERYONE'S glass with sparkling water or the soda of their choice, Mom gave a brief but beautiful and heartfelt tribute to her chef and friend, ending with one of his favorite quotes: "A diner is live theater, where the diners are the most important members of the cast."

I watched as people reached for their coats and a line started to form for them to say goodbye to my mom and me.

The sound of silverware clinking on glass broke through the chatter and the music, and one by one, we stopped what we were doing or saying.

Manny, of Manny, Moe, and Jack, stood on a chair. I smiled, remembering how Moe and Jack, who I just noticed had left early, teased him about his height, or lack thereof, and his age, which was close to retirement status. I thought how nice it was that he wanted to add his own tribute to his friend. He raised his glass and began, in a strained voice that sounded like tears might flow at any minute.

"I just want to say thank you to everyone. Thank you all for filling in for me. For being there for him when I couldn't be. Wouldn't be." He stopped to catch his breath. "I'm so proud of what he became. Oliver was my son."

What? Whoa.

SIXTEEN

AT LEAST I THOUGHT THAT'S WHAT MANNY SAID. HE was too choked up to be really clear.

Then there was another *duh* moment. An I-should-have-known moment.

Manny's real name was Arnold Quinlan. Quinlan, as in eight-year-old Oliver Quinlan. The boy who was adopted by the Burke family after the terrible fire that leveled the group home where he'd been living.

Chris and I were in Anchorage waiting for our second session with Kendra, the one that she bugged out on, when we learned Oliver's birth name. His surname had seemed familiar to me at the time, but I hadn't been able to make the connection with Manny's given name. I excused myself on the grounds that Quinlan was a little more common than, say, Rumpelstiltskin, in which case I would have figured it out immediately.

Oliver had been dead only three days, and so many secrets had surfaced. Who knew how many more were yet to be revealed?

I became aware that my mom, standing next to me, was talking, in a soft voice, as if to herself.

"I thought it was a huge surprise when I learned that Oliver was adopted," my mom said. "I've known him for two decades." She sighed, then continued. "Then again today when Stanley told us he was Oliver's brother." She was fanning herself with a menu—because all the ovens were still sending heat our way, or because she'd had too much excitement in the last twenty-four hours, or however many it had been since she left Vienna? "Now I'm hearing that one of my trusty regulars is my departed chef's father?"

I stayed close to her, worried she might fall over from exhaustion or shock.

Manny maneuvered his stocky body down from the chair. He stood still for a moment, as if he didn't know where he was or in which direction to proceed. Before he could take two steps, Trooper and Chris were on him, my mom and I not far behind. We removed the rope from a booth, guided Manny to one side, and squeezed in around him. I cleared the way for my mom to sit by the window and slid in beside her. Chris, Manny, and Trooper sat opposite us. My mom reached across the table and took Manny's hands in hers. No words were exchanged, but the connection was obvious.

My mom had recovered and resumed her role as healer.

The other guests, untraumatized by Manny's innocuous-sounding announcement, wandered out the door, some waving to us as they passed. We were finally alone in the dining area.

Was it fair to leave all the cleanup to my staff? I thought so, once I scribbled a note and handed it to Nina. We'd close the diner all day tomorrow, Friday, a paid vacation day for any one of them who'd shown up today. Even Tammy and

Bert, who'd pitched in. Tammy had served as the perfect greeter, the job my mom had shunned. But then, Tammy wasn't playing detective. Bert claimed to love the busboy role, which gave him a chance to hoist loaded trays above his shoulder.

I'd figure out the budget for all this later, as well as whether to include Annie (yes, even though she eventually joined us in the booth) and the three volunteers from Annie's inn (maybe, unless I learned that they were wealthy tourists). Annie had leaned in to Pierre, both of them in the kitchen when Manny made his announcement. She must have been as surprised as Mom and I were.

Nina read the note I'd given her to the crew, all of whom gave me a big thumbs-up and seemed to work even faster.

By the time I turned my attention back to my booth mates, poor Manny was being plied with questions.

"Did Oliver know you were his father?"

"Or maybe suspect?"

"How about Kendra and Stanley?"

"How old were you when Oliver was born?"

"Who's his mother? Did Oliver know her?"

"Do you keep in touch with her?"

To break the tension, I asked, "Do Moe and Jack have kids who work here, too?"

Manny smiled at that, which was what I was going for. I also called for a carafe of coffee and the last bits of cherry cheesecake mousse—the best I could do to give Manny a chance to catch his breath and tell his story. Annie transported everything to our table, then took a seat. Her volunteers stayed in the kitchen with the rest of my helpers.

"There's really not much to tell," Manny said.

It was impossible to control our laughter at that sentiment, or gauge whose was the loudest, the most contained, the deepest, the most sustained.

"Okay, okay," Manny said. He cleared his throat. "First, my name is Arnold Quinlan, the father of Oliver Quinlan."

"Did I walk into a Fathers Anonymous meeting by mistake?" Chris asked. Another round of laughs, briefer this time.

"I met Oliver's mother in school, of course. Olivia and I, we were in love the way teenagers can be, I guess. I won't bore you—"

"Bore us," my mom said.

"Well, you know, she got pregnant. Nowadays, you'd say 'we got pregnant,' right? We were barely sixteen and our parents were not happy. Actually, they'd have nothing to do with us. But we were determined to do this, together, have the baby, set up housekeeping. That's what we called it back then." Arnold shook his head. "On less than two bucks an hour, right? Without even a high school diploma between us."

"I can't imagine," Annie said. "No one at the school would help?"

"You have to understand how it was in those days, especially miles from a city, which we were. There was no place in a high school classroom for a pregnant girl. No programs for pregnant teens. No group counseling. No family counseling. No nothing."

Arnold reached for the coffee and we all made a move to pour, Annie winning the contest.

She also moved a menu from the holder on the table to right under his nose. "I'll bet you haven't had a good meal this week."

Arnold looked longingly at the prospects that lay before him, but seemed too frazzled to make a decision.

"Never mind. I got this," I said. I pressed my back into the Naugahyde and called out over Annie's shoulder toward the kitchen window.

"Two dots and a dash."

I heard Victor explain to Pierre, who shook his head, "That means two fried eggs and a strip of bacon."

"Such a long expression," Pierre said, extending his fingers to illustrate.

"Yeah, well, I had French One in high school," Victor said. "I'll bet it would be longer in French."

I noticed Pierre did not volunteer the French translation.

"Here's where it gets tough, to this day," Arnold said, waiting for the kitchen banter to die down. "We made our way to Anchorage, one crap job at a time. Liv had no medical care until we pulled up to an ER at the last minute." He paused, took a sip of coffee to cover his cracking voice. "Bottom line, the baby made it. His mother . . . Olivia didn't."

Annie gasped. We all drew in our breaths, one way or another.

"You'll think I'm a poor excuse for a man, and—"

"Don't you say that, Manny. It's okay if I still call you Manny, right?" my mom asked.

He nodded. "All I said to the nurses before I disappeared was, 'His name's Quinlan. Oliver Quinlan.'"

WHEN MANNY RETURNED FROM THE RESTROOM (WE thought he'd disappeared again), Tammy quickly slipped two dots and a dash in front of him. He moved his fork around in the eggs. I was glad to see that he added a lot of salt, as usual. Not that it was good for him, but I took it as a sign that he was heading back to normal. He ate a few small bites.

"Thanks," he said, to no one in particular.

He was ready to talk again and revealed how he'd found his son two years ago: A magazine article on classic American diners listed his name as head chef at a diner in Elkview, Alaska.

"There was a small photo, and even though he'd changed his name to Whitestone, I knew it must be him. The shape of his face just like his mother's, and he was not far from where he started out. And when I came in here and looked at him, I knew he was my son. I started getting friendly with the other guys, Moe and Jack, so it wouldn't look funny, me hanging out. I thought for sure Oliver would recognize me, and after a while, when he didn't, it just got too awkward to say anything."

We finally let Manny go home, with a "doggy bag" so big it took Victor and Pierre to help carry the boxes to his trunk.

Manny wasn't out the door two minutes when Trooper half stood in the booth, looked at me, then to my mom, then to Chris, then back to me. "You have his home address?"

"We have it," I said. "The three truckers all have tabs here."

"Okay, then." And he sat down.

"Were you going to follow him home otherwise?" Chris asked, with a big grin.

"Darn right."

"I was kidding," Chris said.

"I'm not."

"You don't think?" my mom said.

"You can't think he'd kill his own son," Annie finished.

He scanned our faces. "Any of you know who killed Oliver yet?"

Noes all around. Two of us in particular were especially shamefaced about that.

"Then how else are we going to find out? Everyone's a suspect—" Trooper began.

"Until they're not," Chris and I finished.

"Where's Manny been all these years?" Trooper asked. "He never said, far as I heard."

"But what possible reason could he have?" my mom asked.

"I don't know. Maybe he told Oliver that day. 'By the way, I'm your father'"—Trooper tried to imitate Manny's gravelly voice—"and Oliver got angry that he'd been abandoned. It couldn't have been easy growing up without a father. Or a mother. Group homes aren't always pretty. And before you know it, they're fighting, and things get out of hand. That kind of thing."

"If it was a kind of accident, like Oliver fell and hit his head or something, Manny would have confessed." My mom, playing defense attorney.

"The way he did to fatherhood? Fifty years later?" Trooper asked.

"That's mean," said my mom, who was the only one of us who could get away with talking to Trooper like that.

"Maybe we should all take a breath and come up with a plan to find out the answers to these questions," I said.

"And more," Trooper said.

By now Pierre and the two volunteers had been driven back to the inn by Victor. I'd noticed a tender moment, a lingering goodbye hug between Pierre and Annie before he left the diner. Could this really work out for Annie? I didn't like the picture of her packing up for the Alps, but realized immediately that was selfish.

I tuned back in to Trooper. "Let's go with your idea of a plan, Charlie. Let's see who can do what."

Chris went first. He'd been typing on his phone much of

the time in the booth. I assumed he'd been taking notes, and not answering spam from a mosquito control service or an ad for a home warranty, which accounted for more than half my emails these days.

"I can find out what that magazine article was that Manny mentioned. The one with the list of chefs. See if that holds up."

"Good, Chris. I'd like to know for sure how he found Oliver after all these years," Trooper said.

"I'm on it."

"About Moe and Jack. They couldn't have been called that without Manny. They ought to be interviewed. Find out when that all started," Trooper noted.

I hated to be the one to bring it up, but I did remember one pertinent fact. "Manny came late to dinner that day. Monday. The day Oliver died. Moe and Jack said he'd been running late all day." I left out the part where he'd looked disheveled and upset and had immediately asked where Oliver was. Even so, my mom trained a frown on me.

"You and Chris take the truckers, Charlie," Trooper said.

"Okay," we both said.

"And Stanley came into the Bear Claw twice looking for Oliver. Once he found him working and they had words. Plus, I didn't finish with Gert at the chapel," I said, reporting on her three alibis.

"I can do something," my mom said.

"Me, too," said Annie. "I know Pierre would love to help. If the new car part is the wrong one, he'll have to stay the weekend."

Trooper didn't respond except to raise his eyebrows. Wanting to keep the team local?

"I'll track Gert down. And Lana, too," my mom said.

"And Stanley, Oliver's brother. I spoke to him for a few minutes and he seemed friendly," Annie said. "In fact, he stayed at the inn not too long ago. He'd come up from Anchorage and a storm blew in and he needed a bed for the night. It's a little strange that he didn't mention he was Oliver's brother, or that he knew anyone in town."

"That's probably one of the times he came in looking for Oliver," I said. "You might ask him about that."

"Will do."

"And, Trooper, you can tell us what's going on with Oliver's phone dump, things like that," I said.

Trooper turned his head so he could look at me out of the corner of his eye. His look said, *Not so fast, young lady*, a phrase I seemed to remember from a decade or two ago.

I smiled weakly. "It was worth a shot."

Trooper didn't acknowledge my request for intel, but I didn't think it was a big deal, since Oliver was so unconnected, with no email, no cell phone. The most he had was a landline, and I doubted he used it that much.

Trooper pointed back and forth between Mom and Annie. "You two maybe could work together? I don't like to send my deputies out by themselves."

The two women looked surprised and pleased.

"Deputies," Mom said, a little too euphoric.

Trooper stepped out of the booth and motioned for the women to join him.

"Raise your right hands and repeat after me. I solemnly swear to uphold the laws of Matanuska-Susitna Borough in the State of Alaska, so help me God."

They repeated it.

"Wow, I didn't know this was a thing," Annie said.

"It isn't," Trooper said. "But it felt good, didn't it?"

*   *   *

MOM AND I LEFT THE BEAR CLAW AROUND THREE IN the afternoon. The kitchen was spotless, the appliances shiny, all the food wrapped and put away.

It was the first time I could remember Evelyn and Charlotte Cooke locking the diner doors and hanging a CLOSED sign, with no intention of returning for thirty-eight hours. We'd decided to open at five on Saturday morning to accommodate the weekend truckers, hikers, fishermen, and the occasional eager tourist.

Nina had printed out a new sign with all the information, on paper that had a narrow black border. I'd have to remember to compliment her, and ask her where in the world she'd found that paper.

Mom sat quiet all the way home. I didn't disturb her, with either music or talk. I was counting on Benny to help us both recover from the day.

The last of the memorial service for Oliver Quinlan was over. All that remained was to find his killer.

SEVENTEEN

AFTER THE SADNESS OF THE PAST COUPLE OF DAYS, watching the second joyful greeting between Mom and Benny was almost too much for me. A roller coaster would be a fitting image for my emotions. But my mom did not need to see me break down, so I left the two of them on the recliner—cheek to cheek, Benny perched high on Mom's chest, relishing the rhythmic scratching behind his ears and under his chin—and wended my way to the kitchen.

We were at my place on the way from the Bear Claw, to pick up my mom's luggage, then take her home.

"Maybe I could stay here one more night," she said, shifting her head around Benny's. "It's going to be freezing at our place."

"I'd love that." That was true, and was the reason I didn't remind her that she had a space heater that could be operated remotely to whatever temperature she wanted before she arrived. "I'll bring the food in."

By the time I trekked in from the Outback to my house, Mom was asleep, Benny still on her chest. I couldn't tell whether Benny was asleep without disturbing Mom, so I took an afghan from my sofa and placed it around both of them. If Benny was awake, he was doing a good job pretending otherwise.

I carried the extra food from the day's menu into my kitchen and pulled out a tower of containers with sandwiches and sides of potato salad and slaw. Surely one of the small sacks held a bear claw or two. I rummaged and found them. Whether he heard the crinkle of the paper sack or smelled a combination of delicious aromas, I didn't know, but Benny answered the call and bounded into the kitchen. I looked to his feeder, hoping I hadn't forgotten to fill it. No, that wasn't it; he simply wanted a treat. Or, he thought I might be envious of his attention to my mom and came to give me some love.

I heated up a mug of coffee from breakfast and carried it with a bear claw to the sofa across from Mom. I recognized the very soft sound (not a snore, she'd always insisted) and knew she wouldn't wake too soon, no matter how loudly I chewed. I realized it was the first bear claw I'd tasted since my experiment with chocolate in the middle— the experiment Oliver had ridiculed. Both Trooper and Chris had nixed the samples, thumbs-down, so my final argument with Oliver hadn't needed to happen. Another reminder of my part in sending Oliver out of the diner and to his death. It seemed that burying my hand in Benny's fur was the only way to talk myself out of the overwhelming guilt I felt.

I flashed back to a more pleasant time: Chris's expressed wish to meet Benny. I considered inviting him over for a meal and meet-and-greet this evening. With Mom here, it wouldn't seem like a date to him. On the other hand, it would seem like one to Mom.

Never mind.

"What do you say, Benny?" I whispered. As long as he'd hopped onto my lap to collect his treat, it seemed a good idea to query him. He was silent on the question of inviting Chris—no tail movement at all.

I moved on to the question of Oliver's killer. From our last meeting in the diner, Trooper seemed okay with all of us newly sworn deputies, aka laypeople, carrying out interrogations. As long as we didn't buy ourselves toy store badges, I gathered. I played back the assignments in my head and made a list. It always helped me to write out lists, even if I never consulted them. These days, I used a notes app on my phone.

I spoke softly into Benny's ear and warned him that I was about to use his back as my desk. He settled in and obliged me.

Mom and Annie:
Stanley—why the argument in the kitchen?
Gert—why lie about alibi?
Chris and me:
Manny—check magazine article
verify points of story
why late day of murder?
Moe and Jack—did they know about Manny's fatherhood?
verify Manny's story
? Victor—why take over so soon?
? Kendra—why avoid us in Anchorage?

So many question marks left me discouraged. How did people like Trooper do this on a daily basis?

I hated to include Victor, especially after the way he'd

stepped up this week. Today alone, he'd overseen the gathering after Oliver's funeral, including packaging the food I'd just stuffed into my fridge. He was as competent an employee as one could ask for.

But, according to the oft-repeated phrase, he was a suspect until he was not. I decided to ask Chris to take the lead on that one. Was I a coward? It seemed so. But wouldn't it be better, if he turned up innocent, that he didn't know his boss had suspected him of murder? Thinking of Victor reminded me that I still needed to go through the pile of papers he'd trashed, and that now resided in my tote. Next to Victor's name on my list, I added the word "envelopes," hoping that would be enough to jog my memory.

I could push Benny off my lap and get to work or stay with him and relax. Sometimes when I made a to-do list, I felt I'd actually done the tasks and I could take the rest of the day off.

THE DOORBELL WOKE ME UP. MOM RUBBED THE TOP OF my head as she passed me on her way to answering. For a moment I was in high school again, or even younger, when Mom would wake me for school with that gesture. Combined with a rare nap in the middle of the day, it was enough to disorient me. Chris's voice in the entryway didn't help. The aroma of stew—moose meat, carrots, potatoes, mixed spices—did the trick. I figured out that it was dinnertime and the world's best cook was in my kitchen.

"What's that delicious smell?" Chris asked. "Looks like I arrived just in time."

"You're right," Mom said. "Welcome." I heard her laugh as I turned away from the door and ducked into the bathroom, where I splashed my face with cold water and ran a brush through my unruly hair.

My thought as I approached the living room again: *Glad I didn't invite him. This one's on Mom.*

NOT A DATE, BUT A BUSINESS MEETING. I'D TAKEN A chance that Annie might be available, and she was. Her new assistant—for Annie that meant hired fewer than ten years ago—was working out well, and Pierre was on his way to pick up his car.

"I wanted to drive him, but Max said he'd pick him up since he had some errands downtown anyway." Annie screwed up her face and shrugged. Resigned, it seemed.

I brought out copies of my notes. I'd printed out the page, in case anyone was willing to talk business after a scrumptious meal of moose stew and crusty bread. No one argued about putting off dessert for a while, especially after hearing that Victor had packed an entire pan of cherry cheesecake mousse for us. Apparently, he had been expecting an army.

"Starting and ending with moose and mousse, get it?" Annie asked.

We said we did get it.

As soon as we could drag her away from the kitchen sink, practically by force, Mom started by saying she didn't have a big enough assignment.

"Me, too," Annie said.

It wasn't clear to me what Annie was me too-ing, and before I could ask, she and the others had questions and comments of their own.

The conversation, or more correctly, ersatz meeting, went downhill from there. Why did I assume that four adults could settle a few logistics quickly and amicably? Benny, perhaps the only adult in the room, circled our feet under the table; he was searching for food, no doubt, but also attempting to bring order to the discussion. I felt he clung to my feet more than to the others'. A message?

Overlapping snippets included:

Do Moe and Jack

This will take a trip to Anchorage,

Gert lied,

work on weekends?

Maybe we should

she saw Manny packing

to see Kendra

I don't think

go on Sunday,

This is still Thursday, right?

and Stanley.

less traffic.

it could be Victor.

What envelopes?

so she was covering for him.

Miraculously, everyone seemed to figure it all out, and the one thing we did agree on was that we would keep one another informed about where we were at all times. We'd meet back at my house for dinner Friday evening—there was a pan of meatloaf and gravy for enticement—and report on our findings. If one of us didn't check in and couldn't be reached at home or work, we'd call Trooper.

What could be safer?

I GUESS IT'S TIME I WENT HOME," MOM SAID, WHILE working on a breakfast of OJ and bear claws. I noticed she held on to Benny as she spoke, her fingers never leaving his body—his neck, behind his ears, along his back.

"Why don't you stay here until Dad gets back?"

"Okay."

Okay? I wanted to ask, *Who are you and what have you done with Evelyn Cooke?* I had a hard time reconciling this woman with the one of a couple of weeks ago, who would have relished the chance to have a few days alone in her own home. I could only figure that Oliver's murder had spooked her, the finality of his funeral yesterday cementing that feeling.

Not that I was crazy about being left alone, either.

"Why don't we take your luggage home and pick up whatever you'll need for the weekend?"

She nodded. "Dad will be back Sunday. He always likes to celebrate Seward's Day, and it's this coming Monday."

The last Monday in March. I always thought it interesting that the purchase of Alaska from Russia had gone from "Seward's Folly" to a state holiday. Usually I'd be on top of any celebration, but this week had thrown off both my internal and external clocks.

"Remember that essay contest you won in seventh grade?"

"'Why I Think Alaska is Great.' I remember I had to read it at some meeting on Seward's Day. Sponsored by a veterans' group, if I recall."

"You won twenty-five dollars and a framed certificate. Do you still have that?"

"The twenty-five dollars?"

Laughs turned into giggles, and we had our disconnect with the sadness of this morning.

Mom felt it, too, it seemed. "Let's get going," she said.

* * *

THINGS MOVED QUICKLY AFTER BREAKFAST.

Annie came by to pick up my mom for the trip to Anchorage for talks with Stanley and Kendra.

"Lots of luck," I said, as I waved goodbye.

I picked Chris up in my heated Outback for our follow-up visit with Manny.

In between, there had been games with Benny, a phone call with my dad, and an essential end-of-the-month bill-paying session.

"I feel bad landing on Manny so soon after his heart-rending confession," I told Chris, after switching seats so he could drive.

"It's probably the best time, speaking as a cop," Chris said.

"If we really were cops."

"There's that."

"Did you make any headway on that magazine article that listed chefs?"

"Not yet. I'm hoping Manny will be able to narrow down the date a little."

We'd put Manny's address on North Second Street into my GPS and rolled along, following the nice lady's instructions. The roads were clear of snow, though it was highly likely that the skies would unload at least once more before the mosquitoes arrived for summer.

As we got closer to Manny's address, Chris and I glanced at each other.

"Look familiar?" I asked.

"A stone's throw from Oliver's."

"Coincidence?"

"You know what cops say," Chris said.

"If we really were cops."

I HOPE YOU'RE HERE FOR LUNCH, 'CAUSE I GOT A BOAT-load of food from these friends of mine yesterday," Manny said.

Manny was back to his trucker clothes, jeans and a heavy vest with lots of pockets. I wondered how often he got to wear the suit he had on yesterday, if it was even his. He invited us into a neat living room with mix-and-match furniture. Everything looked tidy and dusted, as if he'd been expecting us. Or maybe I was projecting my own housekeeping habits onto him. Dust before company, vacuum after.

"So did we," I said, in response to his comment about the state of his larder.

"Speak for yourself," Chris said, smiling.

"I expect you have more questions," Manny said. He gestured to a sofa while he took a chair opposite. The coffee table between us had a neat stack of magazines, which, in my house, would be another sign of expected guests. "What can I get you? Coffee? Water? Beer?" A nervous laugh marked the last suggestion, in the middle of the morning.

I opted for water, Chris for coffee, thus giving us a few minutes to settle down and prepare our minds before Manny took his seat.

"As a newspaperman, I'm interested in how you tracked Oliver down," Chris said. "It couldn't have been easy."

Way to not be a cop, Chris. Nice opening.

Manny opened his arms, palms up. "I didn't have a lot else to do. I never married. Thought about it, came close a coupla times, but I never could see myself with another woman, a family even, with Oliver still out there. My baby boy, was how I thought of him."

"Where did you start to look?" Chris asked.

"Figured I'd start with the hospital, but no luck there. Not like it is now. It was like a state secret back then."

I felt another adoption lecture coming on, but from the other side. It was possible, even likely, that birth parents had an entirely different slant from institutions or adoptive parents on open and closed adoptions. But Manny wasn't about to lecture us. Instead, he continued recounting his journey.

"I kept going back, seeing if someone else was on duty. Someone sympathetic. Still no luck, even though I gave them the exact date, down to the hour I brought Olivia in. Then I thought, what if the idea was to send the baby as far as possible from his birthplace? I wouldn't have a chance."

Chris was taking notes at a steady pace, but I could tell he was eager to get to the payoff—what about that telltale magazine article?

Manny told us about the orphanages he'd sought out, the churches and foster care bureaucracies.

"If he even kept his name. My name." Manny shook his head. "I had stacks and stacks of newspapers looking to see if he was on a sports team or got married."

"I can't imagine this kind of search without the Internet," I said.

I also couldn't imagine the pain of this, which seemed to have gone on for many years, only to end in even more heartache. I knew Chris wanted to pick up the pace on the timeline, but I wanted Manny to continue. I was eager for information that was more relevant to the murder investigation. I was also aware that Chris was doing the fun part of the meeting while my questions would sound like what they were: an interrogation. I couldn't jump right into *Why were*

you late for dinner on the day Oliver was murdered? I'd
have to build up to it.

"I notice you live pretty close to where Oliver lived." I
pointed in the general direction of Oliver's house, recalling
the hasty exit Chris and I had made at the wrong end of a
rifle. "Did you visit him at all?"

I chided myself, my jaws tight. Too personal, I thought.
Too cop-like. But Manny didn't seem to mind.

"Nah, I never got up the courage. Like I said yesterday,
at a certain point, the window closes, you know?"

I tried to ignore Chris, in case he was giving me signals
to butt out of the track he was on. "What about Moe and
Jack?" I laughed. "Steve and Dave. Did they know? I'm
sorry to be asking all this, Manny. It's just such an interesting story."

"It's okay. I know Trooper sent you."

Chris and I blubbered, speaking together in something
like a falsetto voice, halfway between confirming and de-
nying.

"I know you gotta ask," Manny said. "Hey, listen, nobody wants to know who killed my son more than I do.
Anything I can do to help—"

A loud knock on the door interrupted him.

The rest was a blur.

Trooper at the door, then stepping in, putting his hand
on Manny's shoulder. Deputy Josh behind him, hanging
back. "You're going to have to come with me, Mr. Quinlan."

"Trooper, what are you doing? We're having a very useful conversation," I blurted.

"Don't need it."

"Why don't you sit down and—?" from Chris.

"Don't need to."

And they were out the door.

Eighteen

AT LEAST TROOPER HADN'T ARGUED WHEN WE SAID
we'd like to follow him to the station and talk to Manny.

"No promises," he'd said.

"We have a good rapport with Manny," I'd argued. "He'll
talk to me."

"No promises."

When had Trooper become a man of so few words? I
was beyond upset at the way Manny had been summarily
dismissed and treated like a common criminal, instead of
a man Trooper had known as a regular in the Bear Claw.

Chris drove us back toward town. "I have an idea," he
said. "Let's drop in on Moe or Jack before we go to the
station."

"But I don't want Manny waiting for us."

"Trust me. It's going to be a while before Trooper lets us
talk to him."

"But—"

"What do you think he meant by 'No promises'?"

"I think I have a lot to learn about police work."

"Did I leave out the part where I was an MP for a while in the army?"

"What? What else don't I know about you?"

He reached over and took my hand. "In due time," he said, and let go.

Hmm.

He scrolled down the list of GPS addresses and clicked on Moe's, which we'd entered, along with Jack's, before we left my house.

After we'd driven for about fifteen minutes, the GPS announced that we'd arrived. Maybe. But there wasn't a house anywhere in sight. There were handmade signs, however, about every five hundred feet, along a rough road that felt like a washboard under the tires. NEXT LEFT. NEXT RIGHT. NEXT LEFT. Then a sign that said TRAIL. Finally, the last sign read STEVE CARTER 2 MI. The small log cabin with a metal roof was at the end of a gravel path. The cabin looked fairly new. So did the outhouse. It occurred to me that it had been some time since I'd visited anyone trailside, with no road access. And no indoor plumbing. Probably since high school. My friends at the time had covered a wide range of levels of income and social interaction, many of them snowmobiling in from remote areas, using that special lane they designated in the winter.

For a tiny house, Moe's was pretty busy today. Three vehicles were on the property. I recognized one as a pickup that Moe drove sometimes on his day off. One of the others also looked familiar.

"Visitors?" Chris asked.

"Moe's other car, and I'm betting the third is Jack's," I said. "Word travels fast even when there are no access roads and no apparent modern devices. And Manny has had his one phone call by now."

"Uh-oh."

"Uh-huh."

I NSIDE THE ATTRACTIVE LITTLE HOUSE WERE TWO AN-
gry men. Unlike Manny, who was short and stocky, but like
Oliver, Manny's two friends were the burly types often associated with men who drove big trucks and lived in the
woods, hefting logs.

It made sense that they'd blame us for Manny's current
predicament. Manny probably did, too. We were Trooper's
representatives. For all he knew, we were in his home to
keep him there until Trooper arrived. One of us might even
have snuck a call to Trooper, telling him he could come now.

"It sure looks like you set him up," Moe said, verifying
my guess. "He told us you dropped in and the next thing he
knew, he was being arrested."

"You can't believe that," I said. "It was only a few days
ago that we bent over backward to get you guys a private
spot when the diner had filled up with Annie's guests.
You've always been special to us."

"You think they give all their customers such unique
names?" Chris asked.

"Yeah, well, that was then," Moe said.

The two men looked sullen, and why wouldn't they?
Their good friend, one third of their world, was missing.

It was clear from our two stops this morning that at least
two of the three men lived very simply. Moe's home com-
prised one room and a loft. From where I sat, I could see
his entire existence. A wood stove and a pile of logs, a sink
and cooking unit, shelves of food and sundries, coolers, a
small table with an empty bottle and a set of keys, a fire
extinguisher, a calendar with days crossed off. There was

no computer, no television set, no microwave oven, no books or decorations except for the calendar and a map on the wall. Not a single photograph that I could see.

He and Jack sat on a recycled sofa from a previous decade. I was offered the only other chair; Chris won the ottoman, decorated with masking tape, cracked open in spots. It was doubtful Moe had ever planned on entertaining three guests at the same time.

"We know Manny is innocent," Chris said. "Maybe you can help us prove it."

"How do we do that? We don't know anything."

"You'd be surprised," Chris said. "Sometimes the smallest thing can be a help."

"Let us ask you a few questions and we'll be out of your hair."

Chris was so tall and the ottoman so compressed that his knees practically hit his chin. He looked so uncomfortable, I offered to switch with him, but he waved it off.

"Okay," Moe mumbled, and Jack nodded.

"Can you tell us what Manny told you when he called from the station house?"

"He thought he should have a lawyer."

"But we don't know any." Moe cleared his throat. "Except for my divorce attorney, years ago, up in Fairbanks."

"I can help with that," I said.

The men brightened considerably.

At the same time I ran through my mental Rolodex of contacts I still had from my one whole year in law school. I was sure I'd be able to come up with someone who'd help us.

Chris moved in. "Did he tell you what they had on him?" He quickly rephrased. "Why do they think he's guilty? Do they have evidence?"

"Nothin'."

"That's not quite true, Jack. We need to tell them everything or they can't help us," Moe said. "On the phone, Manny said Trooper told him his fingerprints were all over the outside of Oliver's house and inside the garage. But we know Manny used to go there and look in the windows."

"And the garage wasn't locked. It's not like he broke in or anything," Jack said. "Manny wouldn't do that."

"When he knew Oliver was working, he'd drive over to his place and, you know, just to see what it looked like."

"He loved that kid," Jack said, his wistful tone suggesting that he wished Manny were his father. It didn't seem to matter that "that kid" was fifty-one years old, certainly older than Jack himself, who was the youngest of the crew.

"So you both obviously knew that Manny was Oliver's father," I said.

They both smiled slightly and gave each other a knowing look. Moe explained.

"We'd stopped at a bar down near Palmer and someone was singing that song that goes, 'Our troubles are all the same,'"—Moe's voice was more mellifluous than I would have guessed—"and it happened to be Oliver's birthday, and Manny just let it all out."

Another barstool confession; perfectly understandable.

"Anything else by way of evidence?" I asked.

"Nothin'," Jack said, predictably.

Moe rolled his eyes, gave Jack a patronizing look.

"Okay, there was the gun."

Our turn for eye movement.

"Trooper asked Manny if he owns a gun," Jack said. "And, of course he does, 'cause he drives a big rig all kinds of places, all hours of the day and night."

"But when the trooper asked Manny to produce it, it was gone," Moe continued, explaining what Manny had related via the station house phone. "Manny knew he had it the last time he drove his rig, which would have been Wednesday night. Then yesterday was all the memorial stuff, so he didn't take it out. And this morning . . ." Moe threw up his hands.

"It wasn't there," Chris offered.

"Nope. And he has no idea where it is. Nobody broke in that Manny could see."

"Someone's trying to frame him," Jack said.

That was a leap the size of Alaska, but it wasn't my place to judge.

"Can you think of anyone else Trooper should be looking at?" Chris asked. "Maybe someone who knew about Manny and Oliver and wanted to settle a grudge against Manny, and took it out on his son?"

"Nah. Maybe if it was him," Moe said, and punched Jack's shoulder. Jack pretended to fall off the couch.

I figured we'd gotten as much as we could get from Manny's pals. I had to get home and call all the lawyers I knew.

"Hey, do you want to come upstairs and see the view I got?" Moe asked, more relaxed now that the heavy questioning was over. "It's spectacular. That's what the Realtor guy called it."

I checked out the so-called stairway that led to the loft. It was a strange arrangement where one section of ladder ended at the wall, forming a kind of landing. A second section adjacent to it spanned the distance from the landing to the loft. I didn't need to see Denali that badly. If I did, I knew of safer lookout spots.

Chris to the rescue. "You know, Charlie, we have that appointment that we're already going to be late for." And to the men: "What if we do that next time? We'll come back with a six-pack and celebrate Manny's release."

We left to cheers, pats on the back.

How lucky I was to be partnering with Chris, the researcher, the army vet and ex-MP, and now the spinner of yarns—an expert at getting us out of tricky situations.

THE GPS HAD A SLIGHTLY MORE DIFFICULT TIME LEADing us out from Moe's property. It wasn't programmed for reversing NEXT LEFT. NEXT RIGHT. NEXT LEFT. TRAIL. Together, though it taxed our memories, we got back onto the road and headed back to town.

"Lunch?" Chris said.

"Is that the appointment we're going to be late for?"

"You bet."

"I can open the diner."

"Nah, let's give the diner a rest. It's had a hard week."

There was only one other choice in Elkview, and it was a good one—Aly's Café, on Main Street. I knew the menu by heart and decided on a chicken and asparagus crepe, coffee, and cookies. All special at Aly's.

After our morning on what Alaskan Realtors called zerobed zero-bath properties, Aly's looked luxurious: a sweeping, bright room with ten or twelve tables and an espresso machine that reminded me of the one in Oliver's kitchen. The overlapping aromas of coffee and melting butter were the perfect welcome after the stress of the morning. I thought of Manny and hoped his stress would be over soon.

I had a feeling Chris's order was also familiar to him— a ham and cheese crepe with mustard sauce. At one time Mom had tried buying cookies from Aly to sell at the Bear Claw, but the investment proved too costly and she returned to in-house baking whatever she offered for sweets. Like the amazing cherry cheesecake mousse that Oliver introduced and then wanted deleted from the menu. That little issue still bothered me.

Since there was no one waiting for a table, we sat for a while with our devices and planned our next moves. I spent some time reconnecting with lawyers I knew. Even if Manny had asked for a public defender, it would be some time before he'd be assigned one. I hoped to head that off with someone I knew and trusted.

Chris worked on a list of questions to ask Manny.

"I'd like to know how Manny got from checking out orphanages and foster homes to a magazine with a list of chefs," he said, as if talking to himself, his fingers attacking the keys of his laptop. I couldn't imagine how that was helping him resolve his issue, but then, I wasn't a researcher.

I struck out with the first attorney, whose voicemail directed me to call the number of her assistant. Then more failures in the form of, "Nice to hear from you, but I'm crazy busy." I was about to give up when I got a call back from Willow Yazzie, a former classmate, and one who'd actually finished law school and passed the bar. She'd set up practice in Anchorage. For some reason, Willow thought she owed me a favor from our law school days and was willing to meet with Manny, and represent him pro bono if it came to that. Whatever I did for Willow back then had paid off, even if I couldn't recall what it was.

Now I was eager to visit Manny and tried to hurry Chris along. But he wasn't ready, so I moved to another table, where there was a nearby charger for my smartphone. I checked in with Mom and Annie, who sent a quick text back, complete with misspellings.

All ok. Here with your mom and gert. Couldn't conect with K and S in Anchorag.

I couldn't put my finger on why, but seeing the text gave me a feeling of relief. At some level, I didn't want my mom to be involved in these interrogations. I wanted her back on the Danube with Dad, or at home, taking a nap with Benny on her lap. Maybe I would just put my foot down and tell her that at dinner this evening. She was too old for this. Or, rather, I was too young, and still needed her.

And me?

What should I be doing instead of acting like a trooper's deputy?

How about some work that would benefit the diner that was now mine? Looking to fill the vacancy left by my head chef, for one thing. What was it that all the books I'd read on management said? Promote and market your business, keep statistical and financial records, assess and improve profitability, network with customers, employees, suppliers, and sales representatives. In general, make improvements to the running of the business and develop the restaurant.

Had I done any of that? Not really. Not with any enthusiasm. I couldn't really blame the investigation of Oliver's death for my shortcomings, however. I'd been coasting on my mom's great legacy.

It was time I took the reins.

Right after I helped Manny get out of trouble.

Nineteen

I COULDN'T REMEMBER THE LAST TIME I'D BEEN IN THE Elkview station house. Like most police and state trooper stations in Alaska, ours was a simple low wooden building marked by an enormous metal tower with a dish antenna at the top. And lots of parking spaces.

When I first arrived in San Francisco after culinary school, people would ask me, "What's the main difference between here and Alaska?" Expecting, probably, "the weather," or even specifically, "ice and snow" or "it rains all year."

But I'd answer, "The parking." My cocktail party line was always, "In SF, there's one parking spot for every one hundred drivers. In Alaska, it's the opposite."

That might have been an exaggeration to get a laugh, but it didn't seem like one when you were driving around a couple of blocks of San Francisco hills four times, hoping to catch someone just leaving a spot.

Chris parked the Outback in one of the one hundred spots open in front of the station house. Again, a slight exaggeration.

"Are we ready for this?"

I nodded. I hoped I wouldn't break down if I saw Manny in dire straits. But what other kind could he be in?

"Do we even know whether Manny has been arrested? Did Trooper just take him in for questioning?" I asked Chris, who seemed so much more in tune with this kind of situation, former MP that he was.

"We don't know," he said, furthering my discomfort. "Trooper didn't handcuff him, but it was two to one, with the deputy backing him up—and where was he going to run anyway?—so that doesn't mean much."

Great.

I bundled up, though it was all of ten feet to the front door. Scarf, gloves, hat, a complete set knitted by Annie years ago when she thought San Francisco might be colder than Alaska. But it was a good thing I was protected, since the sign on the door said USE NEXT ENTRANCE, with an arrow pointing to the right. That meant an extra ten feet.

"They're just trying to make it hard for us," I told Chris. "What if they don't let us see him?"

"What if they do?"

Now he was just being annoying.

WE WERE BOTH RIGHT, IN A WAY. A WOMAN WHO seemed to be falling apart in tune with the building's peeling paint on the outside and shabby furniture on the inside ushered us into a small, unpleasant room that was surely designed to be a deterrent to committing a crime and ending up here ever again. She told us we'd be able to see Manny in a little while and asked if we wanted anything to drink. Water? Coffee?

She seemed relieved that we were both "good, thank you."

I couldn't have been more grateful for that second espresso at Aly's. Or for the diner dessert waiting for us at home.

Happily, she hadn't taken our devices from us, though she did act suspicious of us until she was able to close the door behind her. Chris and I got to the task of making calls, checking boxes on our to-do lists.

I had a text from Willow, reminding me to advise her new client not to talk to anyone, specifically law enforcement. I hoped we weren't too late on that score. Willow promised to leave Anchorage first thing in the morning. I said I'd meet her here, thus committing myself to another stint in this room.

After what felt like hours, I wandered into the hall in search of the woman who came with the building, to try to get a message to Manny. Something like "Don't talk until you see me." No luck, however. I noticed her desk looked to be locked up for the night, though it was only mid-afternoon.

Josh Peters, Trooper's deputy, appeared and caught me reading the bulletin board we'd passed on the way to the waiting room. The notices were a mishmash of good news (a bake sale to benefit the local grammar school and another for law enforcement widows and orphans) and bad news (several overlapping WANTED posters). Did I *want* to know what they were *wanted* for? I decided against reading the fine print.

"Can I help you with something, Charlie?" Deputy Josh asked me.

I supposed *What do you think?* would not be a good response. I needed him on my side. Josh had that fresh-out-of-the-academy, or even fresh-out-of-high-school look, with blond hair and pink cheeks that looked like they'd never felt the blade of a razor.

"I was wondering when we might see Manny? Arnold Quinlan?"

"I know who he is. He should be ready for you in a few minutes."

I didn't like his attitude, but I was trying to be sensible. I realized another not-good response was probably *Can you tell him not to talk to any cops or troopers?*

I settled on "Can you tell him his lawyer will be here first thing in the morning?"

I hoped that covered the law about not questioning someone who's asked for a lawyer. Surely, if I announced that his lawyer was on her way, that meant he'd asked for one. Maybe if I'd stayed in law school one more semester, it would have paid off today.

Josh nodded. He didn't say yes or no. I suspected he wasn't sure of the law, either.

Back in the waiting room, I reported on my adventure to Chris, who was half-asleep, thanks to an overheated room. It was often that way in states that had winter—you were always going from too cold to too warm and back again.

I took a seat, resigned to however long it would take to see Manny. Annie texted again for her and my mom, taking the rules seriously. That was Annie. I felt bad that she had to deal with this at the same time that Pierre was on his way out of her life, but maybe the investigation was a good distraction.

As for me, I wanted him gone, the sooner the better. I needed Annie to come out of this, whatever it was, with nothing even close to heartbreak. *Peine d'amour.* Why did I remember that, and not much else, from high school French with Mademoiselle Martine? Maybe because I'd had some *peine d'amour* myself, not that long ago?

When the lady who'd closed up her desk showed up in

the doorway of the waiting room, alone, her hands crossed in front of her wide midriff, I knew what was going on.

"I'm sorry," she said, showing no such emotion. "Visiting hours are over."

I felt my face redden, even more than it was from the overheated room.

"I don't see hours posted," I said, pretending to examine the bare dingy walls, looking for signs that verified her announcement.

"You'll have to come back tomorrow."

"I'd like to speak to your boss," I said.

I felt Chris's hand on my shoulder, pressing me toward the door. "You know what?" he said to the matron. "We'll be back. What's a good time?"

"Any time," she said.

"This is *any time* and you're throwing us out. *Any time* can be now, right?"

"Thanks," Chris said, nodding to the woman. He continued to steer me in the direction of the hallway that led to exiting the building.

"Is Trooper Graham around?" I asked over my shoulder. One last attempt to gain some respect.

But she had already turned away, her head shaking like a bobblehead doll.

Chris finished his job of keeping me out of jail, his hand on my shoulder until we were clear of the building.

"Charlie. Think about it. Josh What's-His-Name is on duty," he said, when we were in the parking lot, out of earshot. Unless that big tower of an antenna was a listening device. "He's her boss at the moment. He wasn't about to give us access."

"Coward that he is. His name's Peters." Spoken through my teeth.

"I know his name. Why give him any more power? We're coming back with Lawyer Willow, anyway, right?"

"Right."

I buckled into my Outback and crossed my arms over my chest. The memory of Kendra Burke doing a similar thing to us in Anchorage earlier in the week only caused me to fume more intensely. I started on a plan, to tell Trooper what had transpired, to ask him to reprimand his station house crew, to do *something*.

Chris had started the vehicle but left it in park. "Go ahead, scream. You know you want to," he said, and covered his ears with both hands.

I had to laugh. "Let's go," I said. "You're losing valuable steering wheel heat."

THANKS TO THE STIFFING WE RECEIVED AT THE Elkview station house, we were early for the planned dinner meeting at my house. Chris dropped me off at home, transferred himself and his belongings to his pickup, and left to run errands.

I was glad for a little free time to work on two very important goals before the crowd gathered. One, to bond with Benny, and two, to sift through the papers Victor had tossed in the trash as soon as he heard Oliver wouldn't be returning to the Bear Claw. I had a feeling there were only bills, paid or unpaid, and junk mail Oliver hadn't gotten around to dumping in the trash outside the diner. Still, it was a loose end I needed to take care of.

Benny heard my key, of course, and greeted me as if he (a) loved me and (b) wanted food he couldn't reach. The Special of the Day was a treat my mom had whipped up, made of salmon, eggs, and flour and baked in a standard temperature oven. Mom winged it with most of her cooking and baking. If I wanted an exact recipe, with measurements, I'd have to watch her the next time she prepared it. Whatever *it* was. For now, I poured out the last crunchy pieces of the salmon treat into Benny's bowl and watched him enjoy them.

I took out the wire wand with a feather, beads, and bells, the old-fashioned kind without a motor, one he'd had since the day I met him. I waved it around in wide arcs and watched him jump for the neon green feather. Definitely more exercise for him than for me. I was glad he still enjoyed it. After about five minutes, when Benny decided to sit and watch the action around him instead of attacking, I put the wand down and moved him toward the last crumbs of his salmon treat.

I'd read a story in a pet magazine about a cat who'd saved the family silver collection. Taffy, of Cleveland, Ohio, was home alone when an intruder broke in. The thief began stuffing a sack with items from the dining room hutch. A large teapot, a vase, a pitcher, silverware, candlesticks, trays. Even Taffy's silver bowl, taken out on special occasions, went into the sack. Taffy took a flying leap, jumped on the culprit's back, scratched at his neck, and wouldn't let go. Or so the story went, although all the parents saw when they arrived home was a man passed out on the dining room floor. They guessed that Taffy's attack caused the thief to stumble and hit his head on the mahogany table.

I looked down at Benny, now moving toward my lap. "You could do that, right, Benny?" I asked. "It would be a piece of cake for you. Not that you like cake." I lifted him and we sat chatting for a while. Solving the world's problems with my beautiful orange and white tabby seemed easier than solving the local problem of who murdered my friend.

I WOKE FROM A SHORT NAP TO FIND BENNY ASLEEP, having made himself comfortable on top of the box containing the crystal dinner bell Mom had brought me from her shopping excursions dockside. I'd stuffed tissue paper on top of the open box, providing just the right amount of crinkle, thus forming the perfect ad hoc bed for him.

I made myself a mug of coffee and took my overstuffed tote bag to a comfortable chair. I took advantage of the opportunity to clean out the wrappers, cough drops, tissues, and loose change that had accumulated over a week or more, which left me with the papers from Oliver's desk drawer.

I had no expectations of finding anything as interesting as what I'd discovered in the secret drawer at the bottom of Oliver's bedroom chest. We'd yet to follow up on the two-volume potential cookbook, which was on my dining room table. Had Oliver ever published the cookbook? When? Under what name? The to-do lists seemed to keep getting longer, which was not the typical fate of to-do lists.

In keeping with Oliver's spirit of hiding the cookbook volumes, I decided to bury them myself. I kept a long plastic storage box under my bed, junior high style, with things that were private for one reason or another. I slid the box out now and placed the volumes next to my own diaries and letters I'd prefer were kept out of the public eye until I'd left the earth.

The trash from the diner wastebasket had held no envelope as large as the ones Oliver had used for his pseudo wills, the papers leaving his house and vehicle to Kendra. Now that I knew there was a brother as well, I wondered why Oliver had left nothing to Stanley. Nothing we'd discovered so far, anyway.

I went back to my chair and wisely positioned a wastebasket near it. To the personal debris from my tote, I added a catalog of kitchen supplies with items circled that would never be bought. I smoothed folds and wrinkles from several coupons for ten percent off this or five dollars off that at a local grocery store, most of them expired, and scrapped them. I dumped more than one sticky note with indecipherable messages to or from Oliver.

One last bundle remained, this one with more promise: a small stack of handwritten letters. I looked at the date and stopped to do the math. The first one was dated twenty-five years ago. To Oliver, from a Genevieve Moreau, return address in France.

What right did I have to read a personal letter, especially one that Oliver chose to keep handy, so to speak, in his locked desk drawer at work? What possible connection could this have to his murder a quarter of a century later? But I couldn't rule anything out, I reasoned. It wasn't as though I was going to use the contents of the letters for a nefarious purpose, or to embarrass him in any way.

I opened the first envelope and found a letter, in French. So much for that, unless I could catch Pierre before he drove off toward the aurora borealis. There were three more from Genevieve, all around the same date, all in French. The writing was dramatic, as the sentiment seemed to be, with some words underlined, or all in uppercase. The last one, the shortest one, was mostly in English. I smoothed it out on my lap and read:

Ollie dear,

Ah, le livre de cuisine.
I am sorry I can not convaincs *you to stay,* mon amour.
But I understand. You do not feel safe from M. P. M.
I will say it. He is NOT a nice man.
*But why can you not burn the book? Then he would
   leave you alone.*
Surely there are other books de cuisine?
Peut-être *one day you and I will be together. If not in
   this life . . .*

G.

How sad. I hated the fact that Genevieve and Oliver
would never be together. There was no longer any doubt
that Oliver had been running from someone, or had told G.
that he was running from someone, and had still been running. From someone with the initials M. P. M. I didn't want
to dwell on what she might have meant by the last phrase.

A lot of help that was. There was no one on our suspect
list with first initial M, except Manny, and his real name
was Arnold.

Maybe Miss, or Mademoiselle Genevieve was no longer
with us either. Even so, I was very sad after reading the letter and thought hard about whether I needed to have the
other letters translated. Could there be a clue, beyond the
initials of who was after Oliver? Who was to say that M. P. M.
had come to Alaska to murder Oliver? Why now? Maybe
he had never left France? Was he, or she, French or American or some other nationality altogether? Was M. P. M. also
a chef? The culinary school attracted students from all over
the world.

I knew enough French to able to translate the first sentence—who didn't understand that *cuisine* was related to food and cooking? It was practically an English word. It wasn't much of a leap to connect this letter, and the reason Oliver was running, to the cookbook we'd found hidden in his home.

The most immediate question was whether to share the letters with any of the team. Mom, surely, but who else was completely trustworthy? Chris was close. Annie was even closer, but she wasn't always rational when she was involved, or wanted to be involved, with a guy. Pierre would come in handy at this point, translating Genevieve's letters, but his rapport or lack thereof with Benny hadn't been tested.

After my experience at the station house, how could I even trust Trooper? Not that he was untrustworthy exactly, but there was his allegiance to the law to consider. And Deputy Josh was a huge question mark for countless reasons.

Not that any of them were likely Oliver's killer, but there was more at stake if Oliver's personal letters were at risk of going public. Too lazy to return them to my under-the-bed box, I slipped them back into my now clean and orderly tote, their disposition to be determined later.

I thought back on my to-do list. Victor was still a question mark. I couldn't see myself having a serious conversation with him, asking him for an alibi.

All of this mistrust left a bad taste in my mouth. One that might be overcome only by my secret stash of Belgian chocolates. I made sure Benny was out of the room when I opened the cabinet, just in case his superpowers were at the ready.

TWENTY

IT DIDN'T TAKE LONG FOR MY HOUSE TO SMELL LIKE
the Bear Claw at dinnertime. Fortunately, I liked the aromas that filled the air in my diner. Mom had come back
from her travels with Annie and immediately started on the
next meal. I figured that, unlike my dad, she was not crazy
about cruise fare.

"Too fancy," she'd said on the phone the first night.
"Who needs food you can't pronounce?" She'd paused.
"Oh, I know. Your father. I'm hoping he'll have had enough
steak and French sauce for the rest of the year."

Mom prided herself on her many recipes for moose
meat, and mooseloaf was one of her favorites. Throw in red
potatoes and carrots, suitably seasoned, around the sides of
the pan, and it was a meal that was hard to beat for most
Elkview born-and-raised.

While the oven was doing its thing, the other members
of the team checked in, depositing their contributions to the
meal. Annie arrived with a green salad she'd thrown together that looked like a menu photo from a classy restau-

rant. Chris was a little late because he had to finish a story for the morning edition of the *Bugle*, but he'd picked up a loaf of Italian bread and a bunch of flowers on the way. Irises, which I'd admired the day we took that side trip to Eklutna Lake. I told myself not to make too much of the gesture, but it was hard not to.

Trooper came empty-handed except for his hat and a sheepish grin. When he called Chris and me aside, I was pretty sure what to expect.

"I understand things didn't go well for you this afternoon?"

"You mean that we were treated like not even criminals should be treated?" I asked. "Oh, and by a couple of people whose salary I contribute to? Is that what you mean?"

"That's what I mean," Trooper said, while Chris smiled.

"I'm glad you think it's funny," I told Chris.

"Sorry," Chris said. "I was as upset as you were, but I didn't see the point in burning that bridge."

"The old Charlie is back," Trooper told Annie and my mom, who'd come to see what the fuss was about. "For a while, I thought you'd lost your spirit," he said to me.

"Believe me, if Chris hadn't held me back, more of my spirit would have been all over that dingy building."

"Why don't we all have a seat while dinner's cooking?" Mom said.

In other words, *Calm down, Charlie,* is what Mom meant.

Maybe I did overreact, but Trooper had brought up the station house issue. And I had already calmed down a bit, thanks to Benny, who had since wandered off. Although he liked Annie and Trooper and potentially Chris separately, Benny tended to retreat when there were too many people in the house at the same time.

I suspected he was in the back bedroom, Mom's at the moment, where I'd installed his new tree, one more elaborate than I'd ever have bought. A friend from San Francisco had sent it to him when she heard Benny had come to live with me. More of a cat condo than a cat tree, the plush brown residence had a small "house" on the middle level, where he often slept. The other levels had different swinging items. A mouse. A fish. A ball. Very scratchable mesh ladders connecting all the levels. My friend had offered to sign Benny up for extensions if he asked for them. I checked the literature that accompanied the complex and saw that "extensions" meant more levels, another house, more hanging attractions. I declined for now. I wouldn't want to spoil him.

"Let's see if we can make it up to you tomorrow," Trooper said, taking me away from my imaginings about how Benny might be enjoying himself on the elaborate tree in the back room and to what the rest of us had been talking about. "You have an attorney coming in from Anchorage to represent Manny?"

"If they let us in."

"Now, Charlie," Mom said.

"I know. Trooper is playing nice, so I should, too."

"Dinner's ready," Annie called out. She'd slipped away at the first sign of discord, much like Benny.

"Just in time," someone said, as we moved to the chairs around the dining room table.

CHRIS AND I STARTED OFF THE BUSINESS PART OF THE evening with a recap of Manny's fate, which our team, as we liked to call it, had been informed of, one at a time. We agreed we would not spread it around. We reported on the meeting with Moe and Jack. Thinking back, all we'd gotten from them was the content of the phone call between them and Manny. We'd learned what got him pulled into the station house—the fingerprints in Oliver's garage and the missing gun—which, of course, Trooper would have been able to share.

Trooper wasn't talking much, however, at least not right away.

I was tempted to expound in more detail on the travesty at the station house, but what would have been the point? There was always tomorrow morning to set it right.

Mom and Annie had the most interesting and informative day. They were ready with a full report on Lana and Gert, Oliver's most recent girlfriends.

"Gert admitted that she was planning on leaving town with Oliver," Mom told us. "She wasn't sure why Oliver had to leave on such short notice. At first he said he was just getting tired of the cold and asked if she would be interested in moving with him."

"All she knew was that he was headed for one of the lower forty-eight," Annie added. "But she was willing to go along with him wherever, even though she had a feeling he was running away from something. Or someone." She took a deep breath and smiled a longing smile. "It was so romantic."

Sure. Romeo and Juliet *romantic,* I thought. And we all know how that ended.

"Gert was very apologetic. She was especially sorry she lied to you, Charlie. She forgot she'd already made something up about why she was looking for Oliver. And then she was so upset about Oliver's death, she gave out a different reason," Mom said. "She honestly didn't know what had spooked Oliver. I'm tempted to believe her."

"Me, too," Annie said. "And, not that it matters right now, but Gert said she wasn't lying about no longer working on the drive-in theater."

Gert's story would account for the lack of luggage and

clothing in Oliver's house. Since the heavy clothing was still in his hallway, I suspected they were headed far south, maybe diagonally opposite Alaska. Say, Florida? It was impossible to know.

I was sorely tempted to mention the letters from Genevieve, but I wanted to talk to Manny before spilling out any more of Oliver's secrets. If Manny had no clue about M. P. M. or Genevieve, I'd rethink my strategy.

"The same with Lana," Mom added when Annie had finished. "I would definitely cross her off the list. She's practically engaged to a guy who's been helping with her online business and was just coming back from a crafts show in Fairbanks with him over the weekend."

"I just don't see her dropping in on Monday afternoon to kill Oliver," Annie added.

We were inclined to agree.

It was time to get something from Trooper. He did have two helpings of mooseloaf, after all, and was already asking about dessert.

"Did you say that Oliver's vehicle, his new SUV, was found near his body?" I asked.

"I never said."

"Well, can you say now?"

Everyone laughed, which was a nice cover for my total lack of humor.

"I guess I ought to contribute a little to the discussion, huh? If I want some of that surprise dessert you were talking about."

"We didn't talk about dessert," Mom said.

"Well, you could now."

More laughter as Annie confessed that, besides the cherry cheesecake mousse, there was rhubarb pie, a Trooper favorite. "I'll dish it out," Annie said, already on her way to the kitchen. "But talk loud enough so I can hear. I don't want to miss anything."

"We did find Oliver's vehicle a few yards from his body," Trooper said.

"Was it by any chance packed with luggage—clothes and stuff maybe?" Chris asked.

"Maybe."

"Trooper!" I'd been in a dustup with myself not to lose it. Trooper wasn't helping.

"Okay, I guess I owe you that much. Oliver's SUV was packed, all right. But not the way you'd expect if he'd really planned it out. Things were just kind of thrown in a couple of suitcases, some duffel bags. It was almost as if he were going on vacation rather than moving. No household things, for example. No bedding. Bare minimum toiletries."

Chris and I glanced at each other. We'd both already guessed some of that. We'd seen the array of appliances and specialty kitchenware in Oliver's house. The setup looked as complete as you'd find with any major supplier, wholesale or retail. And the bed wasn't stripped. Neither was any small furniture missing, items you might take with you on a permanent move.

"That's not the way Oliver would have packed if he weren't in a big hurry," Mom said. "And in so much of a hurry that he didn't pick up Gert."

"Or he was on his way to Gert's when someone stopped him," Annie said, from afar. She seemed determined to stick to her romance-novel approach.

"Was there any cash?" Chris asked.

"No cash. Not a penny," Trooper said.

"It must have been a robbery, then," Annie said.

"Not a robbery to start with, I'll bet," Mom said. "Once

Oliver was no longer alive, they also took his money? What kind of people are we dealing with?"

It wasn't very often that I saw my mom angry, so angry that I worried about her. I moved to sit next to her and took her hand until I felt her breathing slow, and she assured me with a look that she was fine. Oliver's death had brought out strange twists in the relationships of those he left behind. No one would have predicted that I'd be the stable one for my mom, if only for a moment.

Who was it? Who stopped him? I found myself squinting, as if by concentrating hard, I might be able to see who killed Oliver. Was it a man or a woman? Tall or short? Only one person or a group? I hated that we were barely an inch closer to finding out.

Tonight we had eliminated Manny's two trucker pals, plus Lana and Gert. That was some progress, but not nearly enough to suit me.

As Annie was handing out dessert, Chris turned to me. "Those envelopes you found in the trash? The ones Victor tossed? Was there anything there that could help?"

I held a quick debate with myself as everyone waited for my answer.

I shook my head. "Nothing so far. Bills and things," I said. Another not-lie, like the one I'd told my mom at the beginning of the week.

Luckily, no one pursued the topic and I didn't have to create a bigger lie.

The meeting broke up after dessert. Chris took a call and departed first. Annie left the rest of her salad with us but took a container of mooseloaf with her.

"I doubt Pierre has ever tasted this," she said.

Trooper took whatever we were willing to pack for him.

"Will you be there tomorrow? At the station house?" I asked him.

It was one of those situations—he knew that I knew that he knew what I meant. Would he support our efforts to see Manny?

"What time do you figure?"

I did a quick calculation. Willow had said she'd leave first thing in the morning, which meant around eight. I needed to allow for a bit of rush hour traffic, though she'd be mostly traveling in the opposite direction.

"Around eleven should be good."

Trooper nodded, donned his hat, and left.

As our dinner guests thinned out, Benny approached and headed for my mom's ankles, which were in front of a sink full of dirty dishes.

I urged her to leave the dishes and come to the living room with Benny and me. "Cooks don't do dishes, remember?"

She picked up Benny and carried him to her own old chair. "Don't you wish he could talk?" she asked me, never breaking her scratching rhythm.

"Or at least type out a note," I said.

"We know he'd have great advice."

"I guess we just have to listen."

All three of us sat back to listen to one another, no words needed.

"I SUPPOSE WE SHOULD MAKE A PLAN FOR THE WEEK-end," Mom said. We were ready for bed, saying our last good-night to Benny. "I think I'd like to go home tomorrow morning, get the house ready for your dad."

My parents' home, my childhood home, was less than a mile away, south of Main Street, but I knew I'd miss my mom. It had been wonderful to have her around, even though it wasn't all cheery. I hoped I was mistaken when I thought I heard Benny utter a soft wail. It was going to be hard on him, too. I resolved to be extra attentive to him once Mom was back in her home.

I had one more selfish thing I wanted her to do. "Someone has to talk to Victor," I said.

"Oh, I started to, at what he called the 'funeral party' at the diner yesterday."

"That's so Victor."

"I didn't want to bring it up because I haven't exactly finished with my questions. Maybe I could do it tomorrow morning, if you don't mind?"

Good one, Mom. "What a great idea," I said as we both chuckled.

"I can tell you he's in the midst of switching girlfriends," she said.

"Rachel's the new one?" I asked.

She nodded. "And he spent much of Monday letting the old one down easy."

"That answers one question I had. But I still can't figure why he was so quick to use Oliver's apron, for example, and empty his personal drawer in the trash? And take his name off the new menu?"

Mom shrugged. "I know what you mean. But I suspect there was nothing vindictive about it. He's young, and Oliver's gone. Let me talk to him. You're his boss, still will be when this is all over, so it might be better if you keep out of it."

Whew. Mom knew how to take a load off my mind. I suspected that Victor was guilty of nothing more than ambition, but it would be good to be a little more sure.

Why was this whole interviewing suspects thing so

tricky? So much more than a to-do list. Were we—deputies, that is—supposed make up a point system and figure out a total at the end? Give Victor plus ten points for being a good employee, minus five points for wearing Oliver's apron right away, plus ten for being flexible and coming in when I needed him, and so on? Was there a guide like the ones that came with board games, so it would be easy to figure out who won?

Mom and I cleaned up the kitchen, needing to feel a sense of accomplishment before bed. Dirty dishes at the start; washed and dried and put away at the end.

THE NEXT MORNING, I DROPPED MOM OFF AT HER house, drove back home to mine, and grabbed the *Bugle* from the driveway on the way in. I expected Chris to pick me up in about a half hour for our trip to the station house.

Benny greeted me at the door as usual, but didn't stay long. I figured he needed a little time to get used to the back bedroom being all his again. I made sure his feeder was full and his toys were in plain sight, since some had been inadvertently moved into corners by company the last two nights. I placed the motorized feather-and-bell toy Mom had brought him in the middle of the living room floor. I'd be ready to run it for him as soon as he showed up again.

In the meantime, I sat on the couch and opened the *Bugle*.

And slammed it shut, hoping I'd fallen asleep and had a bad dream. I opened the paper again.

No, that was still the headline.

LOCAL MAN ARRESTED FOR MURDER OF ES-TRANGED SON. By Christopher Doucette.

Chris. How could you?

TWENTY-ONE

HE WAS NOT ARRESTED.

I paced. I read a sentence. I scrunched the *Bugle* pages together. I unscrunched them and smoothed them. I read another sentence.

> Arnold Quinlan, 67, of North 2nd Street in Elkview, was taken into custody, charged with the murder of his son, Oliver Whitestone, 51, a cook at the local Bear Claw Diner.

I paced some more, my jaw tightening, my stomach churning, and read another sentence.

> Quinlan was estranged from his son for many years. The two reunited recently.

They were not reunited.
The reporting was *wrong, wrong, wrong*.
My phone rang its text sound. I glanced at the screen.

Running late. ETA 30 mins.

From Chris. Christopher Doucette of the *Bugle*.
I read one more section.

Whitestone's body was found in the woods near the main
Elkview landing strip. The motive for the killing is unknown. Police are investigating.

I grabbed my jacket, stuffed the newspaper in my tote
without regard for its prearranged folds, ran in for a quick
goodbye to Benny, asked his forgiveness for rushing off.
"I'll explain later," I told him.

I tried to sort it out. First, the big thing. Arnold was not
arrested. I said it out loud, as if Chris and the entire reading
public could hear me. That was *wrong, wrong, wrong*.

And small things. Oliver was not a cook; he was a chef.
"Police" were not investigating. Trooper Graham was investigating. I was investigating. I thought *he* was investigating, not chasing a story, a scoop.

How could Chris get all this wrong?

How could he do this to Manny? To Oliver? To me?

I tried to calm down for safe driving. I'd already decided
not to respond to Chris's text. Let him get to my house and
wonder why I wasn't there. Should I have left a note? No. It
would only have been nasty. I wrote one now, in my head.
*Dear Chris, no more heated steering wheel until you print
a retraction.*

I couldn't believe I'd been so naive. Flirting. *Let's go to
France and taste test the* confit de canard. Thinking he
cared about me. The compliments. The flowers. Watching
kayaks on Eklutna Lake.

Chris had used me, plain and simple. Why, when he was buddies with Trooper, did he need me? It wasn't hard to figure out. Because he knew I wanted to investigate and that would give him a whole other opening into the case, especially since Trooper would be otherwise engaged with the Girdwood issues. And who knew Oliver better than my mom? Another personal contact, with information he might not get from any other source.

Smart. Nice going, Chris. Maybe I'll nominate you for a Pulitzer.

But weren't we friends? Partners in the investigation? Why didn't he just share his plan for releasing the information? Talk it over with me. Was it even legal for him to do what he did in today's story? And why lie?

The pounding in my ears started up anew. I slowed down, tucking the Outback behind a semi with a blue cab, like Manny's, in the slow lane. I wondered when Manny would be driving his truck again.

I called Trooper on my hands-free setup. He answered just as I thought I'd need to leave a message.

"Charlie?"

"Has Manny been charged?"

"No. Of course not. I would have given you a heads-up."

I took a breath. "Is Willow there? Ms. Yazzie, his lawyer?"

"Not yet. I came in early. I'm way behind on paperwork."

"Did you see the *Bugle* this morning?"

"Not yet. Like I said, I'm way behind." He paused. "What's up? Something wrong, Charlie?"

"Front-page story."

"What?"

"By Chris."

"What? Is he with you now?"

"No." I cleared my throat. Almost smiled. "He may be late."

I gave Trooper a quick summary of what was wrong. He clicked off, promising to track down the story.

Another text message from Chris came in.

I'm here. Are you ready? I've been ringing the bell

I thought how ironic it was. I'd been concerned that Annie was being taken advantage of by her Frenchman. I didn't trust Pierre not to use her, whether for a better room at her inn or for his own ego. I came close to warning her several times. And all the while I was one the being duped, being lulled into some romantic fantasy. I felt like apologizing to Annie and Pierre both.

Another message from Chris, this one a voicemail.

"I've decided to drive to the station house myself. I looked in the window of your garage and your car is gone, so I assume you had some other thing. An emergency? I hope not. At least not a bad one. I'm going to call your mom."

No. Not my mom. She'll only worry.

I called my mom, hoping to head that off.

"What's up, Charlie? Are you at the station house yet?"

"No, but something came up and I'm driving alone. Chris might call you to find out what happened. Just say I'm fine and he doesn't need to come."

The silence that followed told me Mom knew there was more to this message. "A spat?" she asked.

"Not exactly. I'm driving, Mom. I have to go."

"I assume you're going to fill me in at the appropriate time?"

"Of course. Love you."

"Love you, too, sweetie. Try to stay calm."

"Of course."

I PULLED INTO THE STATION HOUSE LOT TO THE TUNE
of my cell phone. I had never used the hands-free feature so
many times in one morning. I didn't hit the talk button until I heard Annie's voice begin a message.

"I'm just arriving at the station house, so this has to be
brief for now," I said.

"Oh, I'm sorry to bother you, Charlie. Nothing urgent,
except Pierre and I are getting along so well and I wanted
to share."

"I'm glad, Annie, but can this wait? I'm on my way to
talk to Manny."

"How could I forget? I read that he's been arrested. Poor
Manny. Oh, go, go. I'll talk to you later."

"He has not been arrested, Annie. The *Bugle* was wrong.
Chris was wrong. Don't spread it, okay?"

"Okay. I won't say anything to anybody. Everything is
so mixed-up these days. My head is reeling."

"Mine, too. Later, Annie."

And another call came in, but no message this time, so I
ignored it. I couldn't check for the ID while I was driving and
I wasn't about to take the chance that it was Chris again.

I parked closer to the correct door this time, which
meant my scarf needed to be wound around my neck only
once. My car thermometer said it was thirty-five degrees,
downright balmy, but I didn't trust it. Just as I no longer
trusted reporters for the *Bugle*.

Inside, I stomped my boots on the floor, not because
there was snow anywhere in sight, just because it felt good

to stomp. I glared at the matron who was so unpleasant to us yesterday, and before I could think of something equally unpleasant to say to her now, Trooper came out of an office door.

"Charlie, I was about to call you."

"What? Don't tell me. Visiting hours haven't begun and won't start until sometime after lunch."

Trooper grinned but didn't waste time setting me straight, likely afraid I'd haul off and do or say something I'd really regret.

"Manny's boss called right after you and I hung up. Moe and Jack tracked him down at the company headquarters in Juneau." Trooper pointed to the door he'd just exited and motioned me inside. "It turns out Manny was with him the afternoon of Oliver's murder."

I blew out a breath. If anything could have cheered me up, it was news like that.

I took a seat in the government-issue gray metal chair opposite a matching desk. The office looked like it was shared by a few people. There was nothing personal on the walls or furniture except for a mug that had the misshapen look of pottery made by a kid and smelled like old coffee. The metal bookcase was overflowing with binders containing guidelines for state and federal agencies. Schools. Veterans Affairs. Housing and Urban Development Home and Health Care. I wondered how often they were referred to. They looked unopened, like a set of encyclopedias in a school library in the age of the Internet.

Trooper moved the mug to a credenza and put his feet up on the desk, leaning back as far as the chair would take him.

"'Scuse me," he said. "Long night."

Whether it was the dim light in the windowless office or

my own mood, I thought he looked tired and old. He was my parents' age, I realized, and might be thinking of retiring. I hoped not. I couldn't imagine dealing with Deputy Josh. That alone would be enough to keep me out of trouble.

Right now, at least, he was ready to pick up on his report to me.

"When he got to the Bear Claw that day, Manny told the guys the story about an argument he had with his boss, and this morning they verified it. Good pals, those guys."

I remembered the day, not only because it was less than a week ago and was when Oliver's body was discovered, but also because it was one of the busiest days in the diner. The tourists at Annie's had piled in. They'd filled the place, and Victor and Nina had performed their magic, setting up a separate table with a special meal in the kitchen to accommodate Moe and Jack, and eventually, Manny.

"Manny and his boss had a fight about Manny's retiring," Trooper continued. "You know how the guys are always teasing Manny about getting too old to drive a rig. Well, his boss was not teasing. He was trying to force Manny to pack it in, but Manny has a union rep, et cetera, so they got into it. The funniest thing the boss said, listen to this—'If Arnold was going to kill anyone that day, it would have been me.'"

"Good to know," I said, through a big smile. "So that's all it took?"

Trooper nodded. "That and your lawyer friend. We might have sent him home anyway, but she pointed out, in case we forgot"—Trooper smiled—"that we'd detained him for almost twenty-four hours, so we were going to have to charge him, ask for an extension, or let him go anyway."

Go, Willow.

"His boss has committed to coming in tomorrow and

making a formal statement," Trooper continued. "But yeah, it's over, unless something else turns up."

"Where's Manny now?"

"Out of here. Your friend took him away, offered to drive him home. Nice lady, really. We tried to call you, by the way, but something must be wrong with your phone. Constantly busy."

"I believe it."

"Chris isn't with you?"

"Something came up," I said, and realized I'd better beat it out of there before he showed up. I jumped from the chair. "I'm going to catch up with Willow and Manny. Thanks for this, Trooper."

"Shall I give Chris a heads-up about this before he comes all the way out here?" Trooper asked. "Or are you going to do it?"

"He'll figure it out," I said, and headed out the door, leaving Trooper with a curious look on his face.

I DIALED WILLOW'S NUMBER FROM THE OUTBACK.

The heated steering wheel reminded me of Chris and roiled up my stomach again. I wasn't proud of myself for giving him the runaround, but part of me felt he deserved it. Since he'd left me out of the loop, falsely announcing an arrest in the investigation of Oliver's murder, there was no reason for me to include him in anything I'd learned about Manny's release.

The whole situation sounded a lot like "He started it, nyah, nyah," and that was the part I wasn't proud of. But I wasn't so remorseful that I wanted to give him an update. Let him find out on his own.

Willow's voice, her understanding lawyer voice, soothed me.

"I thought about waiting for you at the station house, but I figured it was better to get Arnold out of there before some higher-up got involved and changed the decision."

"Good thinking. Where are you now?"

"We're almost to Arnold's house. He's anxious to clean up. I figured you and I could take him out for a celebratory meal."

"I know just the place."

"I thought you might."

We made a plan to meet at the Bear Claw in an hour, which gave me enough time to answer messages and, more important, drop in on Benny. I pulled off the road at a safe enough distance to know that Chris wouldn't be on my tail and paid a virtual visit to my tabby. He was lying in his usual cone of sunshine, but upside down, on his back. He probably wasn't sleeping. Missing Mom, I guessed. On the off chance that he could hear me, I told him I'd be home in the afternoon and that I'd be sure Mom and Dad would be at our house for dinner tomorrow evening.

I didn't know exactly when Dad's flight was due. He and the Russells were flying together, and Barney had offered to drive Dad home from the Anchorage airport. Dad would be full of stories about his business stops with Russell in Salzburg and Tyrol, which would prove a nice distraction from the drama of the week in Elkview.

A call to my mom went to voicemail, and I left a brief message about Manny's release.

Since I'd been so short with Annie, I called her back to let her talk.

"I was telling you about Pierre, but really it's not important compared to what we're doing. Investigating, I mean. But Pierre is thinking of staying for a while. He says he can send his article from anywhere, once he gets to the lights when his car is ready, and can come back here. We're getting close."

I'd hardly followed the sequence, and I could hardly believe what I did follow. But I couldn't joke with Annie. Being mean to Chris was one thing; being mean to Annie was untenable.

"Do you have anything else to report, Annie? On Stanley, maybe?"

"I called him, and I'll try again. I didn't want to go all the way to Anchorage without knowing if he's there. I especially don't want to drag your mom there. My deputy partner, you know. She's already spent a lot of time traveling this week, and your dad returns tomorrow."

"That's right. And I know she has things to do before Dad arrives."

"Maybe I'll take Pierre with me to Anchorage. And I know you think I'm just trying to have Pierre time, but really I'm concerned about your mom. Also, that is. And I don't think Pierre's ever been to a big city in Alaska."

Annie meant *the* big city in Alaska, the only one, with about three hundred thousand people. Fairbanks, next largest, had only ten percent of that number. I didn't know the population of Zurich, but since it was a global center for finance, I was pretty sure it topped any city in Alaska. Still, Anchorage had its charms, and a road trip would be one more bonding experience for Annie and Pierre.

Annie was almost ready to finish her Stanley Burke report. As far as I could figure, he might be our last hope. If you could call IDing a killer a hope.

Twenty-Two

WILLOW LIVED UP TO HER NAME. TALL, GRACEFULLY slender, and lithe, just as I recalled, like the lovely tree that inspired her name. Her ultralong hair served to emphasize the parallel. We did a quick review of what we'd been up to since I'd skipped out of law school, leaving Willow behind, and at the top of her class—not that I'd been competition for that position.

"I went the corporate law route, and it felt good not to be poor for a while," she told me. "But once I got myself out of student debt, I made a beeline out of there. A friend and I started Adams and Yazzie."

"From A to Z. And that sounds like diversity in action," I said.

Willow laughed. "That was the idea. We agreed to set limits on what we'd need to succeed, with an eye toward as much pro bono work as possible."

"Lucky us," I said, sincere in my thanks. Willow had helped engineer the best possible outcome for Manny.

We turned our attention to Manny when he exited his

quarters, looking like a man who had a new lease on life. "I'll never take it for granted again," he said. By which I assumed he meant his freedom. Or maybe just his hot shower.

We headed for the Bear Claw in two cars, on a mission for a decent meal for Manny, who rode with me. He was about as chatty as I'd ever heard him. I could have done without some details of his overnight stay in police custody, however. I had no doubt that Moe and Jack would be treated to the same specifics before Manny could put them to rest.

"Every teenager should have to spend a night in jail," he said.

I chose silence on that suggestion, though I understood his point.

We arrived to find my diner crowded but operating smoothly. The late lunch crowd included some climbers I recognized and members of Beth's tour group who had eschewed the Talkeetna zip line tour. I saw that the stacks of Vermont were a favorite today and figured Nina had a way of encouraging that choice. It was always easier to get through a rush hour if you could batch-process a menu item.

I was thrilled to see how well things were going without me. Nina had chosen upbeat country music, and I noticed a lot of fingers tapping to the beat. Maybe I could retire even earlier than Mom had and start my program of seeing the rest of my great state.

Nina immediately offered to set up a special table for us in the kitchen, as she'd done once before for the truckers. Instead, the three of us picked aprons from the stack of clean ones and pitched in.

"This reminds me of summers in college," Willow said, showing adeptness at carrying the Bear Claw's heavy plates along her arms. "But it wasn't as much fun as this is, when you're BFFs with the boss."

"Same here," Manny said. "Like my busboy days until I got my driver's license." He hosed off a tub of cutlery, stacked it all into the dishwasher, and prepared the utility cart for the next load.

When the crowd thinned and we took our turn at being served, Victor approached with a question.

"Ready for something new?"

"Sure," Manny said.

"Of course," Willow said.

"Maybe," I said, with a nod to the absent Oliver and his steadfast adherence to what he knew worked.

"Give me a few minutes," Victor said.

Manny had never gotten the chance to tell us how he tracked down his son, except to tell us that he'd seen Oliver's photo in an article on classic American diners. But how did a long-haul trucker happen upon an article in a food magazine?

When Chris and I were at his house, Manny had been recounting his failure to find his son through the social work system when Trooper had unceremoniously pulled him away from us. He was never arrested, I reminded myself, mentally sending an angry look toward the *Bugle* and its staff. I wondered, but would deny it if asked, where Chris was now. Probably talking to Trooper, learning after the fact that Manny had been released.

Poor Chris. *Not.*

Manny picked up his story now, while we waited for what Victor had promised: something different for lunch.

"I couldn't get anything from the ER, as I told you before, Charlie, but I knew there were only a few places in the city at that time where an orphan—I hate that word. I hate that I did that to my son—where an orphan would be placed."

My heart went out to Manny. I couldn't help thinking

that nowadays young Manny's story would be fodder for a talk show. Or he'd be able to sell it to a tabloid and use the money to hire a private investigator to find his child. Did that make things better? I couldn't say.

"You were a kid yourself, Manny," Willow said. "How were you supposed to take care of a baby with no support?"

I was glad Willow confirmed what some of us had been telling Manny since we heard his moving confession of two nights ago.

"One thing I did have going for me was a driver's license, so I got a job where they weren't too picky about experience, and it was good for me because I could sleep in my truck, and eventually I graduated to a rig with a sleeper cabin."

"You mean trucks have sleeper cars, like trains?" Willow asked.

"Sort of. More like an RV. You have blackout curtains for the cab windshield. You've got a bunk and a microwave and a small fridge. Let's see, what else? Lots of storage for food and clothes."

"Don't forget the pull-down table and television set," I said, showing off, thanks to a special tour I was given by Moe when he was assigned a brand-new big rig a few months ago.

"My knowledge of worlds outside of the law is severely limited," Willow said.

"The rigs saved me during that very bad time. They gave me a home, and driving always calms me down," Manny said.

Willow and I agreed that it was hard to imagine the calming effect of driving an eighteen-wheeler, especially on the wild freeways of the lower forty-eight. I remembered the time a huge semitruck carrying a load of furniture tried to go across the Golden Gate Bridge through a toll lane that was too narrow for its load. The big white truck was stuck, unable to move forward or backward. Eventually, other lanes were opened so vehicles could pass, and San Franciscans hardly paid attention to the odd sight. Just another day of commuting. That was a part of northern California that I didn't miss.

I wanted Manny to get to the clue that brought him to the Bear Claw and his son. But there was one more interruption to our conversation, when Victor and Nina arrived with our lunch plates.

To call what appeared on the plate a sandwich would be only a fraction of the story. Victor wouldn't share the recipe until we'd each taken a bite or two.

"Shepherd's pie?" I asked, hurrying to take another sample.

"Yup. Leftover shepherd's pie between two pieces of buttered toast and cheese. It's a grilled cheese extravaganza."

"That was my idea," Nina said. "I named it. If you want it on the menu, that is."

I smacked my lips. "Why wouldn't I? It's delicious. And a brilliant way to use up shepherd's pie leftovers."

Two thumbs-ups from Manny and Willow sealed the deal; they were too engaged in chewing to comment otherwise.

After polishing off the extravaganza, definitely a Nina word, Manny was back in narrative mode.

"I don't know why, but a church lady took pity on me one of the times I went back to Anchorage."

"You kept going back?" Willow asked.

Manny nodded. "Times were changing, rules were changing, and I kept hoping one of those days it would be okay to tell me where my son was. I don't know if the rule did change or this lady was just sick of seeing me, but she told me she'd see what she could do. Next thing, she calls me and says that she looked through the old files and saw that a few years before, Oliver went to Paris to study. He needed some kind of papers for his student visa. And he wrote 'education at a cooking school' on the form. That was the last thing in his file, and it might have been around twenty years old, give or take, but it was a lead."

"And that's why you happened to be looking at cooking magazines," I said.

"Yeah, anything for a clue. It's not like I could afford to go to Paris, right? And even if I could have, there was no guarantee he would still be there. Then I saw the article with the little photo and I knew. He had changed his last name, but I could tell."

"And the rest is history." I was sorry almost as soon as I said this. Usually the expression refers to a happy ending, and this one was at best mixed, with his son, so recently found, now lost again. But Manny didn't object.

Willow offered to take Manny home so I could hang around the Bear Claw and help clean up. I felt it was about time.

"So this is what 'pro bono' means," I said, teasing, to Willow.

"I'm just glad it all worked out. They're not always this easy, you know."

Willow and I promised to see each other before the next crisis.

I joined my staff in the kitchen until it was picture-perfect, ready for a cooking magazine, like the ones Oliver hated, but had brought his father a measure of joy.

I called in Tammy and Bert, only too happy for the extra time, and sent Victor and Nina home. In between, I called my mom.

"I'm glad Manny is out of the woods," she said. "He's been through a lot. It was nice that you could help."

"It was more Willow's doing, and Moe's and Jack's, but it worked out well."

"The house is all ready for Dad," she said.

I imagined Mom had stopped to pick up their mail and newspapers and done grocery shopping and laundry and fluffed his pillow. It would be as if Dad had never left the full-service cruise ship.

"They'll be taking an early flight, from somewhere," she continued. "I forget his exact itinerary, but the Russells are taking care of it all. He'll be here late tomorrow afternoon. I have everything I need to make his favorite blueberry waffles for dinner."

Was it only diner folk who mixed up breakfast, lunch, and dinner foods? It wasn't unusual for me or my parents to have leftover moose meatloaf for breakfast, cereal and fruit for lunch, and eggs Benedict for dinner.

Speaking of whom, I needed to pay the living, four-legged Eggs Benedict a visit.

"I'm going to head home. Unless you need me for anything?" I asked my mom.

"Nope. Unless you need to talk?"

"Talk?"

"You know. The thing with Chris today."

"Not a big thing at all, Mom. I'll talk to you tomorrow."

"Okay. Let's both get a good night's sleep."

"Works for me. Love you."

"Love you, too."

I was happy the so-called thing with Chris hadn't ruined the rest of my day. Manny's release, catching up with Willow, hearing Manny's story, being back at the Bear Claw in an apron. A lot of pluses.

When Chris didn't come around to the Bear Claw after finding that Manny had been released from custody, I was pretty sure he knew what was up. Otherwise, he might have been on my case about not waiting for him and avoiding his calls.

He wasn't dumb. He knew he'd blown it.

He'd been inconsiderate, printing Manny's name like that. Ambitious, at the cost of someone's reputation. Untrustworthy. Selfish.

All of those things, and more. But not dumb.

I headed home, eager to see Benny. Playing with him would add one more pleasure to the good things that had happened today.

Unfortunately, one bad thing stood out. We still didn't know who had killed my friend and chef. I reviewed the list of suspects in my head and mentally crossed off people as I drove along Main Street toward my house.

The only person I couldn't clear in my head was Oliver's brother, Stanley. My mom had cleared Kendra with a quick call to her office, where her boss verified that she'd been at work that day without interruption. I trusted Mom to be creative enough to fabricate a good reason for her question.

As far as I'd heard, no one knew where Stanley worked, if he did. He looked older than Kendra, who was almost sixty, closing in on retirement age. Maybe he had all the time in the world to murder his brother.

Thinking this way wasn't healthy, I realized, let alone while driving. I admired the law enforcement community, who had to entertain these thoughts day after day and still live a normal life. I was glad this was a one-off project for me.

I waved to Lucas on his porch as I passed his shop. When things got back to normal for me, I'd have to visit him and tell him how his chest with its secret drawer had led to clues that helped solve a murder. If and when it did.

Back to Stanley. What was his alibi? I repeated the question to myself so I wouldn't forget to follow up.

Another important question: what could Stanley's motive be? In the fleeting moment I'd had with him at the memorial service, I picked up that he was aware Oliver had been in some kind of trouble. He may have known that Oliver was preparing to leave the area because of it.

Stanley wasn't mentioned in Oliver's attempt at a will. Another possible motive to fight and ultimately kill his brother?

Mom was occupied with getting ready for Dad's return, and Annie, her deputy partner, was busy getting ready for Pierre's trip to the lights, maybe to join him, so I doubted that team had followed up on Stanley, my last, best hope for a killer.

I'd have to take care of that myself.

I STOPPED AT THE GROCER'S CLOSE TO HOME TO RE-plenish staples that had been depleted by the extra mouths to feed this week. I picked up extra tuna treats for Benny and a bag of popcorn kernels for Annie and me in case Pierre left without her and we needed to stream a feel-good movie. I carried two bulging paper sacks up my front steps, always a challenge since, until June came along, there were bound to be pieces of ice in random spots. I set the bags down in an ice-free zone and unlocked the heavy oak door.

I was surprised to find I had to push the door open against a mess on the floor inside the house. A basket near the recliner that held sewing, catalogs, paperbacks, and other odds and ends had been tipped over, its contents strewn everywhere. A scatter rug had been pushed to the side, not neatly.

Benny? It wasn't like him, even though he had been left to his own devices a lot this week. Maybe something like a loud noise, a bird hitting a window or a vehicle backfiring, had rattled him and he'd done this in an agitated state.

But no, of course not. A dining room chair had been knocked over. Benny couldn't do that.

I left my groceries on the table and walked through the rooms, nearly breathless, finding pockets of upset everywhere. Drawers had been opened, contents thrown around. A favorite vase had been dropped or tossed to the hardwood floor in the hallway, where it had shattered.

Someone was looking for . . . what?

Then I panicked. Benny! Why hadn't he come to greet me?

"Benny!" I called out.

I hurried forward, looking in all the corners, calling his name. I could finally breathe when I found him in the back bedroom where Mom had slept, hiding inside his tree house. He peeked out now and hurried down when he saw me. I picked him up, held him against my shoulder, close to my heart, and ran my hand gently down his back.

"Benny. Who did this? Who came in here and scared you? Who messed up our house?" I stroked his chin, his neck, rubbed behind his ears.

Then I panicked again. What if the person were still in the house? No, I reasoned, there was no car out front. Or yes, I reasoned, that's why Benny had been hiding.

I kept Benny on my shoulder and took my smartphone from my pocket. He wouldn't stop growling. Not a frightening growl, but a frightened growl.

I hit nine-one-one, but what good was that going to do? There was never an officer of the law closer than a half hour away. I left a message with the dispatcher anyway and walked around the house again, alert for a foreign sound or smell. It was deathly quiet until the ice maker in my fridge released a batch of noisy new ice. I jumped, scaring Benny. He leapt out of my arms and raced back to the bedroom, where I found him on the highest level of his tree.

I was convinced there was no one in the house now.

Then I panicked again, for the third time? The fourth? I'd lost count. What if Benny was hurt? I could feel my heartbeat pulsing in my throat. No wonder Benny hadn't calmed down yet. I reached for him, still in the guest room that housed his tree, and held him away from me, looking for bruises, blood. I laid him on the bed. When did he ever allow me to do that? He stayed there obediently while I felt all over his body, running my fingers through his fur, inspecting every inch.

I couldn't feel any bruising and he wasn't flinching at all, but I couldn't take any chances. Fortunately, I had Doc Sherman, our family doctor, part-time coroner-elect, and emergency vet on speed dial.

I explained what I'd found in my house, how I was worried that Benny might be hurt in a way that I couldn't detect.

"Leave the house, Charlie," he said. His tone was serious, no-nonsense.

"I called nine-one-one."

"Listen to me. Put Benny in his carrier and leave the house. Use one of the pills I gave you for Benny if he resists. I'll meet you at my office."

I grabbed my tote-cum-purse and fished Benny's carrier out of the hall closet. I knelt down and had set about unzipping the carrier when something in my peripheral vision caught my eye. I'd missed it in my initial inspection of the house, but now I saw a piece of cloth out of place. One of my dish towels had been thrown over the Bennycam.

The camera system was small and unobtrusive. A black

cube about three inches on each side. The intruder must have known enough to search it out. I pushed away the idea that my home had been invaded by someone who knew me and my residence this well.

Benny had found his way to the hall and entered his carrier without incident. A first. I thanked him for understanding what I was going through and not causing me any further stress.

TWENTY-THREE

Benny was on the back seat of the Outback, buckled in through soft handles at the top and sides of his carrier.

I wished I could reach back and scratch his head, give him comfort, make him feel more at home, but there were the seatback and the latest model carrier in the way. I had to count on that recommended position to keep him safe. I hadn't had time for the usual buildup of treats before coaxing Benny into his carrier. At the last minute I smoothed one of my ragged fleece sweatshirts onto the floor of the container and tossed in two bright squeaking balls. I felt I'd betrayed him, slamming the door to keep him inside. I kept up a constant stream of soothing words to assure him I hadn't turned villain. It wasn't more than twenty minutes to Doc Sherman's, so I felt he would be okay.

I shuddered, thinking of the feeling Manny must have had the night he was in custody, having a full-size, real door slam in his face. I couldn't imagine Deputy Josh caring whether he was comfortable. I was glad I'd been able to play a small part in freeing him.

Benny ran through his whole repertoire of sounds on the way to Doc Sherman's. I heard meowing, purring, yowling, growling, chattering, hissing, and back to meowing. I knew he wanted my attention, but was it more than that?

Yes, I realized, and panicked yet one more time.

Mom!

Benny was reminding me to check on my mom.

I hit the hands-free link to my smartphone and called out Mom's number.

What if Mom's house had also been broken into? She was there, alone, as far as I knew. She'd have been in and out the last couple of days, shopping, looking in on the Bear Claw, straightening up the house. Dad would often tease-slash-annoy her by writing on dusty surfaces every now and then, carving, so to speak, their initials in the dust, complete with a surrounding heart. In my worst nightmare, she'd been home alone, removing all traces of dust, when the intruder came in.

The phone rang through to voicemail and I could hardly breathe. I thought of turning my vehicle in the direction of her house but we were almost at Doc Sherman's. I clicked the phone link off, then on again, redialing Mom's number.

"Hi, sweetie. I see you just called."

At the sound of her voice, Benny settled down, leaning with his back against the wall of the carrier.

I needed to alarm and not alarm my mom at the same time. "Are you busy?"

"I was taking banana muffins out of the oven, which is why I didn't pick up a minute ago."

My dad's favorite muffins. I blew out such a loud breath, I steamed up my windshield. Now what? I was still working out whether to tell my mom immediately that my house had been invaded. Should I tell her the truth so she'd get out of her house in case the intruder was on his way there? Not tell her, and risk her safety?

I thought of a compromise, inspired by Benny's measured meows. "Mom, Benny's not doing so well right now. I'm on my way to Doc's. Can you meet me there?"

"What's wrong with him?" I heard panic in her voice, but that was better than hearing her screams. Or nothing at all.

"I'm not sure. Just meet me there, okay?"

"I'm on my way."

I had just enough time to create a scenario in my mind. With no clear evidence, I decided that someone knew I had Oliver's cookbook. They might even think I still had his will, the sheet with details of the disposition of his cash. It was hard to imagine anyone looking for his letters to Genevieve, but I couldn't rule it out.

The cookbook was in the box under my bed. Or was it? In my rush to protect Benny and leave the house, I hadn't checked on the box. It wasn't out in the room, which might mean it was still in its place. I couldn't imagine the intruder pushing the box neatly back under the bed. He certainly hadn't been careful with anything else as he went through my possessions. The most careful thing he did was cover the Bennycam.

Would this never end? Would there ever be a day when all these loose ends would be tied up? It came to me that I needed Chris. He knew more than even Trooper did what we'd uncovered. I might have to swallow my pride and reach out to him.

Kendra knew Chris and I had been upstairs in Oliver's house. I hadn't expected her to buy the story about my finding Oliver's will in his desk at the Bear Claw. Could Kendra have been my intruder? Looking for the cookbook? Might she have sent Stanley?

I pulled up to Doc Sherman's office. It was time to let Benny know the reason for this rushed trip.

THE GOOD DOC HAD ALWAYS CLAIMED THAT HIS FIRST love was veterinary medicine, and every time I'd seen him with one of my pets during my childhood, I believed him. Doc's exam room sported wall-to-wall posters featuring the anatomically detailed bodies of every animal I'd ever seen or fed. I'd courted as pets a parade of dogs, on the larger side of the pet spectrum, plus rats, hamsters, rabbits, and, briefly, a turtle. As a kid, I'd search for the drawing that matched my pet and try to follow what Doc was doing. For a long time, my parents were sure I'd enter a medical field and perhaps had held out that hope. They didn't know yet that I couldn't stand the sight of blood.

Benny was my first cat, and now I wondered how I'd lived without him.

"How is he, Doc?" I asked again, just before I was politely ushered out of the exam room by his nurse. Apparently, my loud pacing and questioning were interfering with the procedure. I must have been more docile as a kid, since Doc had never thrown me out. Maybe he, too, had been hoping I'd follow in his footsteps.

"Mr. Eggs Benedict here knows us, Charlie," he said. "I think we'll do better if you keep your mom company in the waiting room."

Subtle, but clear. I entered the waiting room, where the posters featured animals in their natural habitats. Bears, bison, deer, elk, mountain goats, a moose with magnificent antlers. None of them with X-ray views showing their innards.

Mom was pacing, but quietly. "You have to tell me what's going on, Charlie."

We took seats together and I started on what I'd found when I arrived home, playing down the panic I'd felt. I didn't get far before the outside door opened and Trooper and Chris walked in. I wasn't ready to talk to either of them, for different reasons, but I didn't have much choice, unless I wanted to revert to what Trooper called my "short fuse" and make a dash past them, out the door. *Not without Benny,* I reasoned.

My mom eased the transition.

"Trooper!" she said. "Did you know about this?" She pointed to me as if I had a blueprint of my house on my face with details of the break-in written on it.

"Not until Freddie told me."

Who knew that Frederica, the day dispatcher in the station house, actually kept track of callers and disseminated information so efficiently? I'd have to keep that in mind for future emergencies, of which I hoped there would be none.

"What are we going to do?" Mom asked, meaning *What are you, State Trooper Graham, going to do?*

"We've already sent a couple of civilian volunteers who are certified in forensics to see what they can pick up at Charlie's by way of fingerprints, tire tracks, that kind of thing." He looked at me. "We'd usually clear that with you first, but I assumed that as long as Benny was out of the house it would be okay with you?"

I nodded, still avoiding eye contact with Chris.

Trooper, doing a great job of taking charge, next instructed Mom and me to stay together tonight, monitored by another of his staff of volunteers.

"We'll get a car there. Your only choice is whose house," he said.

Really, it was Benny who got to choose. Mom and I

thought he'd be better off at her house, where there had been no recent trauma.

"Finally, we're all going to get together"—Trooper swept his hand to include all present in the waiting room—"all you deputies, and pool what we have so far, and solve this thing. I don't care who's not happy with who else at the moment. Forget it for now. Understood? Are we all in?" His tone left no room for anything other than affirmation.

I felt Chris's eyes on me, but I wouldn't look in his direction, as we all nodded.

"One more thing, to clear that elephant out of the room," Trooper continued. "Charlie, Chris tells me he had nothing to do with the article in the *Bugle*, except to fill out a mandatory report to his boss to account for his time out of the office this week."

"But the byline—"

He held his hand up. "Stop, Charlie. Let me finish. Chris told the old man it had to be confidential for the time being. But you all know Wally—he never did understand he wasn't supposed to be putting out Elkview's version of a tabloid. And weasel that he is, he had the nerve to think I'd believe his story that he used Chris's name for the writer so Chris would have all the credit."

"I'm really sorry, Charlie," Chris blurted out. It sounded like he'd been holding his breath for many minutes, perhaps hours, waiting to talk. "The last thing I wanted was to dis Manny or in any way jeopardize the investigation. In retrospect, I never should have told Wally anything, boss or no boss."

To her credit, Mom did not offer an opinion of any kind, but sat with her hands folded, as if to keep from clapping.

I was left feeling like one who had rushed to judgment,

which is exactly what I'd done. I was at least grateful that there was no one else but us in Doc's waiting room.

"I'm sorry, too," I told Chris. "I had every reason to trust you, and I should have given you a chance to explain."

"It's okay," Chris said.

"There, now," Trooper said. "Isn't it good when we can play nice? Apologies accepted all around?"

The four-way laugh was a nice segue to the entrance of Doc and Benny into the waiting area.

"What's so funny?" Doc asked.

"It's a long story," Trooper said.

Doc smiled. "I'll pass, then. My own story is that Benny is fine."

We all joined Mom, who started the round of clapping.

Doc had tucked Benny, who was either sleeping or anesthetized, back into his carrier and set him on the table with the out-of-date magazines.

"I gave him a few antianxiety drops," he said, handing me a small package. "He should be completely calmed down by tomorrow morning, assuming nothing else upsets him. If not, give him another dose of three or four drops. Right now, Benny's as good as new."

That was enough to give me a new spurt of energy.

CHRIS INSISTED ON ACCOMPANYING ME TO MY HOUSE to pick up an overnight bag.

"You missed the steering wheel, didn't you?"

"I missed you," he said as he caught the keys I threw him in midair.

When we reached my house, a queasy feeling came over me. I'd underestimated how hard it would be to walk into my house again, and I was glad Chris was with me. The memory of rushing Benny out was still fresh in my mind. The already rough condition of the place was made worse by the black powder spread around by Trooper's volunteers to collect fingerprints. Elkview forensics people were not afforded the latest in dustless print technology. But if the prints helped identify the intruder, I'd be more than happy to clean up the mess.

"This is awful, Charlie," Chris said. He shook his head. "I hate that you had to come home to this."

Before I could respond, he drew me into a hug. "It was more awful when I thought I'd lost you because of a lack of judgment on my part. I'm not asking for anything more than to earn back your trust."

It was a good start, and even more so when Chris thought of collecting some of Benny's treats and toys and making him an overnight bag of his own, and also offered to come back when I was ready to clean up the fingerprint dust.

"Trooper is asking for us to be all in, no more working around him," I said.

Or each other was in my mind.

"You're thinking we should come clean about our visit to Oliver's house?"

"Maybe if we just show him what we picked up there? I mean the cookbook. Maybe he won't grill us?"

"From your lips," Chris said.

Chris followed me as I dragged the storage box from under the guest bed. Relieved to see the two hefty volumes, I removed them and handed them to Chris.

"What's the rest of that stuff?" Chris asked.

"Kid stuff," I said, and pushed the box with its ticket stubs and angst-laden diaries back into its hiding place. Someday, I was going to have to weed through my teen memorabilia before it was too late. It hurt to realize that "too late" was what had happened to Oliver.

To distract Chris from further queries, I shared another thought. "Let's call Annie," I said. "If Pierre has already left for the Arctic, she may need a distraction."

"And she is a deputy, after all."

A minute later, I heard Annie's typically excited voice. Yes, she'd be happy to join us. She had some news to share about Pierre. I did my best to cut her off gently with the promise of listening to her whole story when she got to my mom's.

I stuffed the two-volume cookbook by Oliver Blanchard into my tote, the one that also held the packet of letters from Genevieve. Who was I to accuse Chris of duplicity when I hadn't been one hundred percent forthcoming with him?

We were almost at the door. "Wait," I said. "I need to show you something. Have a seat."

Chris moved a chair and sat. I took the rocker. I dug the letters from my tote and explained to Chris where I'd found them.

"I just got around to looking at them," I said. In other words, *I haven't been keeping these from you for very long.*

He took a minute to read the only one in English. "Well, there's the cookbook. I wonder who's M. P. M., who's not a nice man? Oliver's killer? Over the cookbook?"

"But look at the date. Whoever it is has waited a long time."

"Sure, but . . ." Chris shrugged. "And what about 'if not in this life'? Do you think she killed herself over this breakup? Wow, it's all coming together, isn't it?"

I took a breath. "A clue that points to Oliver's having to leave Paris because of a nasty man, leave this woman who loved him and whom he loved, I'm guessing. Then, decades later, he's tracked down and killed."

"By this M. P. M."

"Maybe. After almost making it out safely again, from Elkview this time."

"Pretty wild if it's true," Chris said.

"Can all of this be over a cookbook?" I asked. "It doesn't seem like enough. Say the recipes were stolen from this M. P. M. and plagiarized—and I'm not saying Oliver did plagiarize them—why kill him? Why not just sue him for millions of dollars, for example? There must have been some proof of ownership. Some paperwork, or people who could vouch for M. P. M."

"And it wouldn't be too late, since apparently it hasn't been published," Chris noted.

"Plus, wouldn't the guy—I'm assuming a guy—have more recipes than the ones in this book? Why not just publish them? Would these particular recipes be worth killing over?"

Chris shrugged. "It doesn't seem so. But we know people have killed for less."

"Still, I can't help feeling there's something else. Something more personal."

"Like what?"

"I don't know. Maybe it's in the letters," I said.

"I guess we need a way to translate the French," he said.

"We might be able to piece them together with Google."

"We should do that before we show them to Trooper."

"I agree."

"We don't have time now, though. We should probably head out," he said.

I nodded. "I'm feeling the way my Catholic friends did when it was time for confession."

TWENTY-FOUR

CHRIS AND I MADE A SIDE TRIP TO THE BEAR CLAW BE-
fore returning to Mom's house for the meeting Trooper had
called. We picked up an order we'd phoned in from the
car. When you hung around with diner folk, you never convened without food. Tammy and Bert, well trained by Victor and Nina, had filled a large cooler with an assortment
of sandwiches, sides, and drinks. Not that we needed the
thermal container. All we'd have to do is open the windows
to the twenty-degree air, and the car itself would become a
cooler.

When we got to Mom's, I saw that Benny had already
found the nooks and crannies he remembered from the time
he'd lived there. We had a good laugh while we watched him
try to get into Dad's floppy slipper, a feat that would have
been easy for the younger Benny. Once we all started talking, Benny disappeared. I knew he'd be back when the containers from the Bear Claw were opened.

We sat in the living room while Trooper ran through
questions to me. What time did I leave the house this morn-

ing? What time did I return? Had I seen any strange vehicles on the street lately? A new person walking a dog? Any threats by mail? By phone?

I did my best to answer. I estimated the house was empty except for Benny from about ten in the morning until three or so in the afternoon. No strange interactions unless you counted Kendra's rudeness. And the covered-up Bennycam.

"How do you think this guy knew enough to find and cover up a small camera?" Trooper asked.

I shrugged. "Lucky guess?"

Of course, that's what I wanted to believe. Much more comforting than the thought of a stalker following the habits of Benny and me.

"Huh," was Trooper's reply.

He didn't believe it, either.

"Is there anything in your house that might be of value to someone else?" Trooper continued. "Something another person would know about, since it seems he knew about the camera. A piece of jewelry or fur? I'm throwing everything out here. Artwork? A significant amount of cash? Diner money, maybe?"

"No to the jewelry, et cetera. As for cash, we do so little cash business these days, especially from tourists. It's all credit card transactions, sometimes even for small amounts. I just keep it in the safe at the Bear Claw, but no more than a couple of days' worth before it gets deposited."

We'd been skirting around the issue of the connection between my intruder and Oliver's killer. It was time to bring out the cookbook.

Trooper and my mom were impressed at its heft as they passed the volumes between them. I was glad that Trooper didn't question its provenance.

On the other hand, I shouldn't have been surprised that he didn't, since Chris had provided cover by prefacing my action with a likely story.

"Charlie has been going through all of Oliver's personal spaces, to see if there was anything that he left behind that might help the investigation."

Maybe I shouldn't have been so impressed with Chris's ability to come up with a cover so quickly without actually lying.

"I remember you asked if Oliver was writing a cookbook," Mom said. "You didn't mention you'd found a complete draft. Do you think this is why he was killed?"

"I see he's using a different name here. Blanchard?" Trooper noted. "But that's not unusual, is it? Using a pen name?"

We all shook our heads.

When Annie arrived, we gave her a quick summary of what she had missed.

"Should we make sure Manny's okay?" I asked. "If we're thinking that my intruder is also Oliver's killer, couldn't he think that Manny has whatever he's looking for?" I pointed to the cookbook.

"Now that he knows Manny is Oliver's father, that could be," Mom said. "And he'd know if he was at the Bear Claw when Manny made the announcement."

Or if he read the Bugle, I thought, but held back, proud of myself.

Mom shivered visibly. "Oh, I hate that he might have been at the diner. The killer."

"Let's go back to our suspect list and assignments," I suggested. "The only one who doesn't seem fully vetted is Stanley Burke. At the memorial service he said something interesting to me. How Oliver was 'difficult.' That was the term he used, then he said Oliver was putting everyone in danger, or something like that."

"That doesn't sound like he's the killer," Mom said. "More like Stanley's another potential victim."

"Does he have an alibi?" I asked, looking at the paired deputies, my mom and Annie.

"Does anyone know what Stanley does, or did, for a living?" Annie asked, by way of not answering my question. "I didn't think of asking him. Some deputy, huh?"

No one commented on Annie's performance.

"It shouldn't be that hard to find out what he does," Chris said. "I'll check it out in the *Bugle* database. We have a new Anchorage directory that's searchable."

"He seemed like a nice man when I talked to him at the memorial. Nothing like what he said to you, Charlie," Annie said.

"As a matter of fact, I might be able to log in from here," Chris said. "Want me to try it now?"

Trooper kept out of this back-and-forth. I had the thought that he might be overwhelmed. After all, generally he worked with only one deputy, a real one, so to speak, and not four make-believe ones.

When he said, "Anybody hungry?" I knew I was right.

Benny WANDERED INTO THE DINING ROOM AS SOON as we set out all the food from the Bear Claw. It didn't seem to matter to him whose dining room he traipsed through. Mom's furniture was old and dark mahogany; mine was a light contemporary set. Benny found his way around the legs of any table.

It was a good thing Chris had thought to bring Benny's

own food. Chris opened the small duffel he'd used for Benny's treats and toys, trying to entice him to come to him. Once he opened a bag of tuna treats, his strategy worked.

Nice job making friends with my cat, I thought, though I kept my eye on the pair, lest Chris try to make the wrong kind of physical contact. Benny liked to have his chin scratched, for example, and his back rubbed, but his stomach was off-limits. Not to be confused with dogs I've known.

Tammy and Bert had stuffed the cooler with deli meat and cheese sandwiches, potato salad, carrot and raisin salad, and, something new to our menu, a tasty tomato and mozzarella combo with basil and balsamic vinegar.

As much as we'd all declared full disclosure from now on, there were a couple of one-on-ones that looked a little suspicious. And I was part of each pair.

First, Annie cornered me with news regarding Pierre. "What if he really does want to stay, Charlie?"

"It's even stranger that he wouldn't have found another way to get to where he's supposed to be for his magazine article. Why couldn't he have gone into Anchorage to get another rental, for example? It's the wrong direction, but at least he'd have had a car right away. It does sound as though he really wanted to stay around, maybe get to know you better?"

It wasn't the first time I was in a quandary when Annie wanted advice with a relationship problem. I had to tread this narrow line between getting her hopes up and being brutally honest about the chances of success with Tom, Dick, or Harry. Not even my history of a failed engagement held her back in seeking my opinion. Maybe the reason she kept coming to me was that she knew I'd always be there for her no matter which way the chips fell. In the long run, that was good enough for me, and I plunged in with advice.

"Have you tried just asking him outright?" I asked. "How long do you plan to stay in Alaska, and is it because of me?"

Annie gasped.

I guessed not.

The two of them would probably just keep going until they were down to bald tires on Pierre's rental.

The second off-the-books pairing was with Chris, who came up to me in Mom's kitchen when all the others were at the tantalizing buffet spread in the dining room.

"About those letters," he said. "We're still going to try to get them translated first, right? Before we get everyone all excited."

"That's what I'm thinking. In fact, I know someone," I said. "No one remotely connected. I'm planning to try her this evening."

Chris and I had discussed this briefly in the car, how we didn't think it was wise to ask Pierre, or even Nina, who'd taken French all through school. It had to be someone with no vested interest, like my college roommate who worked for the United Nations school project in Anchorage and spoke six languages. I figured one of them had to be French.

As the group was finishing dinner, clearing dishes, talking about leaving, deciding what to do next, we heard a yelp from Chris.

"Aha."

He'd gone off to a corner with his laptop, keyboarding now and then, eyes on the screen. Apparently he'd gotten results.

"Stanley Burke owns Burke Press, a book publisher specializing in home and garden topics. The company is in Eagle River."

"Part of Anchorage," Trooper said.

"Home and garden. That would include cookbooks," I said.

Chris created the story line. "Oliver wants to publish a cookbook with his brother's company. Brother Stanley finds out some or all of the recipes have been plagiarized. Maybe he catches it before he releases it, maybe not."

"That's right," I said, locating my tote and pulling out my tablet. "We don't know for sure whether this was published or not. I'll do a search."

"Back to the drawing board," Chris said. "But for now, we have good reason to believe that Stanley would be angry at being involved in something like this, and he'd be worried that he and/or his company would experience some fallout. Maybe lose his business license. Maybe even be hit with a big lawsuit."

"We might have our motive," Mom said.

"I don't see that it was published, but he could have taken it down," I said. "There are a couple of other places I can search. I'll keep on it."

"Kendra must have known about this," Mom said. "You'd think she would have mentioned it."

"We know Kendra was at work on Monday afternoon," Trooper said. "I need to find out where Stanley was. I'll ask him to come in for an interview." He frowned and looked at Chris. "None of this is on the record."

Chris held up his hands. "This meeting never happened."

"Thanks," I said.

THE LOGISTICS WERE SETTLED WITH RELATIVELY LIT-tle fuss. Trooper would follow Annie home and make sure the inn was okay, though it wasn't a likely target. There were always people moving in and out of the big house and the cabins. One of his volunteers would be on call for her if anything seemed the least bit off.

"I should be fine. I still have six people staying at the main house who are not part of Beth's tour," she said, then screwed up her nose. "Unless one of them . . . ? No, no, never mind."

Annie didn't want to think one of her guests might be a murderer any more than I wanted to think Victor or any of my staff could be guilty.

Following Trooper's plan, I would be staying with Mom, with a volunteer in a car out front all night.

Chris was on his own, which he said was fine with him. Still, Trooper said he'd put someone on call for him, also.

All this because someone had invaded my home. It was unsettling to think the invasion and the murder were connected. If my home had been broken into last month, none of these precautions would have been thought necessary. It would have been a run-of-the-mill incident, confined to the annals of police reports, chalked up to delinquent teens on a spree.

There was no telling what else might happen if we didn't end this investigation soon.

The meeting that never took place broke up at a reasonable hour, leaving time for a phone call. I left Mom playing with Benny and the new wand toy she'd brought back from Germany.

I went back to my old bedroom, where I'd dropped my overnight bag. It had been a good fifteen years since I called this little room home. Not much had changed since I left.

My pastel-colored jewelry boxes were still stacked on my dresser. I wondered what was in them now but was too distracted to take on the project of opening them to find out. It was unlikely that I'd be able to find the keys to the tiny locks anyway. I couldn't remember the last time I'd worn any jewelry since I'd taken over the Bear Claw. I'd even abandoned my watch once the time was more accurately displayed on my phone. I laughed when I spotted the ceramic giraffe, the neck of which held my rings.

On one wall was a collage of photos arranged in the shape of a heart. I took a closer look. Ski weekends. Hikes. Concerts. Dances. I found myself searching for Chris. Would I even recognize him with hair, instead of his current shaved military style? Surely he was in one of the group photos.

Why was I bothering to look?

I moved away from the photo array and sat on my bed, on a comforter I didn't recognize. I figured Mom had pulled it from the linen closet and switched out a dusty one as soon as she knew I'd be staying overnight. Heaven forbid I'd have to sleep on a bed with less than pristine linens. I pulled my duffel toward my feet and unloaded my things.

When I was in high school, Dad helped me create a little nook by pushing my single bed against a wall and stringing up a dark red drapery on a long rod that ran the length of the bed. Strands of lights around the perimeter finished the look, which was basically that of a fortune teller's booth at a carnival. Except that at the head of the bed was a large tribal wall hanging of the Eyak River, evoking an entirely different, tranquil image.

What had I been thinking?

I sat back, cross-legged, phone in hand, my laptop on my lap. Not quite as comfortable as I remembered the position being when I was a teenager. I opened my phone and scrolled for Lacey Thompson's name.

"I hope it's not too late to call," I said when she picked up.

"Nope. Miles to go, as they say. How are things in the hinterland?"

"Meaning any place outside the two thousand square miles of Anchorage?"

"Thanks for the extra thirty-seven."

And that's the way it usually started with Lacey and me. Fun trivia about our hometowns, home teams, or the latest joke we'd heard.

Tonight, since it had been a while since we spoke, we rehashed an old favorite.

"What do you call a penguin in Alaska?" Lacey asked.

"Lost. Penguins live in Antarctica," I answered, and we chuckled.

"Okay, now the reason for the call?"

"I need a favor. But first, do you know anyone in the publishing business in Eagle Creek?"

"No, can't say that I do."

"How about anyone at a real estate firm in Anchorage?"

"No. Is this a riddle? Or a joke? A publisher and a real estate agent walk into a bar?"

I laughed. "We need to come up with a punch line for that one. This time it's serious, though. And for this particular favor, I have to clear you of knowing anyone involved."

"Trust me, if it's anyone over the age of twelve, I don't know them."

"So the project is going well?"

"It's always going well. I love working with minds that are still shapable. But sometimes I miss grown-ups. I hope this is a grown-up favor."

"Very. Is your French still good?"

"Mais oui!"

"Even I know what that means."

I gave Lacey a rundown on what I needed.

"An English translation for three short letters hand-written in French," she repeated. "That's all you've got?"

"Yes, and I will owe you."

"Can you scan them right now?"

I was about to confirm, until I remembered I was at my mom's, not at home where a real scanner was. My phone wouldn't do well with the wrinkled old letters. It would have to be tomorrow, but Lacey promised to get to the letters as soon as she received them. We signed off with an even worse joke than the one about the penguins.

TWENTY-FIVE

THE LONGER I SAT ON MY CHILDHOOD BED, THE MORE comfortable I became. For one thing, no one had invaded this room recently. For another, I'd paid a visit to Mom's kitchen and carried back a plate of small cheese biscuits and stuffed celery to snack on. My fridge at home seldom had anything as tasty.

I browsed on my laptop, looking for an Oliver Blanchard who'd published a cookbook in the last thirty years. No luck. Then I searched for all the books published by Burke Press in that same period. I found that they'd been in business almost thirty years. I scanned their list of specialty cookbooks and, though I hadn't been planning on shopping, ordered one on Alaskan wild mushrooms for the diner.

Nothing by Oliver Blanchard, however, or by any of Oliver's last names.

Even with striking out in my search, I felt a little more confident that we were closing in on the end of the investigation and, hopefully, putting a murderer behind bars.

First, Stanley Burke was now a strong possibility as his brother's killer. The rift went beyond being left out of a will or an obituary in a small-town newspaper. We weren't talking solely about a stolen recipe or two, but a man's business potentially ruined by scandal, accusations of fraud, if our suspicions about the recipes were correct. Trooper was taking care of exploring that angle by bringing Stanley in for questioning. I came close to asking Trooper if I could sit in on the interrogation, but decided not to push my luck with respect to my new deputy status.

I was disappointed but not surprised that Trooper had taken the cookbook manuscript with him. I hadn't had time to read it in detail. When Chris and I flipped through it at the airport in Anchorage, the only recipe that stood out was the cherry cheesecake mousse that we'd been making for years. I made a note to ask Willow about the legality of using other people's recipes, realizing that it would be a moot point if the volumes were relegated to an evidence room for the indefinite future.

The second hopeful development was that civilian forensics techs had been sent to my house. Surely the invader couldn't have been one hundred percent careful, even though he did know enough to cover the Bennycam. I'd read that sometimes all it took was a partial print to ID someone—assuming the person was in the system, which I chose to believe they were.

Third, I had someone reliable and neutral to translate the letters, almost certainly love letters. In other words, probably not useful to the investigation, but one never knew. Maybe Genevieve had spelled out M. P. M. in the other letters. Lacey would be able to start on the English versions as soon as I could get home to my scanner tomorrow.

Besides all those pluses, Mom and Benny were safe,

Chris and I were friends again, and Dad was due home to-morrow, adding to a sense of normalcy. Dad would want to do something special for Seward's Day, which came on the perfect date every year—the last Monday in March, after the serious months of winter weather, and before Alaska's epic swarms of mosquitoes found their way to our picnics. I reminded myself to order a good supply of tiki torches, bug spray, itch cream, and candles before they were sold-out.

I was sure there were more reasons to be hopeful, but that was enough for now. I looked in on Mom, asleep in her bedroom, with Benny curled up at the foot of the bed.

It was safe for me to turn in.

My PLAN FOR SUNDAY WAS FIRST TO STOP AT MY house to scan Genevieve's letters and email them to Lacey. After that, I'd open the Bear Claw to accommodate Annie's tour group. Technically, it was Beth's tour group, but I felt Annie took better care of the members, and not just Pierre. I knew I should cut Beth some slack, since weather had ruined her schedule, but it was Alaska, after all, and weather was always a major factor.

Annie had asked for a special breakfast menu for their last day in Elkview. I'd decided on French toast made from thick slices of cinnamon bread, with two eggs any style and a side of bacon. That ought to get them to Fairbanks, with perhaps a snack stop in Healy.

I tiptoed around the house so I wouldn't wake Mom. Amazing that she was still sleeping at five a.m., especially when she knew I was home and that Dad was on his way. She had a snack covered, with the banana muffins, but I knew she'd be doing more than that. Or maybe with the rich food I'd heard about on the cruise, she'd go back to basics with plain grilled salmon and dilled potatoes. Right now, she was not sweating the menu.

Benny was a different story. He was at my feet in the kitchen as soon as I started the coffee maker. I poured his food into a bowl and asked him to please keep quiet. I explained that I didn't want our mom to be bothered with another task, like figuring out what Genevieve's letters might have to do with the investigation. She'd already done enough, and I wanted her to be able to focus on getting herself and the house ready for Dad. If the Russells were going to stay for dinner, she'd want to do something special for that, too.

I gave Benny a goodbye rub and made sure he had enough food till Mom woke up. I looked out the window at the car parked in front of her driveway. Trooper's men. How difficult was it going to be to go around them? I was about to find out. I grabbed my tote and headed out the door and down the front steps, walking nonchalantly toward my Outback.

Wishful thinking.

One of the two temp officers was asleep, but the other, whom I knew from around town, stepped out of the car and headed me off.

"Morning, Charlie," Buzz said. He looked very official in a navy blue jacket with a patch on the arm indicating his status as a police volunteer. His knit hat with its state logo wasn't quite as elaborate as a regular trooper's, but it was still impressive.

"Thanks for watching out for us, Buzz. I need to stop by my house for a few minutes to use the computer, then I'll be going to the Bear—"

"Let me wake Ferguson over here. Then I can go with you."

"That's not really necessary."

Buzz ran his hand across his throat. "Trooper would have our heads," he said.

"I can set you up with coffees," I said.

He smiled and held his hand out for my keys. "We can stop on the way."

I knew I should be grateful for the extra security with a killer still loose and familiar with my house, but these volunteers were cramping my style. I wondered how detailed their reporting to Trooper had to be.

Or how hard it would be to ditch them.

ARE WE GOING TO BE WATCHED TWENTY-FOUR-seven?" I asked Buzz as we drove past the still-closed shops on Main.

"Hey, this steering wheel is heated."

I took that as a yes, twenty-four-seven.

I had two data points now. If I ever wanted to date again, I'd include "comes with heated steering wheel" in my personal ad for the *Bugle*.

I took a call from Mom, who apologized for not making me breakfast. She'd heard from my dad that he'd be arriving around six this evening and that the Russells would be staying for dinner. She sounded excited and happy. But she didn't know yet that she'd have armed company while she did her grocery shopping.

"Do you think we'll have another meeting?" she asked.

"Maybe a quick wrap," I said. I pictured Stanley in cuffs, though I didn't enjoy the visit to the dank, unfriendly station house, even if it was only in my head.

When we got to my house, Buzz found the right key on the ring, unlocked the door, and uttered a family-unfriendly word, accompanied by a low whistle.

"Pardon my French," he said.

"Funny you should say that." He didn't have to know what I meant.

"Sorry," he said. "I'm sorry someone did this to you."

Seeing the shambles for the third time made it seem almost normal. It was as if the tall gooseneck lamp in the corner belonged on the floor and the soil from the coleus plant was supposed to be spread out on the tile. Only the odor of molding fruit told a story of disorder and inattention.

Buzz made a pass through the house and was satisfied that it was clear of foreign bodies. I blew out a sigh of relief, letting go of fear I didn't know I was harboring. I hoped this uneasiness wouldn't last long. It wasn't like me, or I hoped it wasn't like me.

"I can clean some of this up," he offered.

"I doubt that's in your job description."

"You'd be surprised. I know the techs have been through here, so let me pick up a little. Okay?"

I thanked him and showed him where my cleaning supplies were. I went to my computer in my home office, listed in the Realtor's formal notes as a walk-in closet.

Genevieve's letters were written on small, thin sheets of paper, the kind my parents had used for airmail years ago. Or currently. It had been a while since I'd had that pen pal in Hawaii. As far as I could remember, all we wrote about was homework and the huge gap in temperature as we walked to school. We each envied the other's environment.

Buzz let me roam freely through my rooms and, thankfully, did not stand over my shoulder while I scanned Genevieve's letters. The four of them fit on two pages, which I attached to an email.

I found Buzz sweeping up glass in my dining room. The intruder had made interesting choices about where to look for his quarry, as evidenced by what had been broken or tossed around. If finding the cookbook had been his objective, why would he look in a hutch full of china plates and glasses? Odd. Until I remembered where I'd found the cookbook manuscript to begin with: at the bottom of a trunk in Oliver's home.

I convinced Buzz he'd done enough cleanup. I was eager to get to the Bear Claw, where I knew exactly what needed to be taken care of for a successful day. Unlike police work, especially the faux deputy kind.

I made one more gesture to reclaim my home. On the way out, I pulled the towel from the Bennycam and tossed the offending cloth into the trash.

IT WASN'T HARD TO ALSO CONVINCE BUZZ THAT HE should stay for breakfast with the tourist group. He'd made arrangements for his wife to pick him up afterward, which meant I'd be without supervision for a few hours.

When the familiar white bus arrived with Annie's tourists, happier than usual since they'd be on their way north soon, I was happy, too. Back in my routine with my staff. This morning, it was Victor and Nina again, supplemented by Rachel and Annie. Which reminded me that I needed to post an ad in the *Bugle*. I wouldn't have Annie once the tourists left. And I wasn't sure that Victor's girlfriend, Rachel, wanted to be a permanent fixture here. I wasn't usually this much of a procrastinator, I told myself. These were extraordinary times.

I tied on an apron and joined my kitchen staff, earning thumbs-ups from them. Thanks to the through window, I could hear what was going on in the dining area.

Beth, standing in the aisle between the booths and the stools, had managed to claim the attention of her group.

"All roads are clear and open," she said. She neglected to mention that she meant *all roads that we care about*, but I couldn't ding her for that. Especially since a loud cheer went up, with overlapping applause, whistles, and woot-hoots.

When the excitement died down, Beth answered questions.

"Yes, there's still time for flightseeing if you signed up for it."

"It's practically a given that you'll see moose and bears."

"I'm not sure about mountain goats."

"Glaciers? Of course."

"The jet boat tour? I'll have to check on that."

"No, we're not too late for the northern lights." Beth referred to her official binder. "In fact, they're peaking just about now."

At the last phrase, I noticed a few people reflexively turn to look out the window, as if the shifting greens, purples, and pinpoints of starlight of the aurora borealis were now visible from an Elkview diner.

I looked around for the ultra-blond Pierre, who'd come to Alaska specifically to capture the northern lights for his magazine article, but I didn't find him in any of the booths, nor on the few stools that were occupied. Had he kept track of road conditions and flown off early? Not likely. I glanced over at Annie, who seemed as energetic and merry as the tourists. Keeping track of the Annie-Pierre story was almost overtaking the murder mystery in my life.

Beth had saved the best announcement for last.

"You'll be able to choose dogs from a kennel and mush your own team. Of course, there will be mushers with you."

More hoots and whoops, which happened to occur as Nina was serving food. She took a bow, to more cheers and whistles.

The shock of the morning was when Annie told me that Pierre would not be joining the tour leaving this morning.

"He's giving it another few days, for Max to make good. Or he might just wait for a smaller group to come through and join them. He says those big buses"—she pointed to the long bus in the Bear Claw parking lot—"they give him a headache and he doesn't like the darkened windows."

If my memory served, Pierre had only been on the bus once or twice. I supposed that was sufficient to determine whether you liked it or not.

The French toast was a success, with most of the nearly thirty tourists who came for breakfast choosing that item. It might have had something to do with Victor's declaration as menus were being handed out.

"The bread has been crafted from locally grown cinnamon," he'd said, barely containing his own laugh.

More than one diner yelled out something about Sri Lanka and who traveled the seven thousand miles to get it?

It wasn't the first time I was aware of how much Victor loved interacting with our customers. He enjoyed tossing around diner lingo, teasing about the kind of meat he used in meatloaf, and exaggerating the perils of flightseeing. He'd had to tamp down his enthusiasm when Oliver was around. He now had free reign.

I tried to tamp down the old suspicions I'd had about him and stop them from coming to the surface. What was his alibi for Monday afternoon? I remembered Mom's volunteering to approach him about it, guessing that he was heavily engaged in breaking up with a former girlfriend. I needed to confirm that with her.

At just before nine o'clock, the bus pulled out, hopefully with all passengers, their belongings, and their snack packs accounted for.

Annie fell onto a chair in the kitchen, her arms and legs spread out, as if she'd made a snow angel in the diner air.

"I am so beat," she said.

I believed her. The tourists tired me out, and I didn't have them twenty-four-seven. Annie didn't complain as much as I would have when they needed an extra pillow at three in the morning, or a lemon-scented instead of a lavender-scented bar of soap.

For me, it was a matter of someone needing a bigger or smaller spoon for their soup. Or the occupants of Booth One asking for a shade to be lowered, and those in the adjoining Booth Two wanting it raised. Or any number of small requests that added up to exhaustion, as Annie felt now.

During the rush, I'd checked my phone periodically, looking for an email from Lacey. I was sure she had more to do than the favor I'd asked, but I hoped she'd move me up on the list, for old times' sake.

Nothing from Trooper, either, about his projected interview with Stanley Burke, but it was early yet.

With nothing new to contemplate, I headed for the piles of dishes in the sink. That was one thing that could be cleaned up to complete satisfaction.

TWENTY-SIX

AFTER THE HUBBUB OF ANNIE'S TOURISTS, COMPLETE with the showbiz antics of Victor, Rachel, and Nina, the Bear Claw Diner now seemed like a ghost town at ten on a Sunday morning. All the staff, plus Annie, had split, and the customers who would eventually make their way to the diner for breakfast were still asleep or in church, I guessed.

Leaving me with a much-needed allotment of time and space to myself. Trooper would never have to know that I wasn't properly guarded.

But it wasn't long before the free time disappeared with a rash of phone calls. First, Mom called, with a pronouncement.

"It's official," she said. "Benny is your cat."

"What are you saying?"

"He's walking around looking for you, for his automatic feeder. I think he even misses that camera and red dot game."

"No way. He loves you."

"Sure, but he *misses* you. So here's what I'm going to do. Fergie, the volunteer bodyguard out front, is going to take me grocery shopping. On the way, we're going to drop Benny off at your house. That is, his house. I'll make sure he has fresh water and that all his toys are accessible, that there's no glass, et cetera."

"But I'm not there, and I won't be for at least another hour, until Victor and the girls come back."

"I know, but his feeder is there, and you're there with him through your app. Fergie will make sure the house is clear first, of course."

"Okay, if you really think—"

"I do." She laughed. "I'm really happy about this, you know. For so many reasons. I was afraid Benny would come back here and not want to leave. I'm thrilled you bonded the way you did. And one more thing."

"Yes?"

"Dad has always wanted a puppy."

The truth at last.

I clicked off with my mom, a big smile on my face.

Since I'd already been awakened from my meditative state, I called Trooper to see how his interview with Stanley went, but had to leave a message. I also called Chris to find out if he had uncovered anything I had missed about Burke Press, Stanley's publishing company. Another message left. I hated to bother Lacey, who was doing me a favor, after all, so I went back to my half-awake state and waited until I could contact Benny.

When Tammy called and asked if she could work extra hours during her spring break, I didn't hesitate.

"When do you want to start?"

"Now?"

"Perfect."

Once I knew I'd be going home soon, I had renewed energy and put a pan of bear claws in the oven. Might as well start Tammy off with a good supply, as well as fill the diner with the inviting aroma of melting butter and fresh almond paste for the next customers.

Finally, an email alert sounded on my phone and I found a message from Lacey.

> Hi Charlie,
>
> This was fun! I was reminded of all the exercises in M. Ricard's class. Remember when he took over for Mlle Martine? I've done some political translations for the UN project, but nothing as personal as these. Very sad, as you saw with the one that was in English. Let me know if you have trouble opening the attachment. Call me. I'll be home all day today if needed. Let's have coffee the next time you're in Anchorage!
>
> xoxo
> Lacey

I couldn't wait to open the attachment. But it seemed I'd have to, because I'd left my laptop at home and the icon on my phone had been spinning forever trying to open the file. I almost always carried my laptop with me, and I blamed this failure on Buzz, whose presence had complicated my leaving this morning.

As I moved the warm bear claws to the metal rack for cooling, one of them broke apart. How handy, since I wanted to do a taste test before serving them to my patrons. I took a bite. Something in the delicious pastry activated my brain in a different way, inspiring me to read Lacey's email again.

Lacey was a meticulous grammarian and wouldn't let a

typo pass, even in an informal email. So why was the period missing after "Mlle"? She'd bothered to add it to
M. Ricard's name. While the almond paste took over my
taste buds, I remembered the funny rule Mlle Martine had
taught us. A period is called for after the abbreviation for
Monsieur, but not for Mlle or Mme, the abbreviations for
Mademoiselle and Madame. The reasoning, Mlle Martine
told us, was that Mlle and Mme end in the actual last letters
of the complete word.

"Think of scooping out the inside of the word," she'd told
us. Her version of a mnemonic. "But M. is an abbreviation
that leaves out all the other letters of Monsieur."

Of course! "M. P. M." in Genevieve's letters was "Mr.
P. M." Not three initials as you might have in a monogram,
but a title—"Mister"—and two initials. Now we were getting
somewhere. Another fleeting, wild thought came to me.
What if P stood for our own Pierre? But his last name was
Fournier. Unless, like Oliver, he had several names. Never
mind. Too complicated to think about. There was some
progress, however, and maybe Genevieve's letters held another clue about P. M.

Now I was even more excited to read Lacey's translations. When Tammy arrived, I was packed and ready to
head home to my laptop and Benny. For the first time, it
was almost a tie as to which one I'd greet first. I pointed
Tammy toward the fresh bear claws and the French toast
special of the day. French toast. The irony did not elude me.

I headed out, feeling less guilty abandoning my staff
when I noticed Victor and Rachel pulling in. Three capable
employees would be managing the weekend late-morning
breakfast crowd. I was one lucky diner owner.

About five minutes into my drive, Trooper called to report on his interview with Stanley.

"Can we do a conference call?" he asked. "I'd like to say this once to all my deputies. Chris is on the line. I can't reach Annie or your mom, Charlie. Can you fill them in?"

"Sure. I know Mom is probably still gathering groceries to welcome my dad home. With Sergeant Fergie, of course."

"He'd love to hear that title. I'll have men outside your mom's house for one more night at least. And you're going back there, Charlie. Correct?"

"I'll tell Annie about this report," I said, avoiding the question.

"There's nothing earthshaking," Trooper said, giving up on me sooner than usual. "Stanley the publisher verified that Oliver had come to him with an idea for a cookbook, back when Oliver was still in Paris. He'd won some big prize with one of the recipes and thought that would be a good marketing angle. The two signed a contract and Stanley was ready to roll the presses, then Oliver pulled out of the contract."

"So that's what Oliver and Stanley were arguing about. But so many years later?"

"Stanley doesn't know what got Oliver all excited about it again. Not about publishing it, get this, but to make sure he never did publish it."

"Strange," I said.

"Weird," Chris said.

"Are we clearing Stanley, then, as far as Oliver's murder?" I asked.

"I'm not holding him, but I'm also not satisfied with his alibi. Says he was working in his Eagle River office by himself on Monday afternoon. It was his admin's kid's birthday and he sent her home early."

"That's easy to verify, isn't it?" Chris asked.

"Working on it."

We thanked Trooper for the update, but Chris wasn't finished.

"Charlie, can you stay on the line for a minute?"

Of course I could, and I knew why he asked. I explained that I was on my way home to read the English translation of the letters from Genevieve.

"If you want to meet me at my house, we can look at them together," I said.

"Great. I have a meeting but I'll swing by when it's over. Maybe we can wrap this up."

I was proud of myself for staying within the speed limit, not that there was one posted. I thought again about Pierre. There weren't that many male names that began with P. Or were there? Phillipe, Paul, Patrick—and I remembered one of my law school profs was named Pascal DuBois. There was also the small matter of a different last name. Pierre's was Fournier, decidedly not beginning with an M. Then there was the big matter of my not liking Pierre that much, because I suspected he was leading Annie down a path that was going nowhere, perhaps simply for his own ego.

I had time for one more hands-free phone call. It would be to Annie while I was thinking about her. I reached her and gave her a summary of Trooper's report. She listened, but I could tell she had a report of her own that she was dying to give me.

"I haven't had a chance to tell you the real reason Pierre wanted to stay around. Not that he told me or anything, but I'm guessing, because today is the anniversary of his sister's death and he doesn't want to be alone."

"He told you that?"

"No, no, he's not like that. He almost never talks about personal things, like even family. But I was in his room, just to leave him some fresh towels, and I happened to see something on his dresser and it fell so I had to pick it up and I wouldn't have otherwise or anything."

I questioned the "it fell" designation, but there wasn't always a payoff with Annie's long, convoluted utterances. And I was almost home and didn't want to drag the call out.

"Annie, what did it say?"

"It was one of those cards with a picture of a saint or an angel, they both can have halos, and on the back is information about someone who died. Birth date, death date, and so on. And a prayer, too. You know, it's a Catholic thing."

I did know about that Catholic thing. I knew from Catholic Chris Doucette, for one. Another Frenchman, albeit not one who could speak or read the language. My brain went automatically to Chris's name and initials. Monsieur Christopher Doucette. M. C. D. Not even close.

"Oh, and there was a little newspaper announcement clipped to the card. So sad. It said something like 'by her own hand,' how sad is that?"

"That would be very hard, I imagine."

I wondered which would be worse, a loved one who died by her own hand or one who died by someone else's hand. A foolish question. But it had been a long week, full of strange and sometimes foolish goings-on.

"Her name was Genevieve." Annie sighed. "Isn't that beautiful? And maybe the saint was Saint Genevieve. Is there one? A Saint Genevieve?"

I hit the brake and the accelerator at the same time, skidding into my driveway.

"Did you say Genevieve?" I thought my head would explode. "When did she die?"

"Probably centuries ago." Annie stopped. "Oh, silly, you mean Pierre's sister. She was Genevieve Meunier." After a rocky start at pronunciation, she spelled it for me. "Funny that she didn't have the same last name as Pierre Fournier. Maybe she was married or something, but it didn't say that."

"Do you remember the date, Annie?"

By now, I was unbuckling my seat belt, unhooking my phone from its car holder, grabbing my tote, stepping out of the Outback, and bounding up my front steps.

"The date? Let me think. A long time ago. I don't have it in my hand, of course, but it was a while ago, and this was one of those anniversaries on the fives, like fifteen or twenty or twenty-five. You sound excited, Charlie."

Excited in part because I remembered a French vocabulary lesson and a word that was important for me to learn. *Fournier.* The person in charge of the communal ovens, or the baker. I'd gone home and recited it to my mom.

"Vous êtes fournier," I'd said.

I pictured Pierre helping out in the Bear Claw kitchen on the afternoon of Oliver's service, completely at home with the diner staff, wanting to help in the kitchen.

How incredibly slow and dumb I'd been. I hadn't even put him on my suspect list.

"I'm just unlocking my door, Annie. Do me a big favor and go to my mom's house. Right now. And call Trooper."

I dropped my keys, picked them up, unlocked my front door, and pushed it open.

"Why?" Annie asked.

I stepped into my foyer. "Never mind. I'm inside. I can call him myself."

A pain shot through me. Someone had grabbed my upper arm and squeezed.

Twenty-Seven

"CHARLIE? CHARLIE? ARE YOU STILL THERE? I THINK WE got cut off for a minute."

The pain in my arm and the fear throughout my body kept me from answering Annie's question. I wanted to shout, "Nine one one. Nine one one." into the phone, but the expression on Pierre's face stopped me. If that didn't do it, it would have been the fact that he'd put his index finger to his lips, looking as scary as if he held a gun to my head.

In fact, he was actually holding the gun about three inches from my chest.

He made so many gestures, one after the other, I didn't know where to focus, which of his directives to obey. Should I follow his index-finger-to-the-lips signal, old-fashioned library style, and be quiet? Or his thumb and little finger that were mimicking a phone to his ear. Or his hand, cutting a swath to indicate cut, as in, *end the call or I'll end your life.*

"I have to let Benny out for his walk," I said. "I'll call you later."

Pierre nodded approval and I hung up. I followed the

motion of his gun and took a seat where he indicated, in the family room, not far from Benny's feeder.

Would Annie get my message? My code? Would she remember that Benny never set foot outside unless he was in his carrier? When he went for a walk, it was on the carpet in the living room, the tile in the kitchen, the hardwood floors and scatter rugs in the family room and bedrooms. He walked high up on the beds, the bookcases, the doorframes, or his own condo tree. Surely Annie would know that I never let him out for a walk. She'd understand the code and call Trooper. Wouldn't she?

Where was Benny now? Safe, I hoped. I wanted to ask Pierre, but I didn't dare. Benny was hiding, I told myself. He always disappeared when someone he didn't like was in his space, like our mail person. Maybe Benny hid as soon as he smelled Pierre's aftershave, fruitier than the balm my dad used. I regretted using Benny's name on the phone to Annie and hoped Pierre hadn't been paying attention.

"I found them," Pierre said, thankfully not referring to Benny. "The letters from Genevieve to Oliver. Nice of you to leave them on your scanner. You can thank your friend, you know. Chris. He couldn't wait for you to find a translator, so he told me about the letters and asked me to be ready to translate whenever he could get them away from you."

Chris. Again. I'd deal with him later. If I lived. I closed my eyes tight, until they hurt. I had to believe I'd come out of this, if only to find Benny. Give him a tuna treat.

"You broke in here yesterday to look for the letters," I said.

I needed to keep Pierre talking until Trooper came, in response to Annie. Or Chris, whose meeting might have ended by now. Chris, who was going to get a piece of my mind for not keeping our deal. That we would not include anyone who was remotely connected to the Bear Claw or to Oliver's case.

"That's what it was about, wasn't it?" I continued, unable to bring myself to define what "it" referred to. "Not just the cookbook, but your sister."

Pierre's features twisted into an evil look. If Annie had ever seen that countenance she'd never have fallen for the blond high-fade cut, the hand-knit sweaters and adorable accent.

He pointed the gun at my face, I thought. I'd closed my eyes as the weapon approached, so I couldn't be sure.

"You're smarter than Oliver. Stupid Oliver thought it was just about the money. When I contacted him that first time in Elkview earlier in the month, I told him if he would give me thirty thousand dollars, five thousand more than the prize money he got for my recipe, I'd forgive him and never bother him again. He agreed. He really thought that would do it. He told me he'd probably leave town, just to be sure." Pierre was laughing now, at the stupidity of his victim or at his own genius, or both.

"He took everything from me," Pierre said. "It wasn't enough that he stole my recipe that would have sealed my reputation as a baker. And we were classmates, mind you. And not even the recipe and the prize money were enough for him. He had to take the one person I loved more than anything else."

"Your sister."

"My sweet, sweet baby sister, who was so young, so naive." I opened my eyes. "But Oliver didn't—"

"Worse! Worse than if he killed her." Pierre was swinging his gun wildly now. I tried to see if he had his finger on the trigger. What if he pressed it accidentally? My mouth was as dry as the deserts of the lower forty-eight. "He broke her heart. He took all hope from her. I tried to talk to her about love. That she would find someone else, that she had a lifetime in front of her."

By now, Pierre was pacing in front of me. I thought of jumping up, knocking the gun from his hand. I was taller, I knew, but certainly not heavier or more muscular.

"Five more minutes and I'd have been out of here," Pierre said. He patted his pocket, where I assumed Genevieve's letters rested. "Now I have to do something with you." He jiggled the gun and stopped in front of me. He leaned over, closer to my chest. "What shall I do with you?"

I opened my mouth to suggest he just leave, pretend I didn't show up to spoil his plan.

Instead, I gasped. *Benny.*

Benny was creeping along the hallway, directly behind Pierre.

No, no. Go back, Benny.

But he kept up his forward crawl.

"So you stayed to find the letters?"

"Oliver told me he had them. One of his last pleas to stay alive. He knew I would want them, but I decided to find them myself. I almost gave up. I knew you wouldn't quit."

Stop, Benny. Go back!

"But then Chris told you I had them."

If Pierre turned around, he'd see Benny immediately, and . . . I held my breath, tried not to look at my tabby in case Pierre would follow my gaze, and . . .

Benny ran the last few feet. He jumped on Pierre's back, clawing at the Frenchman's neck as if it were the world's best scratching post. Pierre yelled and tried to shake Benny off, but Benny had hooked one paw into Pierre's collar. Pierre dropped his gun, needing two hands to work at getting free of Benny.

I jumped up and kicked the gun away. It slid along the polished hardwood floor. I remembered the crystal bell Mom had brought me. I scooped it out of its box, still on the floor where I'd unwrapped it. I grasped the long handle, silently asked Mom to forgive me. With one forceful swing of the bell, I clocked Pierre.

Pierre fell in a perfect arc. His head hit the corner of a table across from the Bennycam.

He lay there, unconscious. I heard Trooper's car screeching into the driveway.

All I could think of was how Benny and I had just created the best home movie ever.

TWENTY-EIGHT

WHEN WILLIAM SEWARD, SECRETARY OF STATE UNDER Andrew Johnson, purchased a piece of land from Russia at the bargain price of seven million dollars and change, he was mocked by many.

"Seward's Folly" or "Seward's Icebox," were the slogans, immortalized in newspaper articles and cartoons. Until the discovery of gold revealed the richness of the land a few years later. Since then, Alaska's natural resources have paid back the initial investment many times over.

I was in my twenties when I finally convinced my mom to toss the project I'd done for Seward's Day in grammar school. A clunky papier-mâché Denali with the Alaskan flag stuck on top, hanging from a toothpick. Polar bears, moose, and dogsleds completely out of scale with one another. Lakes and ice made of blue-painted resin arranged in an unrealistic order. I'd won a prize—a pencil case with an image of an elk printed on it—but only because our art teacher, Miss Wyman, believed that every child should win a prize, no matter the quality of the work.

It turned out Mom hadn't completely trashed the project. Instead, she'd memorialized it in a photo and brought out a replica made of a vanilla cake with piles of blue icing.

"Now we're talking," I said.

It had been only twenty-four hours since my heart-stopping dance with Pierre. He was currently at the station house, handcuffed to a cot, according to Trooper, until his status as an international criminal could be determined.

The Bear Claw friends and family community were up for a party. Since Benny was the hero of the hour, we held it at my house so he'd be included without the trauma of another trip in his carrier.

To make up for his lack of judgment in confiding in a murderer, Chris had taken care of the cleanup and recovery of my house after Pierre's trashing. He'd also bought, or found somewhere, a banner with the flag of Alaska printed on it and strung it across the doorway to my kitchen. All that, plus flowers, and I was ready to begin to forgive Chris. Not that I told him right away, however.

The party couldn't get fully under way until we had a complete report and the clarification of some loose ends from Trooper.

"I think Pierre already told Charlie everything we need to know," he said, trying to nab a bite from a passing tray of shrimp.

We disagreed.

"Not me," my dad said. "I didn't know most of this until this morning." He sighed and shook his head. "Geesh, Charlie, he could have—"

Mom rubbed his shoulder. "But he didn't. And I didn't want to spoil your first sleep in your own bed."

Even Annie had already developed a healthy curiosity about the exposing of the man she had thought was Pierre

Fournier, handsome magazine writer, as Pierre Meunier, killer. I'd expected her to have a longer period of mourning, but she brushed aside the idea.

"I only knew him less than a week, Charlie," she said. "I knew it wasn't going to be serious."

She could have fooled me, and did, but I saw no reason to mention it.

"How did Pierre find Oliver?" Annie asked.

Trooper was ready for this one. "The same way Manny did, through that magazine article, except that Pierre already knew Oliver would be cooking somewhere. He scoured cookbooks, magazines, and cooking shows, starting from the first day Oliver disappeared from Paris."

"How come Oliver came back to Alaska, and so close to where he grew up?" Chris asked.

I remembered his conjecture on the topic: that Oliver liked the cold.

"Pierre told me he asked Oliver that question," Trooper said. "He thought it was the last place Pierre would look. He, Pierre that is, traveled to New York, Chicago, Boston, all the big cities of the lower forty-eight, because Oliver always claimed to want to be the head chef at a big-city restaurant."

"Oliver was right that Pierre wouldn't look here first. It took Pierre decades to find him," Mom said. "I still remember a sort of interview I had with Oliver when he applied to the Bear Claw. I asked him, 'Why Elkview, when you've studied in Paris?'"

"What was his answer?" Chris asked.

"That he'd grown up in Anchorage. That was true. And that he always wanted to live in a small Alaskan town. That was not, apparently."

"No, he was hiding, was the reason," my dad said. Always a quick learner.

"Here's something interesting," Trooper said. "I don't know if he was showing off or what, but Pierre told me that after he read that article, et cetera, et cetera, he called around to Alaskan diners, including the Bear Claw, and asked if there was a cherry cheesecake mousse on the menu. He got a lot of noes, but whoever answered at the Bear Claw said, yes, there was, and that's all Pierre needed."

Trooper looked at me when he finished. I looked at Victor, who looked at Nina, who looked at Tammy, who looked at Bert, who closed the loop on me. We all shrugged a "wasn't me" shrug.

"What happened to Genevieve's letters?" Chris asked. "And the translations?"

"I bagged the ones we found in Pierre's pocket," Trooper said. "For evidence. Those were the originals, from Oliver's desk drawer, and that he took from Charlie's scanner."

"What?" Chris asked. A primary source, gone. Not something a journalist wants to hear.

"And I asked Lacey to hand everything over to Trooper," I said. "The French and the English versions. And I deleted the email she sent me with the translations. Without reading them."

Chris heaved a sigh. "Why? I don't get it."

"Genevieve was the only real innocent in all of this. We'd caught Oliver's killer. We didn't need any other clues or evidence. There was no reason to further violate her privacy. To read the letters now, other than for a trial, would have been prurient curiosity."

"If we even need them, with that video confession," Trooper said.

No one disagreed. Not out loud, anyway. And Mom gave me a wide, approving smile.

"Can we eat now?" Victor asked. He'd been silent throughout, as had his sister and friend. I was glad I never had to question him or ask about his alibi. He seemed happy and quite agreeable when I asked if he would be interested in the job of head chef. Now, of course, it was his job to write that ad for someone to work under him.

"I have one more question," Mom said.

Mom's question might have been the hardest one to answer. "How could the Oliver I knew for twenty years have done such hateful things? Stealing a recipe your classmate created. Taking money for that recipe. Abandoning a young woman who loves you. How did I not know this?"

Trooper took it on. "Could it be that we never fully know anyone?"

After a moment of silence, appropriate for Trooper's thought, murmurs passed around.

"Heavy."

"Wow."

"Oh, my."

"Geesh."

"Oh, man."

"Whoa."

"Really."

"Zoinks."

"Uh-oh."

Benny's response was a pleasant trill, during which he jumped on my lap.

"Now?" Victor asked. "The moose meatloaf is ready."

"Not yet. First, we'll have the ceremony," Trooper said.

Not everyone knew about the plan Trooper and I had formulated, but it was clear soon enough.

I took one of Benny's front paws in my hands.

"Raise your right paw," Trooper said, his voice as solemn as he could manage. I helped Benny raise his paw. "Do you solemnly swear to uphold the laws of Matanuska-Susitna Borough in the State of Alaska, so help you God?"

I nodded "Yes," in case Benny's purring hadn't been loud enough.

Trooper pulled out a glittery ball, adorned with a deputy's patch. He tossed it on the floor near my feet. "If a tabby can be mayor of Talkeetna, ours can surely be a trooper's deputy."

Benny jumped off my lap and chased the ball, catching it easily.

The applause was deafening.

BEAR CLAW DINER
FAVORITE RECIPES

CHERRY CHEESECAKE MOUSSE

INGREDIENTS

- 1 lb pitted sweet cherries, fresh or frozen
- 1 1/2 tsp unflavored gelatin
- 1 8-oz package cream cheese
- 1/2 C confectioners' sugar
- 4 oz white chocolate baking squares, melted
- 2 tsp vanilla extract
- 1 C heavy whipping cream

DIRECTIONS

Chop cherries in food processor or blender.
Pour into saucepan; stir in gelatin. Let stand for 1 minute.
Bring to a boil, then reduce heat.
Cook and stir for 1 minute or until gelatin is dissolved.

Pour into bowl. Refrigerate for 45 minutes or until mixture begins to thicken.

In separate bowl, beat cream cheese until smooth. Beat in confectioners' sugar, white chocolate, and vanilla until combined.

Fold in cherry mixture.

Beat whipping cream until soft peaks form.

Fold whipping cream into the cherry cream cheese mixture.

Pour into large dessert bowl or separate dessert dishes.

Cover and refrigerate for 3 hours or until set. Serves 8 to 10.

MOOSE MEATLOAF

INGREDIENTS

- 1 lb ground moose meat
- 1 egg
- 1 small chopped bell pepper
- salt and pepper to taste
- seasonings to taste
- ½ C parmesan cheese

DIRECTIONS

Combine the moose meat lightly with all ingredients except the cheese. Place the meat mixture in a loaf pan, then sprinkle cheese on top before baking.

Bake at 400 degrees for about 45 minutes, or until internal temperature reaches 160 degrees F.

Serves 6 to 8.

ACKNOWLEDGMENTS

THANKS AS ALWAYS TO MY CRITIQUERS: SARA BLY, NAN-nette Rundle Carroll, Ann Parker, Sue Stephenson, and Karen Streich. They are ideally knowledgeable, thorough, and supportive.

A special word of thanks to friends who also provided advice and photos throughout the project: Alaska resident Kris Hutchin, Ann Damaschino, Ellen Kirschman, Nancy Kors, Susan Lawson, Jo Mele, Gail Meyers, Judith Overmier, Lyn Roberts, Leslie Rupley, and Sheryl Ruzek.

Special thanks also to expert ice climber and frequent Talkeetna visitor, William McConachie, who showered me with information and outstanding photographs of the Last Frontier.

My deep gratitude goes to my husband, Dick Rufer. I can't imagine working without his support. He's my dedicated webmaster (minichino.com), layout specialist, and on-call IT department.

Thanks to my agent, Lois Winston, for her hard work and welcome attention, and to the copyeditors, artists, and staff at Berkley Prime Crime for all their work on my behalf.

Finally, my gratitude to my Berkley editors: Michelle Vega, who has been a mentor, support, and friend through a dozen books; and Jennifer Snyder, my dedicated, talented, and newest editor. I hope we also have many projects together!

Ready to find
your next great read?

Let us help.

Visit prh.com/nextread